TEMPTING FORTUNE

TEMPTING FORTUNE

Elizabeth Hawksley

WINDSOR
PARAGON
THORNDIKE

This Large Print edition is published by BBC Audiobooks Ltd, Bath, England and by Thorndike Press, Waterville, Maine, USA.

Published in 2004 in the U.K. by arrangement with Robert Hale Ltd.

Published in 2004 in the U.S. by arrangement with John Johnson Limited.

U.K. Hardcover   ISBN 0–7540–8697–6 (Windsor Large Print)
U.K. Softcover   ISBN 0–7540–9362–X (Paragon Large Print)
U.S. Softcover   ISBN 0–7862–5982–5 (General)

The text of this Large Print edition is unabridged.
Other aspects of the book may vary from the original edition.

Set in 16 pt. New Times Roman.

Printed in Great Britain on acid-free paper.

British Library Cataloguing in Publication Data available

Library of Congress Control Number: 2003110533

To the immortal memories
of
Samuel Phelps (1804–1878)
and
Frederick Fenton (1817–1898)

To all my tutors, especially Professors Andrew
Sanders and Michael Slater, who made the
MA in Victorian Studies at Birkbeck College
so interesting and stimulating; and to my
fellow students, especially those who continue
to share my enjoyment of nineteenth-century
theatre

CHAPTER ONE

The January of 1826 was bitterly cold. A thin, sharp rain had been slanting down all day and by the evening had turned to sleet. The cobblestones on the road outside St James's Church, Clerkenwell, were wet and slippery and already horses stumbled and their drivers cursed. In the portico, a young woman shivered and drew her thin woollen cloak round herself more closely and tried to hush the whimpering child in her arms. The young mother was desperately thin. Her face had the look of someone who has seen too much and was now at the edge of endurance. The expression in her grey eyes was one of utter hopelessness.

The baby, who could not have been more than eight months old, seemed in much better condition. Her cheeks still retained some plumpness and, although her little hands were blue with cold, the wrists had baby creases which spoke of better nourishment than her mother. She stopped whimpering, apparently struck by the glow of the gaslights and the halo around them made by the falling sleet. Her mother stared out apathetically.

There was a sudden swell of organ music and the church doors opened. The evensong congregation, solid, respectable citizens for the most part, came out. Most of them ignored the half-frozen woman and her baby, a few dropped a penny or two into her lap and some pursed their lips and tut-tutted.

At that moment, the mother gave a small sigh and fell, almost in slow motion, in front of a portly gentleman and his wife. The baby, suddenly finding cold stone underneath her, set up a wail.

The portly gentleman poked impatiently at the woman with his cane. 'Seeking attention no doubt,' he said to his wife.

He was pushed out of the way by Miss Henrietta Webster, a stout determined-looking woman of some fifty years of age. 'Well, here's a to-do! Stand aside please, sir, if you can't help. This poor creature needs air.'

The portly gentleman's wife picked up the baby and shushed her firmly.

The vicar, Mr Shepherd, alerted by the commotion, bustled out and knelt beside Miss Webster, who had untied the woman's bonnet strings and was waving smelling salts under her nose. He took hold of the young mother's wrist and felt for the pulse. He looked up at the portly gentleman.

'She's dead.' Mr Shepherd dropped the hand, rose and brushed at his knees impatiently. 'And no ring, I see.'

Miss Webster looked up at the vicar and snapped, 'The unfortunate creature didn't produce the child single-handed. I've no doubt there's a sad story behind this.' She turned back to fold the dead woman's hands gently on her breast.

'And such a pretty baby,' said the portly gentleman's wife. 'You can see she's been well looked after.'

The vicar grunted. Another pauper's burial he'd have to deal with. Last month there had been two beggars who had died outside the church. And the funerals had to be paid for by the parish. The baby would have to go to the Thomas Coram Foundation. He stumped off in search of his churchwarden.

Miss Webster looked down at the dead woman's face for a moment longer, then she bent to cover it with the woollen cloak. As she rose to her feet she noticed a small rush basket by the pillar. Inside was a rag doll, home-made with button eyes and wool hair. She held it out to the baby, who reached out her arms and gave Miss Webster a beaming smile showing two baby teeth.

Miss Webster's eyes filled suddenly. 'Let me hold her,' she said to the portly gentleman's wife. It was a long time since she'd held a baby. The woman handed over the baby and then tugged at her husband's arm and whispered. The portly gentleman sighed, but reached into his pocket and took out a couple of guineas and handed them to Miss Webster.

'My wife doesn't like to think of the woman having a pauper's funeral,' he said curtly.

3

An hour or so later the formalities were over. The body had been removed and the vicar's housekeeper was preparing to take the baby in for the night, when Miss Webster surprised herself by saying, 'Leave her with me. I'll keep the poor mite.' She could feel the baby's warmth against her and one little hand was around her neck, holding on tight.

'Her future must be properly assured,' began Mr Shepherd sternly. Miss Webster was one of the more forceful of his congregation. Her family had come down in the world, he knew. He had seen a really superb late eighteenth-century tallboy in her drawing-room and some good pictures, which spoke of better days. But, whatever the past status of the family, Miss Webster now ran a small lodging-house in Myddleton Square and Mr Shepherd felt that she should treat him with more respect and deference than she usually showed.

'It will be,' said Miss Webster. 'I'll take responsibility for her.' The baby, with her large brown eyes and mop of baby curls, reminded her of her dearest Frederick, who had died during the French wars. Why should she not take in the poor thing? What would happen to her otherwise? The Thomas Coram Foundation, probably. A benevolent institution, deserving of the highest praise, but what the baby needed was a home, somewhere she belonged.

Miss Webster would be fifty-one this year. Her young man had been killed at Cape St Vincent. She had stayed at home in order to nurse elderly parents. She had never had anything for herself. Now she would. Various well-meaning friends had suggested that a woman of her age ought to have a cat. A cat! Hetty Webster had nothing against cats personally, she just didn't like the way they brought in dead birds and mice and left cat hairs all over everything.

No. She had longed for children of her own, and life had denied them to her. Now, a baby had been thrown into her lap and she was going to keep her. In no time at all, the vicar, still expostulating, had hailed a cab, and Miss Webster, the baby and the rush basket were all put in and soon the horse was trotting off to Miss Webster's house in Myddleton Square.

Miss Webster's house, on the south side of the square, was a tall building with two rooms on each of four floors, and a basement. The whole house, which was newly built, as indeed was the whole square, spoke of solid respectability. The steps up to the front door were cleaned daily and the green door, the brass fittings, including the knocker in the shape of a lion's head, sparkled. The back garden faced the New River Head ponds with their weeping willows.

Her lodgers lived on the top two floors. At the top of the house there was Mademoiselle

Valloton, a thin, angular woman, who somehow managed to exude an aura of chic. She was in couture and had a number of wealthy clients who were willing to pay her high prices in order to have clothes designed and made by her. She went to Paris every year (she took care to tell her customers) and always returned with a sketchbook full of the latest fashions. If Miss Webster sometimes suspected that her lodger went no further than Margate, she never let on. It wasn't her business and Miss Valloton always paid her rent promptly.

The second floor rooms were occupied by Mr and Mrs Copperstone. Mr Copperstone ran a number of ironmongers' shops in north London, managed by his three sons, which the old man took care to keep firmly under his own control, visiting each in turn. He had worked hard to make a go of his business and to expand, he told Miss Webster; he wasn't prepared to see his work go down the drain, at least not until he and Mrs Copperstone were underground. He was now in his middle fifties, with a shock of grey hair and a nicely rounded paunch.

On the first floor was Miss Webster's drawing-room and behind that her bedroom. On the ground floor was the dining-room, which she shared with her tenants, and a spare room. In the basement were the kitchen, scullery and washroom and out the back was the privy and a small ill-tended garden, used mainly for hanging out the washing. The coal hole was at the front underneath the pavement. The two maids slept in a small attic room.

Miss Webster gave good value for money. She charged a very reasonable seventeen shillings and sixpence a week each for rooms, breakfast and evening meals and she didn't stint on coals in winter. Her maids were well paid and their beds were comfortable. Miss Webster knew of households where the maids slept on mattresses on the kitchen floor, and had no space to call their own. Miss Webster didn't agree with that. Her maids worked hard and deserved a good night's sleep.

All the same, as the cab jolted its way towards Myddleton Square, Miss Webster did wonder how she was going to explain this baby.

*　　*　　*

That same cold January day in 1826, two young boys were playing with some painted lead soldiers on the floor of an icy room at the top of Hoop Hall, in the county of Hertfordshire. The boys were Charles Fulmar, eight-year-old elder son of Lord Fulmar, whose house they were in, and Jack, the ten-year-old son and heir of Mr Midwinter, owner of the neighbouring estate of Holly Park.

Neither of the young boys noticed the cold.

7

Their play was absorbing and energetic and they had only just discovered the room. It was Jack who had found it.

Jack's grandfather had made his money in the cotton mills of Lancashire earlier in the century. He had arrived in Manchester with little more than the clothes he stood up in, but hard work and a genius for seeing how machinery might be adapted to work to better advantage had enabled him to make his fortune. Jack had inherited his gift for seeing how things worked. The previous day, when both boys were playing outside making a snowman, something had worried Jack. He stared up at the Hoop Hall roof.

The house was Elizabethan. Some fifty years before it had been given a Georgian façade, as was the fashion then, but the older part of the house could still be seen in all the complexity of twisting chimney pots and odd gables. The boys were well acquainted with the attics, which contained such delights as old suits of armour and rusty halberds.

'What is it?' Charlie nudged his friend. Jack had been staring for too long, and Charlie was getting cold.

'That chimney stack. The one with the little window at the bottom.' Jack pointed.

'What of it?'

'That room doesn't exist inside.'

The boys turned to each other in mounting excitement.

'Perhaps it's the priest's hole! Grandfather told me of it once, but he'd never say where it was. Could you find it, Jack?'

Jack looked again. 'I think so,' he said slowly. 'I think it must be behind that attic room where the old linen press is.'

The boys raced upstairs. The attic room with the linen press was panelled in oak and there was no obvious door. Jack went round tapping carefully. He and Charlie listened.

'I think it must be here,' whispered Jack. 'It doesn't sound the same.'

'But we can't get in!' Charlie kicked at the panelling in frustration. 'There's no door.'

'Of course there's no door,' said Jack scornfully. 'If it's a priest's hole, there wouldn't be. But you must be able to get in somehow.' He stood and looked.

After a few minutes Charlie got bored. 'Come on, Jack, it's no use.'

Jack said nothing. When something absorbed him he rarely noticed those around him. After a while Charlie wandered downstairs to play with his little brother, Arthur, in the nursery. Jack went on looking. It wouldn't have to be door-sized, he thought, but it would have to be big enough for a man to get in. It couldn't be too high, but it might be low down. And, from the window outside, it was probably to the right of the chimney.

Jack was a persistent small boy and in the end he found what he was looking for. A piece

9

of beadwork on the panelling contained an ingenious knob. As Jack twisted it, a small panel creaked open. It was quite low down and Jack crawled in. Thin, dusty daylight told him that the room, which was only about seven feet square, was the one whose window he had seen outside.

Jack had hoped for a skeleton at least, but there was nothing, not even a chair and table. He looked carefully at the catch to see if it opened from the inside. When he was quite sure that it was safe to do so, he shut himself in. Then he looked around. Was there another exit? Perhaps one that went down beside the chimney stack to the outside?

Jack spent half an hour in the room, then quietly let himself out and went downstairs to join Charlie and Arthur in the nursery.

He and Charlie never mentioned their find to anyone else. Lord Fulmar, Charlie's father, was not the sort of man one confided in.

'I shan't tell Arthur,' said Charlie. 'He's only a baby, and besides, it's the sort of things that only elder sons know.' Charlie, a thin, nervy little boy, was jealous of the four-year-old Arthur, who was of a much more outgoing disposition and his father's favourite. Charlie's mother had died when Arthur was born and Charlie scarcely remembered her.

Jack said nothing. He had made a second discovery about the priest's hole, which he was not telling anybody, not even Charlie. Jack was good at keeping secrets. He never told his mother, for example, that he had made a proper working mill-wheel in the little stream behind the kitchen garden at Holly Park: she would think it not suitable for a gentleman's son. There seemed to be an awful lot that gentleman's sons shouldn't do.

He was a very good-looking boy, tall for his age, with thick brown hair and hazel eyes. Even at ten, he knew how to twist housemaids round his little finger for some extra jam or cake. 'Oh, you are a one, Master Jack,' they'd say. Jack had learnt very early on that, providing he didn't tell his mother, he could get away with many enjoyable, if ungentlemanly, things.

Charlie and Jack had the priest's hole as their secret room until first Jack and then Charlie went to Eton. After that they gradually forgot about it.

*   *   *

The elderly cabbie clambered down and went to bang on the lion's head knocker of Miss Webster's house in Myddleton Square. He then opened the cab door for Hetty. Polly, the elder of Miss Webster's two maids, a thin, bony young woman of about twenty-six, opened the front door. Hetty climbed out, carefully, and called, 'Polly! Come here quick and take this.'

She dumped the baby unceremoniously in

11

Polly's arms and went to pay the cabbie. Then she took out the rush basket, unfurled the umbrella and trod resolutely up to the front door. The baby, startled by the sudden cold and wet, began to wail.

'Lor!' cried Polly, peering down at the small bundle. 'Whatever are you doing with this babby, Miss Webster?'

The commotion and wails brought the rest of the household to the front hall. Soon a row of faces was peering down the staircase and Leah, the other housemaid, ran up from the basement. There was an excited chorus of exclamations. Miss Webster took off her cloak and bonnet, hung them up carefully, shaking off the water as she did so and turned to take the baby back from Polly. She began to rock her gently. The wailing ceased.

'We need one of the officers of the parish,' said Mr Copperstone authoritatively. 'She—it is a she, I think—will have to go to the workhouse.'

Miss Valloton had come down and was peeping into the shawl. 'Ah, *la pauvre petite*. She has beautiful eyes. What a shame.'

'I'm keeping her,' said Miss Webster flatly. 'Polly, go and put some water on and get down the tub. The baby needs a bath and food. Leah, I want you to heat up a spoonful of the lamb stew with a small potato. Not too hot, mind, and then you're to sieve it.'

'My dear Miss Webster,' cried Mrs

12

Copperstone, 'is this wise? A child of the gutter! I really think you should allow Mr Copperstone . . .'

'I'm keeping her,' repeated Miss Webster stubbornly, holding the baby rather closer. 'Get a move on, Polly. And Leah, too. This baby is cold and half-starved.'

Polly and Leah scuttled back downstairs and Miss Webster, ignoring her disapproving tenants, went upstairs to her drawing-room with the baby and the rush basket and closed the door firmly. She found that she was trembling.

An hour later, the baby was bathed, warm and fed. She lay, tucked up in an old blanket, in a hastily cleaned-out log basket.

Alone once more in her drawing-room, Hetty went through the rush basket carefully. There was a small bundle of baby clothes and baby napkins, an even smaller bundle of women's clothes and a battered wooden trinket box, which held a collection of letters and a pocket book. There was a name inside the pocket book: Maria Beale, and a folded piece of paper saying that Sarah, illegitimate daughter of Maria Beale had been born on 22 May 1825 and christened at St Matthew's Church, Church Row, Bethnal Green, London. The father's name was not given. But on the back Maria had written defiantly: *Let it be known that the father of the babe is James, Lord Fulmar of Hoop Hall in the County of*

Hertfordshire.

As Miss Webster turned the piece of paper over, the pocket book slipped from her lap and a second piece of paper fell out. On it was written in the same angry black ink:

I, Maria Beale, do solemnly curse James, Lord Fulmar, for his cruel neglect of me and our daughter. May he never find peace or happiness. May his sons predecease him and may he have no lawful heirs. May his life be bitter and may he know the burden of shame and anguish that he has forced upon me. May he die neglected and unloved and may his black sins send him to Hell to suffer torment for ever, even as he has tormented and neglected me.

Later, in pencil, she had added, *Oh God, I loved him so much.*

Miss Webster folded the piece of paper gingerly, as though it might sting her, and hid it away in the pocket book. Poor unhappy girl, she thought. Her curse would have had no effect. Betrayed women were two a penny.

Hetty then turned her attention to the letters, which were tied with a blue ribbon. They were love letters. The early ones were brief notes from Lord Fulmar to arrange stolen meetings. It became obvious that Miss Beale was not a servant, as Miss Webster had assumed, but a young guest of Lord Fulmar's.

Maria's eighteenth birthday was mentioned and Lord Fulmar had evidently sent her some trinket. The tone was tender and affectionate—though peremptory too. *Don't be late*, he warned in one. His protestations of love grew as the letters went on. They were full of promises, Miss Webster noted sadly.

Of course, we'll be together, darling. And in another, *How could you doubt my love?* Gradually, the tone changed. *'Don't be tiresome, Maria. It can't be done.*

His final letter was terse and to the point. *Of course I can't marry you. You were a fool to think otherwise. Fulmar.*

The last letter of all was Maria's own. It was a fearful plea for help. She was carrying his child and had nobody else to turn to. She was desperate. Across the outside was scrawled in Lord Fulmar's hand, *Foxton, send the woman packing.* Somebody, Foxton presumably, had returned it to Miss Beale.

Miss Webster sat silently in front of her fire and shivered, though the room was warm. She felt tears on her cheeks and angrily wiped them away. It was an old story, but no less tragic for that. Poor young thing. Maria's pale, half-starved face swam in front of Hetty's eyes for a moment. She had been scarcely more than a child herself, barely eighteen when the affair had started. Now she was dead. Hetty folded up the letters and retied the ribbon. She replaced them, together with the pocket book and its contents, in the wooden box and locked it in a drawer of her bureau.

*   *   *

A few days later, after much careful thought, Miss Webster confided in Miss Valloton, who was much excited by this sprig of the aristocracy found in such romantic circumstances. Together they looked up Lord Fulmar in Miss Valloton's copy of the red book.

'Born in 1783,' read Miss Valloton excitedly. 'Why, that made him forty-one, and a widower, too. Highly eligible!'

'Old enough to know better,' snapped Miss Webster. 'Miss Beale was a guest in his house. I call it disgraceful behaviour.'

'Of course, you must tell him!' cried Miss Valloton. 'Only think, baby Sarah may turn out to be an heiress!' She already had visions of being called on to dress the child.

Miss Webster dampened such flights of fancy. 'He has shown no signs of being willing to acknowledge her,' she said. 'Why should he be told at all? I hold him responsible for the death of that poor young creature.' She sniffed.

'He has the right to know,' urged Miss Valloton.

Reluctantly, Hetty accepted that she was right. That evening she wrote to inform Lord

16

Fulmar of Maria Beale's death; she herself was taking care of Sarah and she gave the baby's date of birth and place of christening. She understood the child to be Lord Fulmar's. Did he wish to make other provision for the baby? She was his lordship's humble servant, etc.

She would expect nothing. Lord Fulmar had not felt obliged to help Maria Beale in her hour of need. There was no reason to suppose he would do anything now.

She was right. In due course, Miss Webster received a terse note from Lord Fulmar's solicitors. His Lordship utterly denied fathering Miss Beale's bastard. Any further communication would be treated as libel. It was signed, T. Foxton.

*   *   *

It might reasonably be supposed that our heroine Sarah, born in such unpromising circumstances, would grow up to be the living image of her beautiful, but fated, mother. She would have a wistful air, and a delicate prettiness suitable to one who was obviously set to suffer, if not a similar fate to her mama, then for it to be a close-run thing.

No such matter. Sarah was a happy, confident and rather large child, with chestnut-brown, almond-shaped eyes and thick, brown, wavy hair. She bounced around the house and jumped down the stairs with scant regard for

17

the sensitivity expected of a heroine.

Furthermore, she had a temper. From when she was about two she would lie on the floor and kick and scream if she did not get her own way. Leah and Polly often allowed Sarah to 'help' in the kitchen, but that day they were busy and Polly shooed her away. Sarah threw one of her tantrums and Miss Webster, hearing the screams, came downstairs to investigate.

'That will do, Sarah,' she said firmly.

Sarah took no notice. Miss Webster picked her up and carried her up to her room, put her in and shut the door.

'You stay there until you can behave.'

Sarah screamed solidly for ten minutes and then stopped. When she came out, she was her usual sunny self. By the time she was seven, she had learned to control her temper.

It didn't seem to worry her that she was the only child in a household of staid middle-aged people. Mr Copperstone, who liked to do carpentry in his spare time, made her a toy theatre out of an old wooden box, and Sarah spent hours playing with it, painting and re-painting the scenery, dressing the wooden actors, who could move along on little grooves cut into the stage, and making curtains which opened and shut properly along a wire curtain rod.

Several years running, the Copperstones took Sarah, together with their grandchildren,

18

to Sadler's Wells for the Christmas Show. Sarah was enchanted by the theatre and came back with her head full of such characters as the Green Knight and Princess Eglantine, which she tried to recreate with the little wooden actors Mr Copperstone had made her. With great good nature, Mr Copperstone made her several more as spares.

Miss Valloton, who had never lost her first romantic fondness for Sarah as outcast heiress, offered to teach her to sew. Miss Webster agreed, privately thinking that it would not last long. As a child, she herself had had to be forced to finish her sampler and she fully expected Sarah to feel the same way. But Sarah confounded her by positively enjoying her sewing lessons.

'I like all the different stitches you can do,' she confided, when she was about six. 'And I can make clothes for my theatre dolls which you can take off. Miss Valloton is going to design a pirate's costume for me. It's going to be very difficult, Aunt Hetty, as it will be so small.'

It won't last, thought Miss Webster. But at least it keeps her quiet.

Sarah continued to enjoy her sewing. Soon, she began to have her own definite views on colour and design. She would beg scraps off Miss Valloton and sit by her side sewing happily and trying out different costumes on her little wooden dolls.

Miss Valloton showed her how to cut out a pattern.

*　　*　　*

The winter of 1834 was a hard one and Miss Webster caught a cold, which went down to her chest. She was extremely ill. Miss Valloton, as senior lodger, took charge and saw that the household continued to run smoothly. She called in the doctor, who looked grave and sent various soothing draughts, none of which seemed to work, and she sat up with Miss Webster during the long nights when she was hot and feverish and the breath rasped in her throat.

'I can't die,' wheezed Hetty, grabbing hold of Miss Valloton's hand one night in her anxiety. 'What will happen to Sarah, if I do?' Her eyes filled with tears which ran down her hot cheeks.

Recovery was slow, and it was not until the following Easter that Miss Webster was anything like her old self again. Those days and nights of lying weakly in her bed, scarcely able to lift a hand, had given her to think seriously. Apart from her niece, Sophy Frampton—and a flibbertigibbet she was, with a husband who was idle and feckless—Hetty had no relations.

There was nobody who could take Sarah. No, decided Hetty, she must recover and then she must tackle Lord Fulmar. Surely, if he saw Sarah, he would be willing to do something to secure her future? So far as Hetty could recall, Maria Beale had been a petite, light-boned woman, with the remains of a fair prettiness. Sarah was sturdy and tall for her age with brown eyes and dark hair. She must favour her father. Perhaps, if he saw a family resemblance, he would relent.

All she was asking was that, if anything happened to her, he would see to Sarah's education and start in the world. She wasn't asking for anything more.

Hoop Hall, Lord Fulmar's seat, was a few miles out of St Alban's and one May morning in 1835, Miss Webster and Sarah boarded the stagecoach in Islington and headed north. Each carried a small portmanteau, for Miss Webster had decided that they would stay at the Woolpack, a respectable inn where she had bespoke a room. They would walk the couple of miles to Hoop Hall the following day.

Miss Webster had said only, 'Now, Sarah, I want you to be on your best behaviour. We are going to visit Lord Fulmar, who knew your mother.'

Sarah's large eyes opened wide. She knew the story of how Aunt Hetty had found her, and she treasured the rag doll, which was all that was left to her of her mother, but any further curiosity was discouraged. She had often thought about it, though. She had once

21

dared to say something to Miss Valloton who had said, in a thrilling whisper, 'I may not say, *ma chère*. But you come from the highest blood in the land! Alas, your papa behaved disgracefully towards your dear mother. We never speak of it.'

Now, as Aunt Hetty had opened the subject, Sarah ventured, 'Is Lord Fulmar my papa?'

Miss Webster hesitated. 'He says not.' No point in raising the child's hopes. Not for the first time, she wondered whether she were doing the right thing.

Sarah thoroughly enjoyed the journey. She was a self-confident child, with a lively curiosity, and this was her first trip on a stagecoach. She liked the way the guard blew the horn and the driver cracked the whip. The bustle of the coaching inn at St Alban's delighted her and, while Aunt Hetty was enquiring the way to Hoop Hall and ordering them an evening meal, Sarah was happy to stand by the window and watch the stableboys running to unharness the steaming horses the moment a coach rattled into the inn yard. One descending passenger, a lady in an extravagantly upturned bonnet with huge ostrich feathers, impressed her so much that she determined that one of her little dolls would have just such a bonnet as soon as she got home. She stood there, trying to memorize every detail.

The following morning, Sarah submitted to

having her hair carefully brushed, her buttoned boots given an extra polish and to being poked and prodded by an anxious Miss Webster. Finally she pronounced, 'You'll do. Now come along.'

This time Hetty carried a small basket and an umbrella in case it rained. The basket held some lunch and, unknown to Sarah, a piece of paper taken from her mother's wooden trinket box and carefully wrapped in oilskin.

The entrance to Hoop Hall had a pair of splendid wrought-iron gates and a small gatehouse with a red-tiled roof, leaded window panes and an arched doorway with a twisted barleysugar column on either side. Sarah wondered if the little house could possibly be made of gingerbread.

The gates, however, were locked.

Hetty stopped in consternation. She had not envisaged this. The gatekeeper was already coming towards them, a forbidding expression on his face.

*   *   *

Earlier that morning two young men had set out from Hoop Hall in the pony trap. Ostensibly, they were going to shoot crows—always a nuisance at this time of year. In fact, they were escaping from Lord Fulmar, who had made himself exceedingly unpleasant over breakfast concerning his son's misdeeds.

23

Earlier that month, Charlie Fulmar, one of the young men, had been sent down from Oxford for drunkenness and insubordination. It was unlikely that he would be allowed back.

His Lordship, who had a blistering tongue, had cut off his son's allowance and forbidden him to leave the estate.

Charlie Fulmar, now nineteen, had still something of the gangling adolescent about him. He was tall, with large almond-shaped brown eyes and a mop of brown curls. He would have been handsome, but his drunken excesses had already given his face a puffy look and his expression was discontented.

He had never wanted to go up to Oxford. The only thing he had ever wanted was to join the army, and that his father wouldn't allow. Lord Fulmar might have been persuaded once, but the death of Charlie's younger brother, Arthur, on the hunting field a few years ago, had made such a dream impossible. Charlie was the sole heir and Lord Fulmar wanted to keep him under his eye and out of harm's way. His Lordship never bothered to explain, he simply ordered.

Charlie, stubborn in his own way, had responded by promptly going to the bad. He drank to excess, gambled and got into debt. Oxford bored him. He had never wanted to go, and he wasn't going to pretend he did. Perhaps now his father would see sense.

His friend, Jack Midwinter, was now twenty-

24

one, and had been master of his inheritance ever since his father had died when he was fourteen. Fortune, thought Charlie enviously, had smiled on Jack. He had fulfilled his early promise and was now outstandingly good-looking; tall, with dark-brown hair, which waved over the edge of his collar, and hazel eyes. From the age of sixteen, droves of women had succumbed to his charms. Jack had never suffered from either adolescent spots or lack of self-confidence, nor had he been kept on a measly allowance. True, before he attained his majority, he had had a guardian and his fortune was in trust, but from the moment he was twenty-one, Jack was financially independent.

Charlie was aware that Lord Fulmar sometimes referred disparagingly to Jack's background as 'damned trade'. 'Heard his grandfather started life as a grazier,' he'd snorted. 'Still, the boy's well-spoken and pretty-behaved enough.' If Jack had had a younger sister, it was doubtful whether Lord Fulmar would have been so happy for Jack to have the entrée to Hoop Hall. His Lordship was very starchy when it came to marriage out of one's class.

Charlie, however, would have willingly bartered his own rank for Jack's ease of manner and financial freedom.

Jack had come over from Holly Park to Hoop Hall the back way, making a small detour through the large walled garden. He had stopped to talk to Salter, the gardener, and when he walked into the stable yard, he was eating strawberries. He offered one to Charlie.

'Early strawberries!' commented Charlie. 'Salter won't allow me to touch them.'

Jack grinned. 'Salter likes me.'

The groom brought out the pony cart. Charlie and Jack climbed up. Jack took up the reins and shook them. The trap set off.

'Where to, Charlie?'

'Hoop Wood. There are several nesting pairs there. We can take the trap as far as Ulthorne's cottage.' Ulthorne was the gamekeeper at Hoop Hall.

It had been a late spring, but a burst of sunshine in the last few days had brought everything on. The chestnuts in the park had all their candles and the hawthorns in the hedgerows were covered with creamy blossom.

'I wish he'd die!' said Charlie suddenly, with barely suppressed passion. 'God, how I hate him. He's like some blasted albatross round my neck.'

Jack glanced across at his friend. Charlie's face had that twisted look again. 'He only wants what's good for the estate.' He had heard Charlie's diatribe before.

'Oh, I know. Nothing comes before the estate,' said Charlie bitterly.

Jack wasn't one to let Charlie's moods spoil

a good day, so he said lightly, 'Why don't you marry? Your father would have to make over part of the estate to you. You'd be free enough then.'

'What at nineteen?' Charlie gave a short laugh.

'Tell your father you want to set up your nursery,' said Jack, grinning. 'He couldn't object to that.'

The morning passed pleasantly enough, though Charlie still thrashed sullenly at the bluebells with a hazel twig as they passed. By eleven o'clock half a dozen crows were hanging from the fence at the wood's edge. Charlie shot at every crow as though he were shooting Lord Fulmar. Every time one thudded to the ground, he grunted with satisfaction and he took a savage pleasure in wringing the necks of a couple which were only winged.

If Jack had been remotely introspective, such ferocity and bitterness might have worried him. As it was, he found himself thinking that if Charlie continued in this mood he wasn't likely to be much of a companion and he, Jack, would leave early and maybe drop in and see the delectable Mrs Ward. Her husband was frequently away on business, and she was one of several women currently in Jack's life. He preferred married women. They were discreet and appreciative, and it was easy enough to invent a moral qualm when he grew tired of them and wanted to break it off.

In any case, he knew his mother had invited a certain Miss Palmer and her mother to tea, and he was well aware that Miss Palmer had been marked down as suitable daughter-in-law material. Jack had no intention of obliging. He much preferred to have an amusing time with Mrs Ward. He was becoming increasingly fed up with his mother's attempts to steer him into matrimony.

He and Charlie walked back to the trap. The pony had been taken out of the shafts and tethered to a tree. It was cropping the grass quietly. Charlie untied the rope and Jack pulled round the trap. The pony tossed its head.

'Stop it.' Charlie hit it on the nose and tried to shove the bit into the pony's mouth. The pony began to shy.

'I'll do it,' said Jack. He didn't like to see any creature roughly treated. He was good with animals and soon the pony quietened under his soothing voice and firm strokes. It was harnessed again to the trap without fuss.

Charlie, with a set face, climbed in and picked up the reins. They returned by the front of Hoop Hall; there might be more crows nesting in the elms behind the gatekeeper's cottage. They reached the gates just as Miss Webster and Sarah arrived.

It was Jack who saw them first. He passed over Miss Webster; it was Sarah who caught his attention. He frowned, staring down at her. There was something about her that was extraordinarily familiar.

Sarah, planted solidly on the ground, with her feet slightly apart, put her hands behind her back and returned the stare with interest.

Jack's gaze travelled slowly over her. Those chestnut-brown eyes, the way the hair grew, even that slightly truculent pose. He turned to his friend and indicated Sarah. 'Well, Charlie,' he said. 'What do you think?'

Charlie turned and his eyes narrowed slightly. There was silence. 'What is your name?' he asked. Like Jack, he ignored Hetty.

'Sarah Beale. I've come to visit Lord Fulmar.'

'Have you, egad. Does he know you're coming?'

Sarah glanced doubtfully at Miss Webster. 'I don't think so.'

Beale, thought Jack. Now where the devil . . . He had a sudden picture of the lawn at Hoop Hall with a pretty, fair-haired girl sitting with Lord Fulmar under the cedar. He, Jack, had only been about nine, but he had remembered her. She had been kind to him and helped him to repair his kite, when it had got tangled up. He had liked the way her fair curls had clustered around her temples as had been the fashion then. Lord Fulmar had liked it too, for he recalled him reaching out and twisting a curl gently round his finger and the girl had

29

blushed. Beale! Yes, that was her name. Maria Beale.

'I would be grateful, sir,' put in Hetty, 'if you'd tell your gatekeeper to let us in. We've come a long way.'

Charlie, a couple of years younger than Jack, did not remember Maria Beale, but he recognized one of his father's begetting when he saw it. She looked not unlike his brother, Arthur, had done at about her age, even to the same way of standing. He had never particularly got on with Arthur, but it was still a pang to see the girl. Charlie pushed the thought away.

Would her presence annoy the governor? Yes, of course it must. He'd gone on at Charlie often enough about his sins as though he himself were whiter than white. Well, Charlie would show him. He'd take this Sarah Beale, or whatever her name was, and her companion, and make sure that his father saw them. He'd enjoy that. They'd be thrown out, of course, but that was no concern of Charlie's.

He turned to Miss Webster. 'Hop in, both of you,' he said, indicating the trap. 'We'll take you up to the house.'

Jack climbed down and helped Miss Webster up. Sarah needed no help and clambered up by herself. She plumped herself down by her aunt and looked around with satisfaction. Jack climbed in after them, told Miss Webster to mind her skirts and shut the door.

'Now I've been in two carriages,' said Sarah happily. 'I like this. What's the pony's name?'

'I don't think he has a name,' said Jack as they started off up the drive.

'No name?' echoed Sarah. 'But that's awful! He must have a name.' Her eyes grew quite dark with anxiety at what it must be like to be nameless.

Jack laughed. 'You must give him a name then.' Nice child, he thought. Intelligent and unaffected.

'Frisky,' said Sarah at once. 'Or do you think he'd like something special? Like Belisarius.'

'Belisarius!' echoed Jack, startled.

'Yes. He was a Roman general, you know. But perhaps that's too grand. Besides, people might call him "Belly" and that would never do.' She giggled.

'Sarah!' cried Miss Webster. 'Mind your tongue.'

'Don't scold her, ma'am,' said Jack. 'I like her chatter.' He smiled at Sarah, who beamed back.

He was curious as to what would happen between young Sarah and Lord Fulmar. She was an engaging child. Would she be able to win him over as doubtless the woman with her wanted? While Charlie saw them in and took the trap round to the stables, he, Jack, would make for the old formal garden immediately outside the library. He could hide behind one of the box hedges. Jack had no compunction about eavesdropping, not, at least, when the situation promised such entertainment.

It had not occurred to Sarah that there might be anything to fear in this trip. So far she had enjoyed it. Even when they reached Hoop Hall, which was bigger by far than any house she had ever been in, she was not afraid. She jumped down from the trap the moment the pony stopped outside the imposing façade and ran to pat one of the stone lions which guarded the entrance.

It was only when she entered the house that things changed. The butler was a tall, dark figure with a stony face. He plainly disapproved of the visitors and something of his chill dampened Sarah's spirits. Then the place was so gloomy. The hall had a black and white marble floor, but any desire to play hopscotch on it vanished. The walls were covered in lifesize portraits of long-dead Fulmars gazing haughtily into the distance. One lady in a huge farthingale caught Sarah's attention. Kneeling in front of her, a black servant was proffering a basket of fruit. The lady was ignoring him. Sarah, who had been well-brought-up by Miss Webster, thought her very ill-mannered.

'They've come to see His Lordship,' said Charlie. 'Show them in.' He nodded at Miss Webster, winked at Sarah, and left.

Sarah gave him a small smile. She caught

sight of another portrait, this time of a young girl, much her own age, holding up a bunch of cherries. Sarah stared. The girl looked exactly like her, except that she was dressed in a very old-fashioned way, in a straight white dress and a shocking lack of petticoats. She dragged her eyes away from the picture with an effort.

They were shown into the library and the door snapped shut behind them.

Jack moved quietly to the window and positioned himself behind a neatly clipped box hedge. He was prepared to be amused. The older woman looked for all the world like a fighting cock, fluffed out and determined to protect her chick. Young Sarah was looking apprehensive. Her large dark eyes, so like Charlie's, indeed so like Lord Fulmar's own, were huge and scared. For the first time, compunction seized Jack. He shouldn't have let Charlie do it. Not with the child there.

A tall harsh-featured man looked up as Hetty and Sarah entered. He had close-cropped grey hair and wore a dark-red silk morning gown over his frilled shirt and fawn pantaloons. He did not rise. He glanced once, dismissively, at Miss Webster, and glared for perhaps half a minute at Sarah.

Sarah tried to stop her lip from trembling and moved closer to Aunt Hetty.

'You child. Sit there and be silent.' He pointed to a hard oak chair in one corner.

Sarah crept to the chair and sat down,

33

cluching at the arms to stop herself from quaking. She bit her lip hard.

On the floor, by Lord Fulmar's desk, was a small tortoiseshell butterfly, rather shabby with frayed wings. Perhaps it had managed to winter in the house? Sarah looked at it anxiously. It was a bit early for butterflies, she hoped it would be all right.

The man began to shout at Aunt Hetty, who was left standing in front of him. Sarah could see that her aunt was frightened, for her hands kept twisting together and her mouth slipped sideways as it always did when she was upset. Why was he shouting? Was he really saying that Aunt Hetty was after money? That couldn't be right. She was not that sort of person.

Something was horribly wrong. In her consternation, Sarah stood up.

'Sit down!' barked Lord Fulmar.

Sarah sat.

Lord Fulmar happened to look down and see the butterfly. He reached out his foot and ground it into the carpet. Sarah gave a small mew of horror.

Hetty turned and looked at Sarah. The child's distress decided her. She reached down into her basket and took out a piece of paper. Starting shakily, but with increasing firmness, Hetty began to read. '*I, Maria Beale, do solemnly curse James, Lord Fulmar . . .*' Her voice steadied. The man behind the desk fell silent.

Suddenly, in Sarah's mind, everything changed. It was as if the very room were listening. Even the clock's tick hushed. Her aunt's voice went on, low and serious. *'May he die neglected and unloved and may his black sins send him to Hell to suffer torment forever, even as he tormented and betrayed me.'*

She stopped. The room was silent. The man's face had paled. Hetty placed the piece of paper carefully on the desk and turned to Sarah.

'Come, Sarah,' she said quietly. 'Let us go.'

*   *   *

Jack, listening outside behind the box hedge, whistled silently. All desire to laugh had vanished.

CHAPTER TWO

Life in Myddleton Square resumed its even tenor—or so it seemed. But things were not the same for Sarah. It was not that she changed overnight, she was still the intelligent lively child who had gone to visit Hoop Hall, but there was now a shadow in her life. She had understood that she should never have been born. Her own father didn't want her. It

35

was a shame she hadn't felt before, but gradually it began to eat into her, like an acid. By the time she was fifteen, she had developed a brooding side which seriously worried Miss Webster.

And nothing had been solved. Miss Webster feared that she had only made things worse. For a while she dreaded a letter from Lord Fulmar's lawyer but there had been no sign. Nothing.

She herself had stayed in good health, thank the Lord. She would not be leaving Sarah penniless. The family money had mostly disappeared, but her dearest Frederick had left her what he had—his prize money of some £2,500, for he had been a young lieutenant.

However, their lives were destined to be upset yet again, this time by Hetty's niece Sophy Frampton, the flibbertigibbet, who had made a runaway marriage with a ne'er-do-well, a man always trying to cadge money off Hetty. They lived a hand-to-mouth existence somewhere out towards Hackney. Their only child, Rose, was about five.

Every now and then Sophy left home on some ill-defined job, 'a lady companion', she said. Hetty had never cared to enquire too closely. Rose was dumped on her great-aunt, sometimes for several months. There was never any word as to how long these 'jobs' would last, or when Sophy would be returning. She would simply reappear one day, with a new wardrobe, smelling of some expensive French scent and with a showy present for little Rose.

Sophy's husband rarely put in an appearance. Had he left them? Sophy never said and again, Hetty felt it best not to ask.

One day, when Sarah was about fifteen, a letter came for Miss Webster. It was short and to the point.

*   *   *

I am Mr Frampton's landlord. This is to inform you that Mrs Sophia Frampton died on Monday, following an argument with her husband. Mr Frampton has fled. If Rose isn't collected by noon tomorrow, I'll arrange for her to be collected by the parish.

*   *   *

Miss Webster fell back in her chair, her face white. Sarah, who was darning stockings, dropped her sewing and ran for the smelling salts.

'Oh, poor Sophy!' Hetty cried. 'I know she was a flighty thing, but there wasn't an ounce of harm in her!'

Sarah said nothing, only patted Hetty's hand soothingly. She had never liked Sophy Frampton who, she felt, had taken advantage

37

of Miss Webster's good nature. That year Aunt Hetty had been so ill, Mrs Frampton had done nothing, not even sent a note or some flowers. She had simply vanished until Aunt Hetty was well again and then that horrid husband of hers had come round asking for money. For the last five years they'd only seen Sophy when she wanted somebody to look after Rose.

'Poor little Rose,' wept Hetty. 'How frightened she must be. I must collect her at once.'

*   *   *

Within a month of her arrival, Rose had the entire household running in rings around her. She was an enchantingly pretty child, delicate and graceful, with golden curls and dancing hazel eyes. Sarah felt large and clumsy beside her. She knew it was wrong to be jealous of a newly motherless five-year-old child, but she couldn't help it. Worst of all, she had to share a room with Rose.

In no time at all, Rose's toys were all over the room and her clothes took up more than half the space. Sarah knew she wasn't being fair, but it felt as if Rose, who was legitimate, had rights that she, Sarah, did not have.

Rose also wanted to play with the toy theatre, which held pride of place, together with her mother's rag doll, amongst Sarah's possessions. Sarah tried to hide it, but in vain.

Rose first sobbed gently and then, when that didn't work, broke into loud noisy wails and ran to Aunt Hetty.

'Aren't you being unkind, dear?' said Miss Webster. 'You don't play with it any more, surely?'

Reluctantly, Sarah took it down from its place on the top of the wardrobe. Half an hour later, the curtains torn off their wires, Princess Eglantine's wand broken and the Green Knight's right arm lost, Rose got bored and, leaving the pieces all over the floor, ran down to the kitchen to coax a sugar plum or two from Leah.

Sarah raged downstairs and brandished the broken Green Knight at a startled Hetty. 'Just look what she's done!' she cried. 'It'll never be the same. Never!' She burst into a storm of angry tears.

'Oh dear, dear!' It had been many years since Sarah had lost her temper. Hetty realized that, in her anxiety to make the orphaned Rose welcome, she had forgotten that Sarah might feel threatened by her great-niece's arrival. 'Now, Sarah, don't take on so. It was naughty of Rose, but she's very little and she doesn't understand. Put it away, dear, and I'll explain to her that she must not play with it again.'

Sarah controlled herself. 'Thank you, Aunt Hetty.'

Mr Copperstone made Rose a hobby horse

and his wife pressed sixpences into her hands for sweets. Miss Valloton ran up little dresses with exquisitely smocked bodices. Even Aunt Hetty, who did her best to instil some notions of propriety into her great-niece, allowed herself to smile at some impertinence, even while she scolded.

Sarah, who felt bitterly resentful at having to share her room, could not help being touched when Rose, her first night in Myddleton Square, crept into Sarah's bed and clasped her arms round Sarah's warm body and whispered, 'Will my mama come back again?'

Sarah turned and put an arm round her. 'Your mother is in Heaven.'

Rose hiccuped once or twice and then sobbed, 'I don't want mama to be in Heaven, I want her here.'

Sarah held her. 'My mama is in Heaven, too,' she said sadly, but Rose didn't hear her for tears.

After that, whenever Rose was at her most infuriating, Sarah could be pacified by a sudden wistful look, even though she came to suspect that Rose turned it on at will.

*   *   *

March 1843 was windy and wet and, as the flagstones to the Fulmar family vault in the side chapel of St Mark's were lifted, cold,

40

damp air engulfed the mourners. Chill gusts made the candles in their sconces on the walls, flare into long, flickering points. Jack Midwinter, glad of his heavy greatcoat, stared sombrely at the coffin which contained the mortal remains of his one-time friend, Charles Fulmar.

He had not seen much of Charlie in the intervening years. Now the poor fool was dead. Inevitable, thought Jack, the way of life he led. Charlie had never gone back to Oxford. He'd married young, hoping thereby to get some independence, but in vain. Lord Fulmar chose him a bride for her child-bearing hips and substantial dowry and refused to allow Charlie to set up his own home. No, he and the honourable Mrs Charles Fulmar were to live in a wing of Hoop Hall. Lord Fulmar did not trust his only remaining son out of his sight.

Charlie's bid for freedom had been for nothing. Lord Fulmar dined with the happy couple twice a week and organized Charlie's day, so far as he was able. Jack only saw his friend occasionally, when he came into Hertfordshire to visit his mother.

'Why doesn't he just bed my wife himself?' Charlie said bitterly, the last time Jack had seen him. 'He doesn't trust me to do anything properly.'

Any hope of Charlie and his wife finding their own way to married happiness was doomed from the start. There was nothing wrong with Charlie's wife. She was a little homely, to be sure, but Charlie, after all his drinking, was no Adonis himself. He had become puffy and corpulent, with a permanently flushed face.

'She's my father's dupe,' he told Jack, resentfully. 'Does everything he says.'

'She's only trying to make things easier,' suggested Jack, shifting uncomfortably. He'd never felt easy discussing emotional difficulties. In his own life, whenever a woman became what he called 'a problem', he left.

'Not she! No, she's always on at me to stop drinking. Damn it, what else is a man to do in this benighted place?'

'You have your son,' Jack reminded him. The evening was becoming a bore, he decided. He'd make some excuse and leave early.

'Pox on him.' Charlie turned and spat into the fireplace. 'James is a milksop.'

James Fulmar was rising five, a timid little boy, who was scared of his father. And who could blame him? Charlie only ever shouted at his son.

'You sound just like Lord Fulmar.'

'Like my father!' Angry colour surged up over Charlie's face. 'You'll apologize for that!' He tried to rise, fell off the chair and crashed heavily.

Jack yanked him off the floor and pushed him back onto the chair. 'Don't be a fool.'

'Like my father,' Charlie repeated,

stupefied.

'Your father's a bully, and so are you.' Jack stood up. He hated seeing Charlie like this, so pathetic and self-pitying.

Jack thought of this as two men lifted up the coffin and slid it, with a certain amount of grunting, onto its shelf next to the body of his younger brother. He had the sudden incongruous thought that somebody should have put a bottle of brandy, something warming, into the coffin with Charlie.

The vicar said a few more prayers, somewhat hastily, for the cold in the vault was intense, and the service was over.

Jack went to offer his condolences to Lord Fulmar.

'Close the vault,' barked Lord Fulmar. He ignored Jack and the other few mourners and stumped off down the aisle. His hair was white now, but otherwise he was unchanged from the stern man who had tried to intimidate Miss Webster and Sarah in the library at Hoop Hall. He was suffering from a sense of burning resentment.

Charlie had been a difficult, wilful child all along, unlike Arthur, who'd been a reckless scamp, but somebody that Lord Fulmar could understand. Now both his sons were dead. All he had left was the boy, James. Useless. Frightened of everything. He'd have to make do with him, though. Try and toughen him up a bit. At James's age, he had been out with his catapult killing sparrows, not hysterical over a few drowned kittens.

Jack didn't bother to follow Lord Fulmar. What could he have said, anyway? That Charlie had turned out the way he had, could be laid firmly at Lord Fulmar's door. All the same, perhaps he should go over and see James, in a day or so. The child was his godson, after all.

Back at Holly Park, the Midwinter family seat, Jack found the London post had arrived. There was a violet-scented letter awaiting him from Clara, the bit of muslin who was taking up a good deal of his attention just now. Sir George Cranborne was planning a masked ridotto, she wrote. Would Mr Midwinter care to accompany her? Cranborne's parties were not for the prudish. There was generally an outrageous theme—one year it had been The Roses of Heliogabalus, where the girls had been covered in rose petals and little else.

Could be amusing, thought Jack. Clara wouldn't have asked him if she did not mean to give him the answer he wanted. She'd had him on a string for long enough.

Mrs Midwinter was not pleased that Jack was preparing to leave so soon. 'I've hardly spoken to you,' she complained. 'You haven't told me whether you went to the Leominsters' dance. I gather Miss Leominster is one of the belles of the season.' She paused hopefully.

Jack sighed. 'No, Mama, I didn't go. I don't

44

care for those sort of squeezes.'

'But Jack, how will you ever meet some nice girl, if you never go to dances? You know, it was your father's dearest wish that you would settle down at Holly Park with some suitable girl.'

Jack sighed again. He knew well enough what was expected of him. The trouble was that he was not interested in some strait-laced debutante, who was anxious to secure a husband. He far preferred the life of a man about town with plenty of money, no commitments and the company of women whose virtue was more elastic.

'I'm sorry, Mama,' he said. 'I have engagements in London. I shall leave early tomorrow.'

Mrs Midwinter knew when it was useless to persist. She said nothing more.

The following day Jack was back in London. He only remembered James a couple of weeks later. I'm a selfish bastard, he thought, remorsefully. He'd forgotten about the child because he'd been so anxious to bed Clara. He should have stayed at Holly Park and done his duty.

He sent James a clockwork soldier, which beat a drum when it was wound up, and was touched when James wrote, in wobbly letters, to thank him.

A few months later, James caught scarlet fever from the gamekeeper's son and died.

Jack, who was spending a few days at Holly Park, going over estate business with his agent, decided that he could not bear to go to the funeral and see the small coffin placed on the cold ledge next to Charlie's. He made his excuses.

'Poor Mrs Fulmar is distraught,' said Mrs Midwinter to her son at breakfast. 'But Lord Fulmar will allow no visitors.'

'He's a brute,' said Jack. 'I heard in the village that he's dismissed the gamekeeper. Poor Ulthorne has to be out of the cottage by the end of the week. He lost a son, too. And I hear another child of his has scarlet fever as well.'

'Jack, couldn't you go and see Lord Fulmar about Ulthorne? He's a good man. It is not his fault his family has scarlet fever.'

Jack shook his head. 'It would do no good. I've asked Ulthorne to come and see me. I daresay I can find some work for him, if he doesn't mind being under Cotham. He could have Sam's old cottage.'

What Jack did not say, because he did not want to upset his mother, was that Lord Fulmar would not take kindly to interference from one whom he regarded a little better than an upstart tradesman, however wealthy. Lord Fulmar's attitude towards Jack's mill-owning grandfather had never worried him, but it would distress his mother if she knew of it. Fortunately, Mrs Midwinter and Lord

Fulmar rarely met.

'Poor James was the last of the Fulmars,' said Mrs Midwinter. 'I wonder what will happen now?' She paused and added significantly, 'It is sad when a great estate has to pass out of the family because there is no heir.'

Jack drained his cup of coffee and rose. 'Time I was off,' he said. 'Don't expect me back for luncheon, Mama.' He left the room.

Mrs Midwinter sighed.

*   *   *

That same year, Sarah was seventeen. She had just left school and was doing her best to help with the running of the house. Her heart wasn't really in it, though. What she really wanted to do was to help Miss Valloton and learn how to be a dressmaker. Eventually, Miss Valloton gave in to Sarah's pleas. One morning, she went downstairs and tapped at Miss Webster's door to beg for the favour for a few words with her.

'I am getting old and I want to pass on my knowledge. My mother, you know, was trained by Rose Bertin herself!' she finished.

Miss Webster's first reaction was to be affronted. The fact that the dressmaker of the ill-fated and extravagant queen, Marie Antoinette, had trained Miss Valloton's mother, was no recommendation in her view.

A niece of hers to become a dressmaker—
even a superior one! The usual apprenticeship
was gruelling; long hours, back-breaking
conditions, and then what? Most dressmakers
eked out a living on an absolute pittance. It
was certainly not what she wanted for Sarah.

'I shall talk to Sarah,' she said, with an
attempt at graciousness. 'Thank you, Miss
Valloton.'

She was surprised to find Sarah enthusiastic.

'It wouldn't be drudgery, Aunt Hetty. I'd
still live here and go up to Miss Valloton
during the day. I think it is something I'd be
good at.'

'Sarah,' said Miss Webster firmly, 'you've
had a good education. I have a bit of money
put by for you, enough to stop you starving at
any rate. I want you to get married. What
respectable man is going to want to marry a
dressmaker?'

Sarah twisted her hands, awkwardly. 'I
shan't get married. I'm far too big and tall.
Who would have me?' She didn't add, and I
am illegitimate. I was not wanted. But it lay
there, at the back of her mind.

'Nonsense,' said Miss Webster. 'You still
have a little puppy fat, that is all. You're a very
well-looking girl. But you shall do as you wish.
Dressmaking is a useful skill, at any rate. One
never knows how life will turn out.'

The next few years were busy ones for
Sarah. She learned how best to disguise one

lady's flat bust and make another look thinner, or taller, or shorter, and which materials were best for what.

'It's all in the cut, Sarah,' explained Miss Valloton. 'That, and the materials. Always buy the best you can afford.'

Soon she was looking at Sarah's own sketches. Sarah's childhood experience of dressing her cut-out theatre puppets, had stayed with her. Her designs were extraordinarily theatrical. They would be wonderful for a masquerade, thought Miss Valloton. She wasn't sure that they would do for everyday life.

'Good, *ma chère*, but don't overload it. I know the fashion is for brighter colours and more flounces, but a large girl like you should beware of them. Too many frills will only serve to make you look like a tea-cosy.'

'Yes, Miss Valloton,' said Sarah, crushed.

Miss Valloton patted her arm. 'You are a very striking girl, and you may best show it off by the quality of the material and the cut. Plain, simple colours, Sarah. Remember that.'

'I'd rather be pretty, like Rose,' said Sarah wistfully.

'Ah, Rose,' said Miss Valloton. She saw problems ahead there. A girl who flirted with messenger boys at six, would be quite a handful at sixteen. She wondered if Miss Webster would be able to cope.

49

Ever since she could remember, Rose Frampton had led a double life. It had started when she was about seven years old. She had begged for dancing lessons and eventually Miss Webster had given in, simply in order to keep Rose quiet. What Rose had never told her great-aunt, or even Sarah, was that the dancing teacher, who came once a week to the little school she attended was a Miss Toller and in private life, the wife of Alfred Frampton, Rose's much-loved uncle.

Rose had recognized her Aunt Bessy instantly, but it wasn't until after that first dancing class, that Miss Toller had said anything to her.

'Rosie, love. So you recognized your Aunt Bessy, did you?' Mrs Frampton, née Toller, was a jolly, well-covered woman, surprisingly light on her feet. 'Oh, your poor ma. How I cried. And your Uncle Alfred, too. He was that fond of her.'

Rose's hazel eyes filled with tears.

'There, there, love. I shouldn't have spoken.' She dabbed at her eyes with a large handkerchief and then mopped Rose's tears as well. 'How are you getting on with Miss Webster, then?'

'She's very kind,' said Rose mournfully. 'But, oh, Aunt Bessy, it's all so quiet!' Life with her parents had been full of noise. Her father enjoyed drinking, her mother liked parties. There were terrible quarrels, which Rose had hated, but also lots of people around who spoilt her and made much of her.

Miss Toller made a wry face. She'd heard from Sophy Frampton of Miss Webster's respectability. She liked a bit of fun herself. Her Alfred worked at Sadler's Wells as dance designer and teacher and there were always folks round at their house in Penton Street.

'I wanted you to come to us, after your ma died,' she said. 'But Alfred said you was too young. We live such a gadabout life, it wouldn't be right for a child.'

'I'd love a gadabout life,' said Rose wistfully.

'Never mind, love,' said Miss Toller. 'I'll tell Uncle Alfred I've met you and perhaps you can come to tea sometimes.'

'You won't tell Aunt Hetty, will you?' Rose begged. Her lower lip began to tremble. 'She called my mother "the flibbertigibbet", Polly says. I don't know what that is, Aunt Bessy, but I don't like my ma being called names. Please don't tell her.'

'I'll ask your uncle,' said Aunt Bessy. 'Now, off you go, Rose. Miss Webster's a good woman, so mind you do as she says.'

Rose made a face.

In the end, neither the Framptons nor Rose said anything to Hetty. Alfred Frampton thought highly of himself as an artist and didn't relish being looked down on by Miss

Webster. His wife loved Rose as the daughter she had never had. She didn't want to lose touch with her. Somehow, things were allowed to slide. If Bessy didn't altogether believe Rose's accounts of the strictness of Myddleton Square, she had no objection to undermining Hetty's authority a bit. She had met Miss Webster once, and found her starchy in her notions: she would never allow Rose to come visiting.

In this she wronged Hetty, who would have felt it her duty to see that Rose kept in touch with her father's family, whatever her private feelings might have been.

By the time she was sixteen, Rose Frampton had very definite ideas about what she wanted from life. It did not include dull respectability at Myddelton Square.

She wanted pretty clothes, parties, a house in a good part of Town and marriage to a rich man, preferably a lord. The fact that indigent great-nieces of lodging-house keepers, however respectable, could not usually command such a lifestyle, did not worry her in the least.

Already, she was attracting numerous male admirers.

Hetty was at first amused and then alarmed at the number of young men who called and claimed acquaintance with Miss Frampton.

'Where does she meet them?' she asked Sarah. She had just seen off one admirer. 'My great-niece does not receive visitors who are unknown to the family.' The young man had raised an eyebrow in what Hetty thought was a most impertinent way and left, whistling.

Sarah didn't answer. She was fond of Rose—it was impossible not to like her—but she couldn't help thinking that, at twenty-five, nine years older than Rose, no young man had ever asked to see her. She felt a giantess beside Rose's fairy delicacy.

Sarah, at twenty-five, still saw herself as the overgrown girl she had been ten years earlier. In fact, she had slimmed down and the figure, which had so embarrassed her as an adolescent, was now pleasingly curvaceous, and her large golden-brown eyes looked out on the world with intelligence. She was tall, but after years on the backboard and nagged by both Miss Webster and Miss Valloton, she held herself well.

There were, in fact, a number of young men who saw her in church, who would have been delighted to have come calling, had they received any encouragement to do so. Sarah had never noticed them.

Rose, when questioned about her visitor, would only laugh. She didn't remember. She met so many people. Perhaps he was the brother of one of her friends at dancing class. She couldn't help it if boys wanted to see her, could she? She darted over to Miss Webster, who was looking anxious, and kissed her.

'Dear Aunt Hetty! Whoever he was, he was very rude to call in that way. You were quite right to snub him. Please, don't be cross with me! How could I help it?'

Hetty smiled uncertainly. 'I'm concerned for your reputation, Rose,' she said. She worried about Rose. Her school reports always spoke of inattention and complained of work ill-done. Rose had a butterfly mind, thought Hetty. Never stayed in the same place for more than a few minutes. 'You surely don't want to get the reputation of a fast girl?'

I wouldn't mind, if it got me what I want, thought Rose rebelliously. She was pretty certain who the caller was. Unknown to Miss Webster, Rose, with her Aunt Bessy's connivance, had skipped dancing class and gone with him to White Conduit House.

'You're only young once, love,' said Aunt Bessy. 'You go out and enjoy yourself. Just be sensible, mind.'

There had been nothing to worry about, thought Rose. Wine and cakes and a kiss or two. She'd left when he became too spoony.

*   *   *

1851 was to bring changes into their lives. It started well. Miss Valloton introduced Sarah to a friend of hers, a Miss Bailey, who designed and made the costumes at Sadler's Wells Theatre. Miss Bailey was a woman of

54

uncertain age who only lived for her work. She was small and dumpy, with greying hair, fastened out of the way in a bun, surprisingly nimble fingers, and bright blue eyes.

Her room, up a creaking wooden staircase, leading from the stage door to the various scenery workshops at the back, was whitewashed and Miss Bailey's table was directly underneath the window, so as to get the most light. There was a small fireplace in one corner. On the walls were Miss Bailey's sketches for the production she was currently working on, and there were rails of costumes in varying stages of completion and a dressmaker's dummy which held Katherine of Aragon's black velvet dress with gold embroidery, for the dream scene in *Henry VIII*.

Sarah took a deep breath in sheer delight. This was it: this was what she had been wanting to do all along. She knew her designs were too bold and startling for everyday, and she had always tried to tone them down for Miss Valloton. But here they fitted in. Hanging on a hook was Cardinal Wolsey's deep scarlet, almost crimson, robe in a wonderful rich velvet, with fur trimmings. She would love to design and make something like that.

She was quiet during the visit, but she was thinking hard. A few days later, she knocked at the stage door with a portfolio of sketches under her arm, and asked for Miss Bailey.

There was a small room, scarcely more than

a cubby hole, to the left of the stage door, and in it sat an irascible little man, with scrubby grey hair and fierce grey eyes under bushy eyebrows. An old, rough-haired dog, with one leg bandaged, lay on a rug in one corner. He lifted his head as Sarah asked her question and growled.

Mr Williams, known in the company as Pepper because of his uncertain temper, looked up from his newspaper and glared at her. 'Who are you?'

'Miss Beale,' said Sarah nervously. 'I came to see Miss Bailey last week.'

'Miss Bailey doesn't want anybody wasting her time.'

'I shan't waste it . . .' At that moment the dog stood up, tried to take a few steps and fell. 'Oh, your poor dog!' cried Sarah.

In spite of himself, Mr Williams was mollified. Most of the company called Spot, 'that moth-eaten cur' and worse. At least this Miss Beale was sympathetic.

'He cut his leg bad on some wire.'

'I'm so sorry.'

Spot, hearing a kindly voice, thumped his tail. Pepper Williams grunted. 'I can see he likes you. Go on then. You know where Miss Bailey is?'

'Yes, thank you.' Sarah ran upstairs before he could change his mind.

That evening Miss Webster was horrified to hear that her niece had been offered a job at

Sadler's Wells Theatre at twenty-five shillings a week. The fact that this was good money did not console her.

'A niece of mine to be working in the theatre!' she wailed. 'Oh, Sarah! How could you have done such a thing? I shall have to go down tomorrow and tell them that I cannot allow it.'

Sarah went and sat beside her and held her hand comfortingly. 'But Aunt Hetty, it's not as if I should be acting. I shall be working backstage. Nobody will see me. It is perfectly respectable. Only last week you were talking of how Mr Phelps has banished the rowdy element from the theatre. They do Shakespeare! Surely you cannot get more respectable than that?'

In fact, Sarah had been told by Mr Phelps, actor-manager of the theatre, that, if asked, she would be expected to do a walk-on part. He had taken one look at her shocked face and added, 'Everybody here does what is needed. Mr Williams, who I daresay you met at the stage door, prompts for us and acts old men—very well too, I might add.'

'But . . .' stammered Sarah, 'Mr Phelps, I really cannot act. I have no talent for it, I am sure.' She noticed that his eyes were almost colourless and this somehow made his stare more alarming.

Phelps smiled. 'There is no need to take on so,' he said kindly. 'You would not have to

57

speak, a walking-on part only. Maybe a lady-in-waiting, something of that order.'

Sarah said nothing of this to Miss Webster. She had told Mr Phelps that she really did not want to act and she hoped that would be the end of it. If she had to, perhaps she could hide at the back of the stage where nobody would notice her. Just the thought of being seen by hundreds of people made Sarah feel large and clumsy again.

All the same, the thought of working with Miss Bailey on the costumes filled her with a sort of heady delight. The first day she started work at Sadler's Wells, Sarah brought Spot a bone as a thanks-offering.

*   *   *

That, however, was to be the last pleasant thing to happen that year. Mr Copperstone died and his widow went to live with her eldest son and his family. The pleasant little household, which had always been part of Sarah's life, began to disappear. Then, shortly after visiting the Crystal Palace with Sarah and Rose one Saturday afternoon, Miss Webster herself fell seriously ill. Rose at once insisted on leaving school and nursing her. Miss Valloton left her dresses unmade and took her turn. Every day for a week, Sarah went to work with a heavy and anxious heart, and often came back for half an hour or so during her lunch break to see how her aunt was.

Hetty was seventy-six. It was a good age, but Sarah didn't want to lose her just yet. Surely, she would pull through? Her aunt had always been strong. In fact, apart from the dreadful winter when Sarah was nine, she never remembered Aunt Hetty having anything worse than a cold.

What would they do without her? Who else had any influence over Rose? Who would run the household and find some respectable lodgers to replace the Copperstones? Sarah did not want to leave her job to become housekeeper and she doubted whether Rose would be either willing or able to take on such a task.

'I'm not worried about you, Sarah,' whispered Miss Webster, one night when they were alone. 'You are a sensible girl. I'm proud of you.'

Sarah's eyes filled with tears. She took hold of Miss Webster's thin hand. 'Thank you, Aunt Hetty. I know what I owe to you.'

'You don't owe me anything.' The voice was so low that Sarah had to bend to catch it. 'Your coming was a blessing for me. A real blessing.' The hand pulled gently at Sarah's.

'Yes, Aunt?'

'Sarah, go to the dressing-table and fetch me a small packet of letters wrapped up in red ribbon.'

Puzzled, Sarah did so.

'They are the letters from my dear Frederick who was killed at Cape St Vincent.' Hetty took them in her worn hands and kissed them gently. 'When I'm gone, Sarah, you're to burn them. They are not for other eyes.'

'I promise, Aunt Hetty.'

'And Rose, Sarah, try and see she's all right. She's not steady.'

'I'll do my best.' All that Rose will let me, she thought.

Hetty died peacefully in her sleep with Rose and Sarah by her side the following evening. Rose at once burst into a storm of weeping and Sarah quietly drew down the blinds.

*   *   *

There was nothing, Sarah realized, more exhausting than grief. She wrote at once to Mr Phelps, who gave her a week's leave of absence, organized the funeral, got in touch with Miss Webster's attorney, Mr Wood, and Miss Valloton helped her run up some black dresses for herself and Rose. She did all this as though she were an automaton.

'Time will make it easier, my dear Sarah,' said Miss Valloton.

'I hadn't realized there would be so much to do,' sighed Sarah. 'People to write to. Documents to sign. There seems to be no end to it all.'

Something must be done about Rose,

thought Miss Valloton. And quickly. She doubted whether Sarah had noticed, but Rose was absent much of the time.

'I have to go back to work next week,' went on Sarah. 'I've had no time to do anything about replacing the Copperstones, and I must.' It could wait a week or so, it was not pressing. Aunt Hetty had left Sarah and Rose £1,000 each, Rose's to be in trust until she was twenty-one. The house had been left to Sarah. There was some financial leeway. But all the same, if Sarah were to continue with letting out lodgings, then it were best to settle something soon. The Copperstones had brought in thirty-five shillings a week.

*   *   *

Rose had taken advantage of the upset surrounding her great-aunt's death to sneak out. She was going to tea with an actress she had met, and she was aware that it was a friendship of which everybody at Myddleton Square would disapprove. Amy Rush, as Rose suspected, was an actress only in name. True, she appeared on the London stage from time to time, mostly in burlesques—which allowed her to show off her magnificent legs—but she relied for her income on her male admirers.

Amy was discreet about what favours she allowed in return, but Rose was not deceived. Her rooms, just off Piccadilly, were far more

61

expensive than could have been afforded on a chorus girl's salary. There was a bedroom with a large four poster bed, a huge looking-glass, a number of expensive knick-knacks and a couple of prints on the walls which made Rose blush. The drawing-room was specially opulent, with swagged velvet curtains and a *chaise-longue*, whose width and comfort suggested amorous intrigue.

Amy had a maid, too, who slept in an attic room. At the back was a small dining-room. Any meals she wanted were brought in from the chop house round the corner.

'I'm not often here,' said Amy, enjoying Rose's admiration. 'Most evenings I'm out with my friends.'

She showed Rose round, then took her into the bedroom and allowed her to open the wardrobe and see the rows of gowns.

'Oh,' gasped Rose. She took out a yellow silk evening gown reverently and held it against herself and turned to look in the glass. The dress was cut tantalizingly low. 'It's beautiful!'

'Would you like to try it on?'

In a trice Rose was out of her dress and standing in stays and petticoats, her arms held out. She was of a slighter build than Amy and the dress hung a little loose, but the general effect was magnificent.

'I need to be fuller . . . you know . . . up here.' Rose tried to push up her breasts to make a more satisfactory show.

'You are charming just as you are!' An amused male voice spoke from the doorway.

Rose flushed pink and put her hand up to cover herself. She peered at him from under her lashes. This must be Amy's 'friend'. Lucky Amy! Tall, dark, disturbingly good-looking, and the expression in his hazel eyes gave her a flutter of excitement somewhere in the pit of her stomach. She stood like a naughty schoolgirl caught out in some misdemeanour.

Amy rustled over to be kissed. 'Jack, I wasn't expecting you. Have you come to tea?' She raised her eyebrows coquettishly.

'Won't you introduce me to your little friend?'

'Miss Frampton, Mr Midwinter,' said Amy ungraciously. Rose's expression was of a cat who has just spotted the cream, and Amy gave Jack a little push. 'Go away, Jack, for a minute or so, while Rose takes off my gown.'

She couldn't help suspecting that if she hadn't been there, Jack would have had no hesitation in helping Rose off with the gown— and probably everything else besides.

Jack looked from one to the other and laughed. 'Don't be long,' he said. 'I'll ring for tea. I hope you'll stay too, Miss Frampton.'

Amy bit her lip.

So her name's Rose, thought Jack, as he rang the bell. 'Tea please, Hannah. And get some cakes from Gunter's. Cream ones.' Rose looked scarcely more than a schoolgirl. He could just imagine her little pink tongue whisking up a dollop of cream. The idea set up a train of intriguing erotic possibilities.

*   *   *

Sarah had had a tiring first week back at Sadler's Wells. The season was drawing to a close. Over the summer the theatre would be let out. Mr Phelps was going on tour and the acting company dispersed. The key backstage staff stayed. The Fentons were hard at work on the scenery for the autumn schedule and Miss Bailey and Sarah were busy designing for the new shows.

Still, some things had been sorted out, like the problem of the Copperstones' vacant rooms. Mr Greenwood, the lessee of Sadler's Wells, had introduced her to the Johnstones, who were looking for rooms, and Sarah liked them both. In his youth, Mr Johnstone told her, he too had worked in theatre, though now he was in the tea business. It was a relief to have money coming in once more.

'Mrs Johnstone was telling me that when her son was a baby, he slept in one of the theatre hampers,' she told Miss Bailey. She remembered Aunt Hetty's story of her own first night at Myddleton Square, sleeping in a log basket.

'That's not unusual,' replied Miss Bailey. 'I

64

once knew an actress whose first role was as the infant Princess Elizabeth in *Henry VIII*. She was christened anew every performance!'

Sarah wondered what would have happened if her mother had found work in the theatre. Surely they would have accepted her there? 'What a childhood she must have had, always moving on, never a proper home.'

'You don't miss what you've never had,' said Miss Bailey. She shot Sarah a sharp look. Miss Valloton had dropped hints about Miss Beale's background. A foundling, she'd said, but Sarah had never said anything and Miss Bailey didn't want to pry. 'You would never be lonely, at any rate.'

'There is that,' said Sarah. One of the worst things for her poor mother must surely have been having nobody to turn to. Aunt Hetty had told her that the doctor's verdict was death by starvation and exposure. She swallowed hard and surreptitiously wiped her eyes.

Miss Bailey came over to look at Sarah's sketches for *Harlequin and the Yellow Dwarf*, which would be the 1851 Christmas pantomime. 'Yes, I like those. We need something really imaginative for the giant Grimgrumhumblebumble.'

Sarah giggled. 'What a name! Where does Mr Greenwood find them?'

'Oh, I think he spends most of the year thinking them up! And we must design a giant's costume worthy of his name. Don't

65

forget, this is mainly for children. It must be magical.'

'You're right about the magic,' said Sarah. 'When I was a child, Mr and Mrs Copperstone took me to the pantomime. I quite believed in it all. I remember having nightmares about a character called Sharktooth. I think he was a demon. I must have been about eight.'

'Good Heavens, did you?' cried Miss Bailey. 'I designed the costume for Sharktooth! It was in a little piece called *Jack Sprat*, I think, in '34.'

Sarah laughed. 'I can assure you that it was most effective. My poor aunt was up with me that night, soothing me with hot milk and honey.' She gestured to the sketches of *Harlequin and the Yellow Dwarf*. 'There's nothing like proximity for destroying the illusion.'

'But that's the glory of theatre,' said Miss Bailey seriously. 'It's the illusion, the magic. Just look at the world nowadays. Machines to do everything. Railway locomotives. I've heard they have invented sewing machines. It's all so mechanical.'

'You think we need illusion?'

'It gives the mind a holiday,' said Miss Bailey. 'Reality can be so . . . harsh.' She thought of her crabby old mother at home, always complaining about something. Miss Bailey was aware that she sewed her dreams into her costumes.

'Yes,' said Sarah. She thought of the drabness of her own position. Overgrown, plain, illegitimate. No wonder she loved designing clothes that fostered illusions. 'I wish Mr Phelps didn't want me to be in the pantomime,' she said. 'I'm so huge and awkward.'

'Nonsense!' Miss Bailey looked up, genuinely surprised. 'You're just right for the stage.'

Sarah shook her head.

'How is your sister coping with your aunt's death?' asked Miss Bailey, tactfully changing the subject.

'She's supposed to be helping Polly run the house.' Sarah frowned. When questioned, Rose was evasive. She seemed to have been out a lot, but Sarah could never quite pin down exactly where or with whom. She was too tired by the end of the day to pursue it as she knew she ought.

She could not have guessed that Miss Amy Rush, fearing that Jack might prove susceptible to her little friend, had just introduced Rose to young Lord Byland.

CHAPTER THREE

Lord Fulmar had decided to marry again. With his grandson's death he'd lost his last surviving heir, and he needed another son, preferably several. But, unaccountably, all his applications to the fathers of suitable ladies failed. Back in 1816, when he had married Lady Charlotte Wyld, he was a young man of thirty-three, good-looking, wealthy and a catch. Now he was an old man of over sixty, of uncertain temper and with a fearsome reputation in the county. Local opinion had it that he had driven Lady Charlotte to her early grave. If he were not directly responsible for his sons' deaths, then Arthur's recklessness and Charlie's drinking could surely be laid at his door, and his dismissal of poor Ulthorne after James Fulmar's death was widely condemned.

Poor Mrs Charles Fulmar remained at Hoop Hall. Lord Fulmar had control of her dowry and he liked to have her around to shout at. Once a year he grudgingly allowed her to visit one or other of her relations. In the summer of 1851 Mrs Fulmar left Hoop Hall on one such visit. She meant to visit the Great Exhibition in Hyde Park and perhaps buy some new clothes. She stayed with her sister Lady Rundell at her house in Berkeley Square.

'Oh my dear Jane,' confided Mrs Fulmar that first evening, when the sisters were sitting in Lady Rundell's boudoir. 'What a relief it is to be here.'

'Away from Lord Fulmar, you mean?' said Lady Rundell bluntly. She had only met His

Lordship on a few occasions, and found him quite odious. He was overbearing to a degree and, if it hadn't been for her fondness for her sister, Lady Rundell would have dropped his acquaintance.

'Such a difficult man,' confided Mrs Fulmar. 'If it weren't for the unfortunate settlement Papa made, I'd have left long ago.' Lord Fulmar had bullied Mrs Fulmar's father into placing all his daughter's dowry under Lord Fulmar's control.

'Papa was a mouse when it came to dealing with Lord Fulmar,' said Lady Rundell forthrightly. Thank God, Sir Richard, her husband, had been more accommodating. He knew his place in the scheme of things, which was to allow her to spend her own money and to leave their children to her superior management. Consequently, they were on the best of terms.

A notice was placed in *The Times* to the effect that Mrs Charles Fulmar was staying with her sister Lady Rundell in Berkeley Square, and a gratifying number of people called. If most of them wanted to hear if Lord Fulmar was really as impossible as rumour had it, at least Mrs Fulmar was invited to a number of dinners and theatres in return.

Jack Midwinter called as well. He didn't really want to; he'd always found Mrs Fulmar very dull. But, however selfish, he was not an ill-natured man, and Charlie had once been his

69

best friend. His current mistress was becoming tedious, so Jack was prepared to spend an afternoon escorting Mrs Fulmar and Lady Rundell to the Great Exhibition.

He had visited the exhibition several times earlier, twice with his uncle-by-marriage from Manchester, Josiah Pinks. They had both been interested in the Machinery Court—for Jack had not lost his youthful interest in how things worked. Josiah, the brother-in-law of Jack's father, still ran the family business in Manchester, in which Jack himself had shares.

'Tha shouldst come up North more often, lad,' said Josiah. 'I reckon as you've a good head for the business. It's a pity your father ever left.'

'His health wasn't up to it,' said Jack. 'But I'd like to come up, Uncle Jos.' It was true. Jack liked the energy of the place, the raw vitality.

'It's your ma as doesn't like it, I daresay,' said Josiah.

Jack made a face. 'She and my father struggled to get out. She can only see my interest as perverse. But sometimes, Uncle Jos, I tell you, I wish they'd never left Manchester.'

'Not cut out to be an idle gentleman, eh?'

'It's too damn easy, that's the trouble,' said Jack.

Josiah laughed and clapped him on the back. 'You're welcome any time, lad. You just send word.'

Jack took Mrs Fulmar and Lady Rundell to the Crystal Palace with a good grace. They would certainly not be interested in the Machinery Court, and he was amused to see that both ladies ignored Mr Hiram Powers' female nude statue of *A Greek Slave* and averted their gazes from *Andromeda Exposed to a Sea Monster*. Jack had no objection to looking at statues of naked women. Indeed, most of the statues were surrounded by groups of admiring men, but he doubted whether it could be called art. Instead, the ladies enjoyed Plouquet's 1,500 stuffed animals arranged as *'comical, humorous and interesting scenes in animal life.'* Here, stuffed kittens had tea-parties, and stuffed rabbits went to school and were chastised for inattention by a stuffed stoat.

Jack was thankful when both his guests had had enough and he could offer them tea and buns in one of Messrs Schweppes' Refreshment Rooms. He escorted them back to Berkeley Square, bowed gracefully over their hands and escaped.

That evening Lady Rundell said, 'What a good-looking man Mr Midwinter is, to be sure.'

'Not quite out of the top drawer, though,' said Mrs Fulmar. 'They say his grandfather was a grazier.'

'My dear, with looks like that—and his

71

wealth—it scarcely matters!'

'He's the despair of his poor mother. We are on visiting terms, and she often laments his single state—though, between you and me, I suspect she enjoys being mistress of Holly Park. That would cease if Mr Midwinter took a wife.' Mrs Fulmar added, 'He must be thirty-six at least, for he was a couple of years older than my poor husband, and there's no sign of him getting married.'

'He likes women, though, if rumour be true,' suggested Lady Rundell. She knew his name had been linked with a number of married ladies.

'Too much so, I fear. My dear, he has had scores of actresses in keeping—not that I ever mention that to his mother, but it's common knowledge.'

'Dreadful,' said Lady Rundell comfortably.

Mrs Fulmar returned to Hoop Hall at the beginning of August. Lord Fulmar so far unbent as to ask her if she'd enjoyed herself. He even seemed pleased to see her and remarked, 'You look well, Mrs Fulmar. Your holiday has done you good.'

By the following morning, though, things were back to normal. An unlucky observation by Mrs Fulmar on the glories of the Great Exhibition led to an explosion from His Lordship.

'Damned waste of money. Always said so.'

'Surely not, My Lord.' Her short holiday

72

had made Mrs Fulmar bold. 'Why, it is praised on every side. They call it the Crystal Palace, you know, and one can see why . . .'

'Crystal Palace, faugh!' exclaimed Lord Fulmar, beginning to snort with rage. 'It's that damned German, Albert's, fault. Good God, do we really want to see pieces of machinery, of all things? They'll be displaying housemaid's buckets and brooms next. I shouldn't be surprised if they have riots, as I hear they are allowing in every Tom, Dick and Harry. What will happen with all that glass about? Tell me that?'

'The crowds seemed very . . .' began Mrs Fulmar timidly.

'You are a woman, Mrs Fulmar,' stated Lord Fulmar with finality. 'Your opinion is of no value at all. I suggest that, if you have finished your breakfast, you retire to your sitting-room and amuse yourself with whatever trifles ladies like.'

When his daughter-in-law had gone, Lord Fulmar retreated to his library. He was feeling particularly put out because he had just received in the morning post a curt rebuff from the Earl of Ryedale, declining his offer for the hand of Lady Margaret. The Earl made it quite plain that his daughter could look far higher than a mere baron over forty years her senior, with an unsavoury reputation.

Automatically, Lord Fulmar's hand went to unlock the top right-hand drawer of his desk.

Inside it, tucked away at the back, was a worn piece of paper. *May his sons predecease him and may he have no lawful heirs*. The idea of that minx Maria Beale, a person of no importance whatsoever, whose seduction had beguiled away a tedious summer, having any power over his life was laughable.

He pushed the paper back into the drawer. The estate was not entailed. He could leave it to any one of a number of distant cousins. It was absurd to think that they would all predecease him. Mere superstition.

He wasn't in his dotage yet. He was sixty-eight. Many a man had fathered children at that age. Perhaps he would have to lower his sights a little and maybe a woman of less exalted social standing would be better. She would be grateful to him. It was always better to excite gratitude. Lady Margaret might expect him to dance attendance on her. No, he must find a woman who knew her duty and who would give him sons. He was not beaten yet.

*   *   *

Jack was sitting sprawled in a leather armchair in his rooms in Half Moon Street. Unlike most gentlemen, who took rooms for the season, or for a few months, Jack had his on a long lease. He had been there for twelve years or so. Apart from his valet, Archie, who had come south from Manchester with Jack's father, nobody else ever went there. His mistress had her own apartment, paid for by Jack. If he wanted to meet friends, he did so at his club, or in a nearby coffee house.

It was only in Half Moon Street that Jack felt he could be truly himself. There were no sporting prints on the walls, no notices from Tattersalls on forthcoming sales, none of the things one might expect to find in a bachelor gentleman's apartment. Instead, there were prints of machinery—a working design of an early railway locomotive, for example. A rare sixteenth-century German nef stood on the mantelpiece and there was a broken clock on a tray on the sideboard, its various cogs, wheels and springs beside it. Jack was mending it in his spare time.

Jack glanced again at his mother's letter. It appeared that Lord Fulmar was to remarry. Doubtless, what was at the back of his mother's mind was that if Lord Fulmar could do so, why not her son? *Rumour will have it that Lord Fulmar has at last found a second wife—Miss Fell is mentioned. Poor creature, if so. Her father is deep in debt, so it cannot be supposed that he would object, but Miss Fell must be forty years younger than His Lordship.*

Jack considered Miss Fell briefly. Plain, almost on the shelf, with very little dowry. It would probably be her only offer.

He laughed suddenly. It would be quite

ridiculous. He could just picture a gouty and furious Lord Fulmar stumping up the aisle and Miss Fell, with her long, pink nose, at the altar. The estate wasn't entailed. If he wanted an heir that badly, why didn't he adopt Sarah Beale?

He recalled that scene long ago, maybe ten, eleven years with himself concealed behind the box hedge and little Sarah, solemn-faced, with huge scared eyes, sitting rigid on the chair. Then the curse. He could still remember how the hairs had stood up on the back of his neck.

Later, he'd watched the child and the woman trudge back down the long drive and disappear.

Sarah Beale was undoubtedly Lord Fulmar's daughter by pretty Maria Beale. A bright, engaging child. He had enjoyed the confiding and chatty way she talked when they were in the pony trap. She would not have disgraced the family. But she had obviously been frightened by Lord Fulmar and Jack did not want to think about his part in that. She was only young; she'd have forgotten soon enough.

Jack did not believe in curses. So far as he could see, it was Lord Fulmar's bullying which had driven Charlie to drink and to his death, and Arthur's and James's deaths had been tragic accidents. If there were any curse on the family, it was Lord Fulmar himself.

He roused himself and rang the bell for his

76

valet. No point brooding on it. Jack did what he usually did and pushed away unpleasant thoughts.

'Yes, sir?' Archie glanced down at the letter on the table and recognized Mrs Midwinter's writing. She was a pleasant-enough lady, but he did wish she'd stop going on at his master about being a gentleman and asking when he was going to settle down. It only served to put his back up.

'Lay out my evening clothes. I'm going to the opera. And you can take a note round to Lady Hingston for me.' Lady Hingston had offered Jack a seat in her box any time he cared to use it. Jack was well aware that she had a *tendre* for him—as well as an elderly husband who spent much of the day dozing in his club. He would accept. If he ended up in Lady Hingston's bed it would serve as a warning to Amy, his current mistress, whose extravagance was becoming a bore, that he could amuse himself elsewhere.

*   *   *

The second half of 1851 was a bad time for Sarah. There had been Aunt Hetty's death and then, only a few weeks later, a second, completely unexpected blow. It was a Saturday. Sarah worked only until two o'clock. Once the season started at the end of August, there would be no such indulgence. It was a pleasant day, not too hot, and Sarah was looking forward to getting home and having her tea in peace and quiet. She arrived to find Miss Valloton wringing her hands on the doorstep and Leah, apron over her head, having hysterics in the hall.

'Oh, my dear Sarah!' cried Miss Valloton. She reached out to undo Sarah's bonnet and take her cloak.

'What is it?' Sarah was seriously alarmed.

Miss Valloton ushered her into the drawing-room, pushed her gently down onto the sofa and sat next to her.

'I'm afraid it's Rose.'

'Rose!' Sarah turned white. 'Has there been an accident?'

'No, no! Oh my dear Sarah! Rose has left! It was just after two this afternoon and a carriage drove up. Very fine it was, with a powdered footman. Everybody in the square was looking,' went on Miss Valloton despairingly. 'A carriage with its owner's arms emblazoned on the doors is not seen in Myddleton Square every day. Naturally, everybody rushed out.'

Sarah closed her eyes for one agonized moment. She guessed what was coming.

'Rose was obviously waiting, for she just opened the front door, ran down the steps and into the carriage. She didn't take so much as a bandbox with her!'

'She left no message?' Sarah was trying to

grapple with the news. Thank God Aunt Hetty was dead, she thought. Though perhaps, knowing Rose's mother's wanton ways, it might not have surprised her too much.

Miss Valloton reached into her pocket and produced a letter. 'This was in the hall.'

Sarah broke open the seal.

Dearest Sarah
Pray don't worry about me. I am quite all right and have gone with the best of men. I'll write when I'm settled. I am going to Paris and shall buy everything new. I'll bring you back some pretty thing. I couldn't have stayed any longer. It was all so flat and dull. I know what I'm doing.
Fondest love, Rose.

Sara read it and silently handed it to Miss Valloton. *I know what I'm doing*, thought Sarah. Poor girl. She cannot know, of course. How long does she think this new life of hers with its tawdry glamour will last? At one stroke, and in the most public way, she had cut herself off from respectable society. There would be no way back.

Miss Valloton opened her mouth to exclaim 'Like mother, like daughter', but remembered just in time what had happened to Sarah's own mother. From the look on Sarah's face, she was remembering that, too. Miss Valloton had come prepared to comfort, but Sarah's face

79

was stony. Perhaps some Gallic common sense was called for.

'Rose's mother always seemed to land on her feet,' she said at last. 'You probably don't remember but she was away sometimes for months . . .'

'I have not forgotten,' said Sarah dryly. Rose, a bewildered and wailing baby, had been dumped on them, and Sarah had had to share her room with her. 'It's plain that marriage is not on Rose's mind at all.' Perhaps better so, thought Sarah. At least she would not be betrayed by false promises as Sarah's own mother had been.

'We know she is not dead. That's some comfort,' said Miss Valloton, briskly. She rather admired Sarah's stoicism—so very English—in the face of social disaster. She saw that Sarah had regained some of her colour. 'Shall I ask Polly to bring you some tea and something to eat?'

'Thank you.' There was no point in starving herself. If only Rose had been more discreet in the manner of her going away, then they might have salvaged something of her reputation. As it was, no concealment was possible.

*   *   *

Over the next two years, Sarah heard occasionally from Rose. Some kid gloves arrived at Christmas, and later a warm pelissemantle with astrakhan trimming. Rose sent her address, a handsome set of rooms in Regent Street, and urged Sarah to visit, but Sarah did not do so.

She thanked Rose for her gifts and said that she thought it best if they didn't meet. Rose was to be assured that Sarah was there if she ever needed help. It was more than had been offered to her poor mother, she thought.

Perhaps Rose resented the tone, for she wrote back that she was there if Sarah ever needed any help and that she could look after herself very well, thank you.

The correspondence dwindled. Sarah always remembered Rose's birthday and sent her a present. Rose never remembered Sarah's but, from time to time, a few scrawled lines arrived.

*　　*　　*

By 1853 Sarah was well established at Sadler's Wells. Miss Bailey allowed her to do some of the costumes for the minor characters and Sarah had overcome her reserve far enough to be on good terms with the backstage staff. She particularly admired the Fenton brothers, who seemed to be multi-talented. Mr Frederick Fenton, the older and quieter brother, designed and painted the scenery, as well as being responsible for the lighting. His younger brother Charles was more extrovert and acted

81

as well as painting scenery. In the forthcoming season he would be Flute, the bellows-mender, in Mr Phelps's new production of *A Midsummer Night's Dream*. Both had theatre in their blood. Mr Frederick had started off as a page at Drury Lane and had also, in his time, written pantomimes. There was very little about the theatre that he didn't know.

The first two weeks of August at Sadler's Wells was chaotic. The theatre was being converted from candles and oil lamps, to gas lighting. The place was full of scaffolding, half the floorboards were up and there were planks missing, which made walking backstage particularly hazardous. Frederick Fenton, however, was in his element.

'I have something really spectacular in mind for *A Midsummer Night's Dream*,' he told Sarah. 'You can do so much more with gas lighting.'

'It smells awful,' said Sarah, 'particularly by the footlights.'

'Oh yes, chorus girls have been known to faint.' He did not seem too concerned. He spent most of his time, when not working on various models of the scenery, with the gas fitters. He had a number of original ideas to use the new medium to its fullest advantage.

Sarah could only admire his self-confidence.

It was Mr Fenton who helped Sarah to overcome her anxieties about appearing on stage. He taught her how to breathe properly,

82

how to move with confidence and how to stand more effectively.

'I am to be in *A Midsummer Night's Dream*—one of Hippolyta's attendants,' said Sarah with a grimace.

'You'll do very well,' Fenton assured her. 'I believe Miss Portman will be Hippolyta. She likes you. She complains that some of the others try to upstage her.'

'I shouldn't dare!' Sarah laughed.

It was a pity that Miss Beale disliked the thought of acting, thought Fenton. She had just the right sort of features for the stage— well defined and with large brown eyes. She had a good, clear speaking voice. Still, there were plenty of ladies wanting to be actresses, God knows, and all too few who could design costumes with Miss Beale's flair.

However, the new season was still a week away and there was much to be done. The air was full of sawdust and the upheaval had disturbed an army of mice. The theatre cat was working overtime and insisted on bringing his offerings to Miss Bailey. Every morning Sarah could expect to find a neat row of dead mice outside the small wardrobe room. Now, as well as the usual smells of candlewax and paraffin oil, there was the faint, sweet smell of gas.

Sarah was busy and content and she told herself that she wished for nothing more. For most of those who worked at Sadlers Wells, it seemed to be a way of life as much as a job.

Even the dour and grumpy 'Pepper' Williams, who prompted, was a really good Old Man on stage. Mr Williams, like the Fentons, had spent most of his life in the theatre, and had been assistant stage-manager at the Wells for years—long before Mr Phelps's time.

Sarah rather liked Pepper Williams. Ever since she had given his dog a bone on her first day working there, he had been grudgingly appreciative. When she had had a spot of bother with a young man who had seen her as Marian, in *The Lady of Lyons*, Mr Williams became a veritable dragon. Sarah had (most reluctantly) taken over the part from Miss Young, who had sprained her ankle. The part of Marian was tiny, and Sarah was not on stage for more than a few minutes, but this was enough to inflame the young man.

At his second attempt to waylay Sarah after the performance, Mr Williams cut in.

'Now that's enough, young man,' he said firmly. 'Miss Beale will thank you not to come a-bothering her.' Spot, leg fully recovered, took a step forward, growled and bared his teeth.

'Can't a fellow admire a girl, then?' cried the youth indignantly.

'Nothing to stop you admiring,' said Pepper. 'But I won't have you pestering. Now go home and cool off.'

'Thank you, Mr Williams,' said Sarah gratefully. The experience had confirmed her in her dislike of appearing on stage.

Financially, she could have stopped work. The £1,000 Miss Webster bequeathed her brought in fifty pounds a year and she could easily have supported herself on that and the income from the lodgings, as Miss Webster had done. She had thought, when she started at Sadler's Wells, that working there would satisfy her, and to a great extent it did. She enjoyed using her talents and learning her craft.

Then, too, she had the liking and respect of her colleagues, like Pepper Williams, and that counted for much. But somehow nothing could quite erase that painful feeling, which had been there ever since that trip to Hoop Hall, that she was an outsider, illegitimate and a foundling. She had a shameful secret which must be kept hidden.

She had just had her twenty-eighth birthday and life was passing her by.

'Why don't you ever talk to the young men in the theatre?' asked Miss Bailey. 'Mr Thorpe, now, he's a good, decent man. He admires you, I can see that.'

'And he's about a foot shorter than I am,' retorted Sarah.

'Nonsense. Maybe an inch or so. But what's that to say to anything? Don't you want to get married?'

'I'm married to my work—as you are, Miss Bailey.' Just keep out, she thought. I don't

85

want to talk about it.

Miss Bailey recognized a rebuff—even one so gently spoken. She sighed. 'I have my old mother to look after.' Mrs Bailey was a difficult old lady, quarrelsome and crotchety. Miss Bailey was on the shady side of fifty and had never been pretty. She had always known that her chances of marriage were very slim.

Sarah had never spoken to Miss Bailey of her parentage. What would any man, Mr Thorpe, for example, think if he knew the truth? She would have been a workhouse child if it hadn't been for Miss Webster's charity. She was a bastard. The very thought of telling her history to any man made her feel sick with shame.

Would she have felt differently if she had never visited Hoop Hall, she wondered, not for the first time. Before that journey, she had been a happy child, loved and cherished. After it, she had known at some deep level that she should never have been born. Even her own father didn't want her. Somehow, from the first moment she saw him, Sarah had never doubted that Lord Fulmar was her father. There was that portrait of that young girl in the hall who looked like her. She remembered Charlie, her half-brother, saying as she jumped down from the dog-cart, 'Come along, Sister Sarah,' and he had laughed at her and she had smiled back. He knows, she thought. I have a brother and he knows me.

But then it all went horribly wrong. Every time she remembered the bit in the library her mind shied away. All she could recall was her own fear and Lord Fulmar's humiliation of Aunt Hetty. For the man on the other side of the desk, Sarah herself simply did not exist. Worse, she felt that he would have stamped out her life as he had killed that butterfly and never given it a second's thought.

Afterwards, during the long, exhausting walk back to St Alban's neither Sarah nor Aunt Hetty spoke a word. Sarah glimpsed Charlie and his friend in the distance, but neither of them came near, not even to say good-bye.

Sometimes she thought about Jack. She did not remember his other name, perhaps she never knew it, but he was the only bright spot of that day. He was not part of the awfulness as Lord Fulmar and Charlie were. He was like a prince in a fairy-tale; tall, dark and handsome. And he'd talked to her as though he enjoyed it. Afterwards, when she was safely back home, she tried to draw him and failed. But those dark good looks stayed with her as her standard for what a man should look like.

She ignored Mr Thorpe's hopeful overtures.

*   *   *

Jack Midwinter was at Holly Park paying a visit to his mother and sorting out some estate business. He dealt with the estate efficiently but without much interest. He was fond of the place, it was his childhood home, but he had always had a sneaking suspicion that his interests might have been better served if they'd still been up in Manchester and he'd been allowed to have a share in running the cotton mill with Uncle Josiah Pinks. But there was no use repining. Jack had always known that his part was to become a gentleman. His parents had sent him to Eton and then Oxford, and encouraged his friendship with Charlie Fulmar with that in mind.

Not that Jack had any real objection. Some of the fellows at Eton had teased him for being a mill-owner's grandson, but Jack had ignored them. He would have an income of £7,000 a year; they were probably jealous. Most of his school-fellows were only too pleased to call him friend; he was rich, handsome and good company, and generous if a friend had overrun his allowance. No, Jack had no complaints about being a gentleman. Then, he could have any woman he wanted. When in bed, none of them had ever complained about his background—or anything else for that matter.

A day after he arrived at Holly Park the news came of the new Lady Fulmar's death in childbed only ten months after the marriage. Mrs Midwinter had heard rumours from her maid a day or so previously, but Lord Fulmar discouraged visitors and enquiries of any kind, so it was not confirmed until the morning after Jack's arrival.

Mrs Midwinter took the paper Jack handed to her and looked at the notice. 'Poor thing.' She put down *The Times* and sighed. 'Not much of a life. Rumour has it that he treated her most cruelly.'

'I wonder what will happen now?' Jack helped himself to some more coffee. 'No direct heirs and Fulmar's getting on. He must be seventy now.'

'They say his health's not good.' Mrs Midwinter spoke with a certain satisfaction. She was not a vindictive woman, but she couldn't help feeling that it served Lord Fulmar right. 'The family name will die with him.' She suppressed a sigh.

Not quite, thought Jack. Sarah Beale must be in her mid twenties by now. Married to some respectable tradesman, probably. Doubtless there were children. But he couldn't see Lord Fulmar welcoming a pack of tradesman's brats to Hoop Hall.

'Shall you go to the funeral?'

Jack grimaced. 'I suppose I'd better.' He didn't want to. He hated the thought of descending into the old dank vault and seeing the row of coffins, Arthur's, Charlie's, James's, and now Lady Fulmar and her baby's. Jack rarely did what he didn't want to do, but his mother was friends with the Fells, Lady Fulmar's family, and they at least would be offended if he were not present.

The service was as bad as he had feared. The parson was evidently terrified of Lord Fulmar and stumbled through the service. The Fells, Lady Fulmar's father and her two brothers, were standing stiffly to attention and ignored Lord Fulmar. Jack had heard that Mr Fell had threatened to horsewhip Lord Fulmar for his neglect of Lady Fulmar. Now, Fell was tapping his foot impatiently at the parson's fumblings. One of the brothers saw Jack out of the corner of his eye and nodded curtly.

They descended into the vault. Jack tried to think of something else: his latest mistress, a pert eighteen-year-old blonde, whose fresh young body he was currently enjoying. She would soon pall, like all the others. Delia's high round breasts would be succeeded by somebody else's dimpled bottom, then another's pretty lips. Jack couldn't remember the number of women he'd had. Still, at the moment it was Delia. He fleetingly acknowledged the decadent pleasure of thinking about her in so unsuitable a place.

He'd drop her a note to say that he'd be back a day or so later than he'd thought. She was not to go out. He wasn't having some other man sniffing around, at least not until he'd tired of her.

Eventually the committal was over. They came back up into the Fulmar side chapel. Lord Fulmar, Jack noticed, was looking grey and worn, but also furious. Mrs Midwinter had related that His Lordship had shouted at his wife for fainting in church. Doubtless, he was now thinking that her death was all her own fault.

Lord Fulmar shot a sharp look at Jack and crooked a beefy finger at him. Jack reluctantly went over and began to murmur his condolences.

'Never mind that now,' barked Lord Fulmar, cutting him short. The parson, who had just been about to embark on the closing prayers, stopped short in consternation. 'I want to talk to you afterwards. Come up to the house.' Lord Fulmar turned to the parson. 'Get on with it, man.'

Jack sat and switched his mind back to Delia's charms. She was eighteen and he was now thirty-eight, and part of her attraction was her youth. Jack enjoyed the fact that his mistresses were always young. He liked showing her off to his friends. He was the only man with so young and pretty a mistress, and made sure that that fact was noticed. He took her out to be seen; to the races, to Cremorne, and to any number of private parties among the *demi-monde*.

At last the service was over. The parson droned the final blessing and the few guests departed. Jack spoke briefly to the Fell party and then moved across to Lord Fulmar, who jerked his head in the direction of his barouche. Reluctantly, Jack climbed in.

The library at Hoop Hall was as it had always been. The day was chilly but no fire was lit. The servant lit a branch of candles and left.

'Sit down.'

Jack sat.

'You spend most of your time in London nowadays.' It was a statement rather than a question. 'I want you to do something for me.'

Jack frowned. Now what?

'Remember Maria Beale? You'd be about ten. Pretty, fair young thing. Came with the Cranbornes one summer. Some sort of cousin.'

'Ah, yes,' said Jack non-committally.

'She had a daughter. I want you to find her.'

'Why?' Jack asked bluntly.

Lord Fulmar was just about to blast him for his impertinence but, with an effort, shut his mouth. The man in front of him was quite capable of walking out. Instead, he reached into his desk drawer and handed Jack a letter.

'Read it.'

It was from a Miss Webster, dated 1826, and informed Lord Fulmar of the death of Maria Beale and said that the baby, named Sarah, was now residing with the writer. Miss Webster understood that Sarah was Lord Fulmar's daughter and did he wish to acknowledge her? She remained His Lordship's humble servant.

So, thought Jack, that time he'd met Sarah and Miss Webster wasn't the first knowledge Lord Fulmar had had of her.

'I threatened the female with a lawsuit if she ever attempted to lay the child to my charge.'

'But if she is yours . . . ?'

'Of course she's mine. But at the time I had two sons living. Naturally, I didn't want this bastard.'

'And now you do?' The contempt in Jack's voice was plain. What sort of man was it who wouldn't provide for his bastard? Good God, it would only have needed a few shillings a week.

Lord Fulmar made no attempt to justify himself.

'She'll be, what, twenty-eight by now. Probably married,' said Jack, looking at the date on the letter again.

'I want to know her situation. If she's married she may have a son I can adopt. If not, she must be made presentable and I'll find her a suitable husband. Mrs Fulmar can tell her how she should go on, polish her up a bit.'

'How do I go about finding this Sarah Beale? This address is from twenty-seven years ago.'

'That's up to you. Start with that address. Chalk up your expenses to me.'

'Suppose she's not interested?'

Lord Fulmar gave a harsh laugh. 'What? In her position? She'll jump at it.'

'I'll let you know,' Jack said shortly, putting the letter into his jacket pocket. He wondered whether Lord Fulmar remembered that curse and whether he was acting to negate its effects.

93

Or had he forgotten all about it? Lord Fulmar wasn't saying.

The barouche took him back to Holly Park. Part of him was resentful at being treated as Lord Fulmar's lackey, but another part was curious to see what young Sarah was like now. He was bound to be disappointed. She'd be a stolid matron, probably. Should he tell his mother? He had never mentioned Sarah's visit as a child, but if there were a possibility of Lord Fulmar adopting her, then his mother should be warned. At any rate, it would take her mind off trying to find him a wife or lamenting his lack of interest in living on the estate.

Unknown to him he was shortly to have other matters to deal with, for Delia had just met young Bertie Claremont.

*   *   *

Rose Frampton sat in her half-tester bed with its prettily swagged curtains and plucked at the silk coverlet. There was a looking-glass with a couple of upside-down gilt putti on top, which hung opposite the bed so that the occupants could see themselves. It reflected her discontented face. She'd been living with Lord Byland now for two years and the gloss had worn off.

She hadn't realized how much he was under his father's thumb. True, he had taken these rooms for her, and her allowance was generous, but he now spent less and less time there, sometimes only one night a week and she'd heard from at least three friends that he was about to marry some dull, well-bred girl he'd met at Almack's. And what would happen to her?

In an agony of anxiety, Rose set about finding out all she could. The debutante in question was the honourable Penelope Camden Hargeaves. What a mouthful. Her parents had taken a house in St James's Square for the season and Rose sneaked out to look at it. It was the sort of house she could never hope to enter, she thought resentfully— unless she did so as a parlour-maid. But she couldn't keep away. She wanted to see this creature who was preferred to herself. Eventually, by dint of bribing one of the footmen, she found out when Miss Camden Hargreaves would be going out.

And what did she see? A thin, brown stick, of no looks whatsoever but, if the footman were to be believed, with a dowry of £18,000.

Her friend Amy had said to her, when she'd first met Lord Byland, 'Get him to buy you an annuity. Then you'll have something when it finishes.'

Rose had taken no notice. Why get him to settle a couple of thousand pounds on her, which would only bring in a hundred pounds a year, when he was happy to spend four times

95

as much on herself without? Anyway, it seemed inconceivable that the affair would ever end. Now, she wished that she'd taken Amy's advice. Lord Byland could easily have come down with a hundred or so a year and scarcely have noticed the difference. Now, Miss Camden Hargreaves was in the offing and Rose could no longer ask him.

The rent of the rooms wasn't cheap, she knew. What would she do if Lord Byland gave her her congé? No doubt he'd see that she was all right for a few months, but he'd expect her to find herself another lover.

And who was there? Rose ran her mind over the possibilities. There was Mr Tamworth who kept giving her bottom sly squeezes whenever he could. He had fat little hands and just the thought of allowing him greater intimacies made her feel sick. There was Lord Maurice Walmsley, who had expressed an interest more than once, but he was notoriously mean and besides, she couldn't stand his braying laugh.

The only one who appealed was Jack Midwinter. She had been aware, ever since meeting him at Amy's two years ago, that he liked her. But Amy, she now realized, had seen the danger and manoeuvred her very neatly into Lord Byland's arms. She didn't blame Amy; she was entitled to do the best she could for herself. Soon after Rose and Lord Byland returned from Paris, Amy and Mr Midwinter parted company. Now, several mistresses later, he was with Delia Sharpe. Sharpe by name and sharp by nature, Rose thought. The one time Rose had tried to stir Mr Midwinter's interest, just a bit, Miss Sharpe had deliberately stuck a pin into her and whispered, 'You keep off. Understand?'

There had, however, been a rumour that Delia was seeing something of Bertie Claremont . . .

*   *   *

Jack got back to London on a cold, drizzly day, which exactly mirrored his emotions. The thought of traipsing around Clerkenwell trying to find this missing Beale woman, depressed him. It was too delicate a task for him simply to pass it over to his man of business. No, he would have to do it himself. Not for the first time, he damned Lord Fulmar, who had always treated him as a sort of superior upper servant. He would leave it for a day or so. He decided to go straight to Delia's rooms in New Bond Street. She would cheer him up. He instructed Archie to take his luggage on to Half Moon Street and said that he didn't know when he'd be back.

Archie sniffed, but made no comment. He was perfectly capable of telling Jack straight out what he thought—he hadn't known him since he was a baby for nothing. A day or two with Mrs Midwinter always made his master edgy and Archie couldn't blame him for going straight off to his piece of cherry-pie.

Jack allowed his mind to ponder on Delia's charms. Her body was always warm; even on the coldest night her toes radiated heat. Yes, he'd take her to bed and maybe later, when he'd rested, they'd go to the theatre.

The rooms Jack had taken for her were above a tobacconist's, and the entrance was to the left of the shop's bow-fronted window with its blue and white jars of tobacco and neat rows of pipes. He poked his head around the shop door. 'Miss Sharpe upstairs?'

The tobacconist's wife gave him a long look and then said, 'I believe so, Mr Midwinter.'

Jack's brows snapped together. Something was up. Half ashamed of his suspicions, he took out his key, quietly opened the front door and tiptoed upstairs. Delia was in. Alone. She greeted him, Jack thought, with surprising restraint. She didn't ask about the funeral. In fact, she seemed unconcerned about what he'd been doing. Even while Jack was telling her, her mind was obviously elsewhere.

Jack stopped his narration. 'Come on, Delia. What is it? Cross with me for staying away so long?'

Delia shrugged. 'Nothing.' She gave a bright smile and pulled herself together. 'If you must know I was thinking about Rose Frampton.'

'What about her?'

'Lord Byland has just announced his engagement to Miss Camden Hargreaves. Miss Frampton is at her wits' end.' She gave Jack a mocking smile. 'So she will be on the look-out. She has always fancied you, you know. You couldn't find a prettier girl. Lots of men will be putting in their bids, I daresay.'

Jack laughed. 'What's this, Delia? Has Rose put you on commission?'

Delia tossed her head. 'If you must know, I'm leaving you, Jack.'

There was a pause. Jack moved over to the sofa and sat down. 'May I ask why?'

'Oh, I don't know.' Delia began to fiddle with an ornament on the mantelpiece. 'It's been wonderful and we've had a lot of fun, but . . . But, Jack, I want somebody younger. Someone who wants to do all the silly things I do.'

She didn't see Jack's look of shock.

'Well, you're thirty-eight. You could be my father.'

'I see. And who's the lucky man?'

Delia turned to look at him. He was sitting relaxed, one arm along the back of the sofa, but there was something in his voice that made her feel uneasy. His face was, for once, expressionless.

'I'm not sure I shall tell you. You might . . .'

Jack gave a short laugh. 'Believe me, Delia, in spite of your comments on my advanced age, I have no notion of doing anything so antiquated as calling him out. I am simply curious.'

Delia bit her lip. 'It's Bertie Claremont.'

Claremont! That weedy youth! Jack was both incredulous and outraged. Why, the fellow was scarcely out of school. He'd just come into a fortune, though, and doubtless Delia would like that.

'Whatever you think, it's not his money,' snapped Delia, reading his mind. 'We enjoy each other's company. He's a dear boy and I love him.'

Jack rose and went to put on his coat and hat. 'I'll say good-bye then. I'll cancel your allowance as from the end of this month and you'll let me know when you'll be out of here?'

Delia nodded, relieved that he wasn't making a fuss, and gave an inward sigh of relief.

Jack walked back to his rooms in Half Moon Street and, in a few terse words, told Archie what had happened and sent him out to fetch a meal and a bottle of brandy from the nearest chop house. He had never felt so mortified. He went over to the looking-glass above the fireplace and scrutinized his reflection. No grey hairs. No receding hairline. There were slight lines round his eyes, but they were negligible. His handsome face stared back, mockingly.

Too old! No woman had ever called Jack's attractions into question before. Angry and incredulous he paced about the room. Was he really on the way to becoming like old Naseby, the club bore, with his anecdotes of amatory conquests which nobody believed? Jack remembered thinking on one such occasion, he really ought to shut up and recognize that he's no longer young. Recalling it now, he winced.

Jack only picked at the food but drank his way steadily through most of the bottle of brandy and had only the faintest recollection of Archie putting him to bed.

The following day found him with a pounding head and a dry mouth. What he needed was fresh air. Preferably somewhere where he would see nobody he knew. After some coffee and a slice of toast—whose crunching echoed through his brain in a most unpleasant manner—he set out northwards. He would go to the zoological gardens, he decided. He couldn't imagine that anybody he knew would be there.

Some forty minutes later he entered Regent's Park by York Gate, skirted round the Botanic Gardens and the Toxophilite Society butts and up towards the zoo. He paid his shilling and went in. There was nothing he particularly wanted to see, so he shook his head at the man selling bags of buns for the bears or elephants and moved instead towards the giraffe house, which at least looked quiet.

There were several benches in front of

the enclosure and Jack sat down and contemplated the giraffes. They reminded him of a couple of davits from the stern of a ship that he'd seen once in the Pool of London. The giraffes held their heads at a similar angle to nibble some leaves from a tree. There was a young giraffe with the two adults, which gambolled around on its ungainly legs. He sat for a while, admiring their elegant markings. The giraffes were content to be who they were, he thought. They didn't forever chase after the chimera of youth.

Jack bent his head on his hands. He could see his life stretching out into a dreary future, always the same. Some new eighteen year old, perhaps Rose Frampton, who had made her interest in him pretty clear, and then another and another. And maybe they would all feel the same—that he was too old. He would never be sure now, not after what Delia had said.

And what was the point? What was it all for? How much did he really enjoy the parties, the drink, another new mistress? Those boring rooms, with that inevitable plush, gilt, mirrors and *risqué* pictures.

Looking back, Jack could see years of self-indulgence. When somebody bored him, he moved on. He'd help out a friend financially, but real trouble, as with poor Charlie Fulmar, he passed by. He hadn't wanted to know.

He'd failed as a friend and he'd not been a

good godfather to young James Fulmar. If he'd done as he ought and taken the boy under his wing a bit, would James still be alive today?

What the devil was he doing with his life? He didn't seem to be able to make up his mind. He did neither what his mother would have preferred, to get married and settle down as a country gentleman—a perfectly reasonable wish on her part, he admitted, nor did he do what he wanted to do. Whatever that was. The trouble was that he had never had to think seriously about his future. It had all been handed to him on a plate.

Looking down at his hands—thirty-eight-year-old hands—Jack realized with a sense of shock, that he didn't like himself very much; that he was callous, selfish and self-indulgent. He wondered, suddenly, whether Maria Beale's curse had been extended to himself. He'd always known he was good-looking and maybe this, far from being a blessing as he'd always thought, allowed him not to grow up. A chance arrangement of features saw to it that he was indulged in all his whims, allowances were always made and he could evade responsibilities and never be called to account.

He had used his looks very much as Lord Fulmar had used his wealth and position. And he didn't like what he saw of the result.

He straightened up and looked again at the giraffes. There they were, strange creatures to be sure, but with their own beauty and content to be themselves. No, he thought, he would not go after Rose Frampton, as Delia so temptingly suggested. A spot of celibacy wouldn't hurt him. He would wind up his affair with Delia—and be generous. She had taught him something about himself, and he would learn to be grateful. Perhaps he should then return to Holly Park and do what his agent was always urging on him, take some personal interest in his tenants' concerns? But before that, he'd fulfil Lord Fulmar's request, and try and find Sarah Beale.

CHAPTER FOUR

The following day was a Saturday. Sarah's work at the theatre finished at two o'clock and she was able to get home early. She still had some sketches to finish for Oberon's attendants, but she could do those at home in peace and quiet. The wardrobe room was frantically busy just now with organizing costumes for the new season, and there were several extra seamstresses working in the large wardrobe room and needing constant supervision, so peace was at a premium.

She arrived home to find Polly in a state of high excitement.

'A gentleman called to see you, Miss Sarah! Ever so handsome he was.'

'A gentleman!' echoed Sarah, bewildered. She took off her bonnet, hung it on its peg, peered anxiously into the hall mirror and smoothed her hair. Polly helped to untie her cloak. 'Did he leave a name?'

Polly indicated the card on the hall table.

J.M. Midwinter, Esq.,

The name meant nothing. 'Did he say what he wanted?'

'No, Miss Sarah. He said he'd call again.'

'Very well.' Sarah dismissed the unknown caller from her mind and went to her room to change her shoes.

She worked on her sketches for a couple of hours, spreading them out on the drawing-room table by the window. At four o'clock Polly came in with the tea. Sarah had just poured herself a cup when she heard the door knocker and a few moments later a flustered Polly ushered a dark, good-looking gentleman upstairs to the drawing-room.

'Mr Midwinter, Miss Sarah.'

'Miss Beale?'

Sarah bowed. He looked somehow familiar, but she couldn't place him. 'Do sit down, sir.'

'Thank you.' An attractive woman, thought Jack. Well-spoken, too. Miss Webster had obviously taken her self-imposed responsibilities seriously. As Sarah seated herself, he looked around.

The fashion of the 1850s was for dark-patterned wallpaper, fat-buttoned armchairs and plenty of knick-knacks and tables to put them on. This room was different and Sarah noted that Mr Midwinter was taking a covert look around. Miss Webster had inherited a number of good pieces of furniture, relics of her family's better days, and Sarah saw Jack's eyebrows lift at the tallboy and an Italian marquetry table. The room was painted in a clear yellow and was remarkably free of clutter. The few pictures on the walls were eighteenth-century watercolours. Good ones too, thought Jack, who had an eye for such things.

She saw him glance curiously at her sketches by the window, but he said nothing.

'How may I help you, Mr Midwinter?'

Jack took out a folded piece of paper from an inside pocket and handed it to her. Sarah took one look, turned white, and scanned it briefly before handing it back. She felt as if somebody had ripped the court-plaster from a wound and left her exposed and bleeding. Desperately, she tried to hold her thoughts together.

'I have not seen this before,' she said at last. 'But, of course, I know about it.' And if her hands trembled, her voice did not.

She now recognized him.

Jack seemed to be nervous too, for he tugged at his collar before saying, 'I think it best to be straight, Miss Beale. Lord Fulmar is now without an heir. He has asked me to find you as his last living child.'

'What does he want?' asked Sarah coldly. 'I scarcely need bringing up now.'

'He intends to dower you suitably and find you a husband fitted to your new station.'

'What?' She rose jerkily and moved over to the window.

Jack, perforce, rose too. 'He is an old man, Miss Beale. He wishes his estate to stay in the family.' He could see from the tension in her back that she was struggling with some emotion. Excitement perhaps? Relief? The house they were in contained some surprisingly good pieces, but he had just offered her a fortune.

Sarah turned round. 'No, thank you.'

There was a pause. 'Is this the answer you want me to give Lord Fulmar?' He could scarcely believe he had heard correctly. Lord Fulmar was a most unpleasant man, but all the same, a Miss Beale, a nobody, to turn down such an offer? It was inconceivable.

Jack went across to her. He looked down at the table and appeared to be studying the costumes for Oberon's attendants. *A Midsummer Night's Dream. Sadler's Wells Theatre, 1853,* he read.

'I am not obliged to give Lord Fulmar any answer at all,' returned Sarah. 'If I had realized that that was what you wished to say, I'd have refused you the house.'

'Miss Beale, I don't think you understand.

Lord Fulmar is a very wealthy man. He is offering you a position befitting your birth and your new prospects.'

'Which I am refusing,' said Sarah steadily.

'But why?'

Sarah turned and faced him. They were standing quite close together and he could see the hostility in her eyes.

'I recognize you,' she said. She sounded contemptuous.

Jack took a step back. 'And I you.'

'I've thought a lot about that day. I was so excited when we set out. It was like an adventure for me. And then I met you and . . . Charlie, wasn't it? My half-brother. It was wonderful to think I'd found somebody who was family, who belonged to me. I thought you both the most magnificent young men I'd ever seen. And so kind to be giving Aunt Hetty and me a lift. It was like a fairy-tale to be whisked up to the house in that carriage.'

'Pony-cart.'

'But you weren't kind, after all, were you? You and Charlie were enjoying yourselves at our expense—I can see that now. You knew how we'd be greeted by Lord Fulmar.'

Jack swallowed. He felt suddenly mean and shabby. She was right. He'd known well enough. He remembered his pang of guilt on seeing her through the library window; a small, brave figure, sitting on that oak chair, her legs in white cotton socks and little black boots,

108

dangling.

'I'm sorry.' It sounded inadequate.

'I-I've read Lord Fulmar's letters to my mother,' went on Sarah, unheeding. 'They were found with her when she died of starvation and neglect. I have never read such cruel and unfeeling letters. He killed her, Mr Midwinter, as surely as if he'd cut her throat. He seduced and abandoned her without a trace of regret. If he'd given her so very little help, she would probably be alive today.

'It is Lord Fulmar's fault that I never knew my mother. And that is why I cannot accept anything from the man who was responsible for her death.'

Jack took a turn about the room. He wasn't used to such intensity of emotion and it unnerved him.

'Come, Miss Beale. Melodrama is all very well, but Lord Fulmar is your father.' He hadn't meant to sound so dismissive of her feelings.

Sarah's eyes flashed. How dared he! How dared he come with such a proposition and expect her to fall in with Lord Fulmar's wishes? It had simply never occurred to him that she had any rights in the matter at all.

'I do not acknowledge Lord Fulmar as my father,' she said with restraint. 'If you find that melodramatic, I am sorry. It does not change my mind.'

'But . . . but what message shall I take back

to Lord Fulmar?'

'Give whatever message you please,' said Sarah. 'I simply don't care.' She turned and resumed her seat. Her hands were trembling so much that she had to clasp them together.

Jack, feeling more of a fool than he had ever done in his life, had no option but to leave. She heard him go downstairs and then the front door slammed behind him. She unclasped her fingers, which were white with the pressure, and sank her head into her hands.

*　　　*　　　*

Lord Byland, horribly embarrassed, stood by the window of the rooms he had taken for Rose, and wished himself a thousand miles away. He had just announced his engagement to Miss Camden Hargreaves and Rose had burst into tears and begged him not to leave her.

'Come on, Rose,' he said, with an attempt at heartiness. 'What's there to weep about? We've had some jolly times, ain't we? At least I got you away from that old great-aunt of yours. Just as well she died when she did, eh?'

Rose's tears spilled over. Dear Aunt Hetty! For the first time in two years Rose thought tenderly of Myddleton Square and all she'd left behind.

'You ruined me!'

Lord Byland laughed. 'And you were eager for it, my dear. Why, you practically begged me! No, no, Rose, that won't fadge. It was good for both of us. M'father was anxious I should get some experience of women before I settled down, and you . . .'

'Your father wanted . . .' Rose looked up, appalled.

'Of course. I was a greenhorn. The governor gave me plenty of money and told me to find myself a pretty girl. "A clean, fresh one", he said. "Sow your wild oats". By gad, we did that, eh?' He looked at himself complacently in the glass. His father had even commended his choice. 'Like that filly of yours,' he'd said, when they were dining at White's.

Rose flushed with mortification. She had allowed herself to believe that it had been a sort of elopement, and all the time she'd been used as an instrument for Lord Byland to learn on. If the truth were known, he hadn't learnt much.

She opened her mouth to tell him so and then shut it again. She needed Byland just now. Let Miss Camden Hargreaves find out for herself just how selfish a lover her betrothed was. It would serve her right.

'Oh, we had a wonderful time,' she managed. 'You were so good.'

'You'll find somebody else,' said Lord Byland, pleased that it was going more easily.

'Not for a while.' Rose cast her eyes down.

'After you . . .' She dabbed at her eyes.

Lord Byland, flattered, moved across to pat her shoulder. 'You are not to worry, Rose. I'll see you're all right. The rooms are paid for until the end of August. I'll keep up your allowance—for a while at any rate.'

'Oh, Byland!' Rose hoped she sounded grateful. She noticed that he hadn't offered to pay for Lizzie.

When Lord Byland had gone, Rose looked round the room. How she'd relished it all only two years ago: her wardrobe full of gowns, her own maid, all the pin money she could spend. It had seemed like a fairy-tale. It now felt like a prison.

Aunt Hetty had run her household on just over two pounds and ten shillings a week; an income beyond most working men. Even senior clerks usually earned less. She, Rose, had got used to having about eight pounds a week, and her lodgings and maid paid for.

She never appeared in the same gown more than half-a-dozen times—and she thought herself economical when she made Lizzie change the trimmings to give some dress a new lease of life. She gambled a little, but was careful never to lose too much, and she drank only for company.

She must face it, shortly she wouldn't have eight pounds a week, or anything near it.

That evening she rang the bell for Lizzie. 'Lord Byland is keeping things as they are for the moment,' she said. She ignored Lizzie's look of scepticism. 'All the same, Lizzie, it's as well to be prepared.'

'I made enquiries about Mr Midwinter, as you asked, miss.' Lizzie was well aware that Rose had him marked as a possible future protector.

'And?'

'Miss Delia has left him for Mr Claremont. But Mr Midwinter hasn't been seen anywhere.'

'Has he left his rooms in Half Moon Street?' Rose was alarmed. Pray God he had not gone back to that estate of his.

'No, miss. But his valet says that he's not going out as he used to.' He's avoiding the likes of you, she might have said, but that wouldn't be tactful. Lizzie had done a bit of work on her own account. If Miss Frampton didn't find herself a new protector soon then she, Lizzie, would be out on her ear. She, too, was looking out for a new situation.

Furthermore, Lizzie knew some unwelcome news that Miss Frampton had not yet allowed herself to realize. Shortly, her mistress was going to be in a very tricky situation indeed.

*   *   *

Jack had decided to say nothing to his mother beyond the fact that Lord Fulmar had asked him to make a private enquiry. Time enough for explanations, he thought, when and if he found Sarah Beale. Mrs Midwinter had been most indignant that her son should have been treated 'like a messenger boy'.

'I know,' said Jack. He shrugged. 'But it's his way.'

Mrs Midwinter was silent. Lord Fulmar had never fully endorsed the Midwinters' claims to gentility. If only Jack would marry suitably! When Jack returned to Holly Park, she asked only, 'Was your enquiry after Miss Beale successful?'

'I'm not sure,' said Jack. 'I'll have to see what Lord Fulmar says.' Jack had received a peremptory summons from Hoop Hall—a curt note had arrived at breakfast. 'I'll take the gig, Mama, unless you want it?'

'Well,' barked Lord Fulmar. 'What did she say?' He had spent the morning pacing impatiently up and down. The clock had already struck half past eleven. Where the devil was the man? His visitor was shown straight into the library and Lord Fulmar wasted no time, not even pausing to offer Jack any refreshment.

Jack resented being treated like a lackey. 'She refused,' he said, abruptly.

His Lordship seemed to have some difficulty in breathing.

'She did what? Speak more intelligibly, man.'

'She refused,' repeated Jack. 'I told her very clearly that you wished to dower her and marry

114

her suitably as befitted your heir and she said no.'

'You must have muffed it. She can't have understood you.'

Jack's lips tightened but he said nothing. It was hot and airless in the library. The only sound was the angry buzz of a wasp that was crawling up one of the window panes.

'Did she give a reason?'

'She said that she regarded your behaviour towards her mother as directly responsible for her death and she wanted nothing to do with the man whom she sees as her mother's murderer.'

'Nonsense. The girl's mad.'

Jack didn't reply. He could see Sarah's face clearly in his mind; those striking eyes, her contempt. Whatever else she was, quixotic possibly, she was not mad.

'Well?'

'She has a point. Miss Maria Beale died of starvation and neglect.'

Lord Fulmar waved Maria aside as of no importance. 'I am her father. She owes me her duty.'

'She does not acknowledge it.' It crossed Jack's mind that Miss Beale had something of Lord Fulmar's own stubbornness.

'She must be made to acknowledge it. I should not have asked you. Might have guessed you'd make a mess of it. I shall write to the girl myself.'

'In that case, sir, I'll take my leave.' Jack rose.

'Not so hasty. Sit down, damn you. What sort of girl is she?'

'She looks more like Arthur than Charlie. Tall, good figure. She has a temper.' Much like yourself, he thought.

'Respectable?'

'Undoubtedly.'

'Well-spoken?'

'Yes.'

'She'll do. I'll write. I'll have the housekeeper make the south room ready for her.'

Lord Fulmar had come out of his temper. He smiled quite pleasantly at Jack and said, 'Thank 'ee, Jack. Daresay you couldn't help it. Always thought that ladies' man reputation of yours a bit overdone myself.' He nodded dismissal.

Jack was still seething as he climbed into his gig and drove himself back to Holly Park. Whatever his mother might feel about the importance of belonging to the gentry, in Jack's view Lord Fulmar's behaviour was not that of a gentleman. And that slur on his way with women rankled. Delia's parting words had left Jack feeling vulnerable.

When he now looked back on his relationships with women, they were all retrospectively coloured by this new, unwelcome, knowledge. Delia had been one of

116

a long list of women, Clara, Amy Rush, Delia, he had forgotten half their names. They were never around for very long. They were all very much the same, young, blonde and pretty. He had prided himself on treating them well while the connection lasted: expensive clothes, handsome rooms, a maid. He hired a barouche for them to ride in the park. He didn't stint them.

In return he expected them to be attentive to his wishes, be faithful, and pleasant, though not too pleasant, to his friends. When the time came to part, he was generous. No old flame, down on her luck, ever asked in vain for help.

Then there were the married women with whom he'd had affairs. Scores of them; women with husbands complaisant enough to look the other way, providing their wives were discreet. He avoided widows. He did not want to find himself trapped into marriage.

The Hertfordshire countryside bowled past, the trees heavy and green, but Jack scarcely noticed it.

For the first time he began to wonder whether this obsession with remaining single wasn't, in some way, an avoidance. Why hadn't he wanted to settle down? Most of his contemporaries were married now, with young families—though it was true that a number of them had mistresses as well.

He was greatly attracted to women, so why had he never found one he wanted to marry?

He loved their soft, rounded bodies—it was their messy, over-indulgent emotions he couldn't stand. One of his mistresses, Clara, always used to fly into petty rages. She changed her mind forty times a day. Her concentration span could be counted in minutes. She'd been only sixteen when he'd taken up with her and, at first, he found her wilfulness and irresponsibility charming. She was like a pretty little kitten. But it soon began to pall. He'd been first amused, then irritated, and finally, exasperated. When they parted after only eight months, he'd heaved a huge sigh of relief.

So why hadn't he learnt from that? Why was his next mistress a similarly empty-headed creature? Surely all women weren't like that? His mother wasn't, for example. Putting aside her maternal anxieties on his behalf, she was a sensible woman, who ran her household efficiently; charitable too, who did what she could to help those less fortunate than herself. Jack was aware that it hadn't always been very easy for her, coming from so different a background.

Nor could Miss Beale be thought of as empty-headed. From what he'd seen, she, too, ran her household well. Her work was obviously respected at Sadler's Wells and she had an undoubted talent for design. It was true that her attitude towards her good fortune had angered him but, on reflection, he could scarcely blame her.

What Lord Fulmar's reaction would be if Miss Beale persisted in her refusal to fall in with his wishes, he daren't think.

That afternoon, when Jack took tea with his mother in her pretty green and yellow drawing-room, he found himself telling her about Sarah Beale and his first meeting with her.

Mrs Midwinter was very shocked. 'Poor Maria Beale!' she exclaimed. 'I remember her, of course. She was a pretty girl, but a trifle forward. I could see that she had a *tendre* for Lord Fulmar—and he was a very good-looking man in those days—but I never dreamed that he would behave in so ungentlemanly a fashion. A guest in his own house!

'And she had a child by him! What a disgrace.'

'Sarah was a lovely little girl,' Jack found himself saying, defensively. 'I remember thinking how quick-witted she was. Charlie and I should never have been so thoughtless.'

'You could not have known that Lord Fulmar's reaction would be so violent.'

Jack shook his head. 'I might have guessed. I have felt badly about it.' After some hesitation, Jack told her about his recent meeting with Sarah and its aftermath.

'It sounds as if Miss Beale is well able to take care of herself,' Mrs Midwinter said repressively. She was not sure that she liked

119

the sound of this Miss Beale.

'She was certainly very emphatic. But I am concerned for her, Mama. Lord Fulmar is so intemperate when crossed. I'm worried about what he may do. Still, she may change her mind.'

'If one of Lord Fulmar's rages carried him off, the whole county would cheer,' observed Mrs Midwinter.

Jack laughed but said, 'Miss Beale ought to be warned. The problem is she took so against me, that I fear I would be forbidden the house.'

Did she indeed, thought Mrs Midwinter, affronted. Surely this lodging-keeper's niece was hardly a suitable person to become heiress to Hoop Hall, whatever her birth.

*   *   *

It took Sarah several days to recover from Jack's visit. She realized, with a sense of shock, that apart from Lord Fulmar, he was the only other living person to know about her visit to Hoop Hall, and one of the few people to know the truth about her parentage.

There was something else: ever since that visit to Hoop Hall, Jack's image had remained with her. He was the shining hero of her childhood, whose looks had charmed her and who had talked to her on the drive up to Hoop Hall as though she really mattered. He had enjoyed it, as she had. To realize that he had been indulging in a piece of mischief-making and was now at Lord Fulmar's beck and call, was a cruel disillusion.

Sarah had drawn on her memories of Jack many times in her work. He was the source of her costume designs for Theseus's attendants. She imagined them tall, dark and good-looking, as she remembered him, and had given them peacock blue and green Greek tunics to set off Theseus, who was to be dressed in gold. The Jack of her childhood would have looked wonderful in peacock blue or green.

She was, she realized, both angry at his treachery and bitterly disappointed. Looking at him, she could see that he was no longer the man of her childish dreams—if he ever had been. Now, his charm was calculated—she had not missed Polly's gratified smirk when he had smiled at her—and his attitude self-congratulatory. He obviously knew her story, so why had it not occurred to him that she might resent Lord Fulmar's sudden intrusion into her life? There had been a brief apology, but no sympathy with her viewpoint. Nothing.

She struggled to accept the alteration in her view of the past which Jack's coming had brought. She scarcely thought about Lord Fulmar's offer. It seemed, frankly, unbelievable. What on earth did she, Sarah Beale, brought up in the homely respectability of Myddleton Square, and working at Sadler's

Wells, have to do with Hoop Hall? She had no pleasant memories of the place, nor of Lord Fulmar.

One morning, about a week after Jack's visit, Sarah came in to breakfast to find a letter by her plate. She so rarely received any post, for the tradesman's monthly bills were delivered by hand, that she stared at it in some consternation. She was sitting at the head of the table she shared with the lodgers, and Miss Valloton and Mr and Mrs Johnstone were all looking at it, and at her, with undisguised interest.

Sarah turned the letter over. She did not recognize the seal, but the paper was heavy and of good quality, she noted. She slipped it into her pocket and turned her attention to her toast and coffee. She was sorry to disappoint everybody, but she preferred to keep her correspondence private. As soon as she could she excused herself and sped to Aunt Hetty's drawing-room.

The letter was short and to the point.

Lord Fulmar has instructed me to inform you that your presence is required immediately at Hoop Hall. His Lordship reminds you of your filial duty towards him. A cheque for the sum of fifty pounds is enclosed for your travel expenses.
Yours etc.
T. Foxton

122

Sarah read it through twice, the first time in disbelief, the second time in outrage. This was Mr Midwinter's doing, she felt sure. Doubtless he thought she could be bribed with fifty pounds. It was a large sum of money, as much as her aunt's legacy brought in in a year.

Her first thought was to send the cheque back with a curt note. She even crossed to her writing desk, but then stopped. No, it would be better if this came from a third party, a lawyer. She would go to Mr Wood, who had dealt with her aunt's Will. He was a man Miss Webster had trusted. She was sure he would keep her confidence.

She would return the fifty pounds and Mr Wood would frame her refusal so that there could be no possibility of Lord Fulmar misunderstanding.

*   *   *

'What shall I do?' whispered Rose. She had just finished retching into a bowl held by her maid, Lizzie, and her face was white and covered with sweat. 'Oh, Lizzie! What shall I do? And I was so careful.'

Lizzie straightened up and went to put the bowl on the wash stand. A sour smell filled the room. Miss Frampton with child, she thought, and Lord Byland newly engaged. He's not going to like this. Things were difficult enough as it was. Her mistress had been very weepy the last few weeks and Lizzie had seen how it irritated Lord Byland. Her being with child would look as though she were trying to trap him.

'Perhaps it was just something you ate, miss,' said Lizzie. 'You did say the fish tasted odd, last night.'

Rose shook her head. 'I'm five weeks late. You know that as well as I do.' She lay back against the pillows and mopped her face with a towel. 'Make me a cup of tea, Lizzie.'

The maid left the room. The moment Lizzie heard that Lord Byland was getting engaged, she knew that it was the end for him and Miss Frampton. He might mount a mistress later on, many gentlemen did, but not immediately after his marriage.

She was well aware that the days of her own job were numbered and had put out a few feelers elsewhere. Judy, Miss Amy Rush's maid, might be moving on soon. Lizzie had slipped Judy half a guinea and was hopeful that she'd be recommended. She had had to promise Judy another two guineas, but it would be worth it to be safely employed. She'd easily make that up in tips. Miss Rush knew what was what. She'd never let herself get caught this way.

Lizzie was sorry for Miss Frampton, of course she was, but a girl had to look out for herself.

Rose took a few cautious sips of tea. Her nausea was subsiding. She had to face it: she was pregnant. There was no point in hoping otherwise.

'I must get rid of it,' she said. 'Lizzie, do you . . . ?'

'No, miss.' Lizzie shuddered. A friend of hers had gone down that road and died in a pool of blood on the kitchen floor.

'Then I shall have to ask Miss Rush.' Amy, she felt, would be sure to know. 'Fetch me my writing desk, Lizzie. I'll ask her to come and see me.'

'I'll go round for you, miss, if you'd like,' offered Lizzie. 'Best not to put such things in writing.' She would rather Miss Frampton and Miss Rush didn't meet, not while things with Judy were at such a delicate stage. If she went round herself then she could demonstrate how devoted she was to her mistress's interests at the same time. It would do no harm for Miss Rush to see that she could be trusted. Whatever happened, Miss Frampton would be taking it quiet for a while and she, Lizzie, would be dismissed. She knew that Rose could not afford her wages once Lord Byland stopped paying them.

'Oh, thank you, Lizzie.' Tears of relief came into Rose's eyes.

The relief was short-lived. Miss Rush either could not or would not help. Lizzie softened the message when she passed it on, but Amy's reaction was unequivocal. 'Silly cow,' she said. 'No, I can't help her. I don't want the law on me, thank you very much. She'll have to tell Lord Byland. He won't like it, but he'll support her until she's had it. Then it can be farmed out.' It would probably die, she had added to Lizzie, most farmed-out babies did, and that would be the end of the problem. Perhaps it would teach Rose to be more careful in future.

Rose turned so white at Amy's message that Lizzie was seriously frightened. 'There, there, don't take on so, miss. Lord Byland ain't a bad man. He'll see you're all right. Here, 'ave a drop of brandy.'

Rose pushed the brandy away, pettishly. 'Go away, Lizzie. I just want to be alone.' Oh God, how had she ever got into this mess!

'You ain't thinking of doing nothing silly now, miss?'

Rose shook her head. She didn't have the courage. Besides, she felt too ill. 'I'll write to Lord Byland in the morning.'

When Lizzie had gone, Rose dragged on her dressing-gown and went to sit by the window. She would not write to Lord Byland unless she absolutely had to. She had been humiliated enough there. There must be another way. Amy, she hoped, would be discreet, but if Rose asked around any more then word would soon get out and she didn't want that. There were plenty of girls who would gloat at her downfall.

No, what she needed was a solution that got

126

rid of the baby and kept her out of circulation for a while, just until she recovered her nerve. It had not occurred to Rose before, but she realized that, while part of her enjoyed the easy living and the pretty clothes, another part of her resented the uncertainty and loss of consideration it brought. As Byland's mistress, she had to do whatever pleased him; be obliging and attentive at all times, and go gracefully at the end. Her own feelings didn't count. Maybe Aunt Hetty had been right after all. A good name was worth something—and she had lost it.

Rose put her head down on the window sill and sobbed bitterly.

It was some twenty minutes later that a thought struck her. She sat up, wiped her eyes again on the sleeve of her dressing-gown and blew her nose on her sodden handkerchief. The Framptons! Aunt Bessy and Uncle Alfred. Why hadn't she thought of them before? She had kept in touch with them in a desultory sort of way over the last two years. The last time she had seen Aunt Bessy was six months ago when they met by chance at the theatre.

Aunt Bessy had not seemed shocked. She had kissed Rose, admired her dress, chatted for a while and then said, 'Now you look after yourself, love.' There had been a smile and an anxious look, but no recriminations.

Yes, thought Rose, tomorrow she would go and see Aunt Bessy. Surely she would help her niece? If Uncle Alfred were still working at Sadler's Wells, perhaps he could find her a job there, just for a while? She was pretty and she could dance well. Of course, she wouldn't want to spend the rest of her life on an actress's wages, and she'd be lucky to get thirty shillings a week, but that added to what Lord Byland gave her would be all right for a while. If only she weren't with child.

She got back into bed and fell asleep almost immediately.

*　　　*　　　*

Jack ran up the steps to Sarah's house in Myddleton Square with surprising eagerness. He had handled it wrongly last time. He had assumed that Miss Beale would be willing to have a fortune thrust upon her. Most women would. Having spoken to his mother and thought it over, he could now see Miss Beale's point of view.

He did not know what Lord Fulmar would do, but he wouldn't put it past him to come to Myddleton Square himself and try to bully Miss Beale into doing what he wanted. Once at Hoop Hall, she would have no option but to go along with whatever Lord Fulmar had in mind. She should be warned.

He was looking forward to seeing her again. When he'd come out of his temper, he realized that he liked her openness and admired her

128

stance. She had been a frank and intelligent child and it pleased him that she had not changed.

He knocked and Polly came to the door. Jack gave her his card and said, 'I wonder if Miss Beale could spare me a few moments of her time? Tell her it's a matter of some importance.'

Polly looked at him doubtfully and turned the card over in her hands. 'I'll ask, sir. If you'll just wait a moment.' She closed the door on him.

Sarah was upstairs in the drawing-room and the window was open. Jack could hear Polly enter and then Sarah's voice came clearly through the open window, 'Drat the man. Why won't he leave me alone? Tell Mr Midwinter I'm not at home.'

A few moments later Polly came back down to the front door.

'It's all right,' said Jack, glancing up at the drawing-room window. 'I heard her.'

'I'm sorry, sir,' said Polly. 'Miss Beale has a deal on her mind just now.'

And could well have a lot more, thought Jack, as he went back down the steps. He could not leave it there. There must be some way he could see her, if only for a few moments.

*　　　*　　　*

The following morning Rose woke up with the usual nausea and with a dull ache somewhere in the small of her back. Her face felt pinched. She rang the bell for Lizzie and, the moment she came, gestured for the bowl.

When her sickness had passed and her maid had mopped her face, Rose said, 'Bring me my walking dress, Lizzie. I'm going out this morning. I'm not sure when I shall be back. You could be mending the tear in my silk petticoat while I'm away.'

'Yes, miss.'

Rose dressed slowly and carefully, put on her mantle and bonnet, and took her purse. 'Call me a cab, please.'

The cab had once been a gentleman's carriage which had seen better days. It was malodorous and uncomfortable and it jolted and lurched over the cobblestones as it wound up Pentonville Road towards Islington. Rose could hear the horse snorting and the cabbie cursing.

By the time they arrived at the Framptons' lodgings above a tobacconist's in Penton Street, Rose was feeling really ill. Dizzy and sick, she pulled out her purse, thrust the one shilling and sixpence fare at the cabbie, and stumbled out of the carriage. She barely made it to the pavement before nausea overtook her and she clung onto a tree in front of the tobacconist's and retched helplessly into the gutter.

It was there that Bessy Frampton found her. She had been looking out of her window and seen the cab draw up, but had not at first recognized her niece. Then Rose's bonnet fell back and Bessy caught a glimpse of fair hair. She ran down the stairs.

'Rose!' She took the situation in at a glance. 'Come inside, love. Careful now.' She put an arm around her and helped her gently up the stairs.

Twenty minutes later Rose was in Mrs Frampton's spare bed clutching a stone water bottle wrapped in a piece of cloth to her stomach. Her aunt was sitting by the bed with a steaming tisane.

'Sit up a minute, love. I want you to drink this. It will make you feel better.'

Rose pulled herself up. 'I don't want this baby,' she whispered.

'And by the looks of you, you won't be having it,' said Aunt Bessy. 'Your ma was just the same. You were the only child she brought to full term. She couldn't hold them.'

'What is it?' Rose sipped cautiously at the liquid.

'Raspberry leaf, pennyroyal, some others. There, now you go to sleep and stop worrying.'

Aunt Bessy was right. Rose started bleeding that evening. As soon as she realized, she burst into tears of relief. She could go home. Everything would be just as it was. But she knew it wouldn't be.

'You still look a bit peaky, love,' said Mrs Frampton, the next day. 'I've discussed it with your uncle and we think you should come and stay with us for a while. Uncle can see about getting you a job at the Wells, if that's what you would like.'

'Oh, Aunt Bessy!' wept Rose. What she wanted, she realized, was to be looked after for a while, not to have to be on show all the time. She would dismiss Lizzie, get what settlement she could out of Lord Byland, and have a rest.

*   *   *

Sadler's Wells was now two weeks into the new season and rehearsals for the new production of *A Midsummer Night's Dream* started on 9 September. This would be a major production and it was already being advertised as having *new scenery, dresses and decorations*. The gas pipes were now laid and the scaffolding had all gone. The smell of sawdust, paraffin oil and candlegrease was superseded by gas, overlaid by the smell of paint and size, for the Fenton brothers were hard at work on the flats and scenery for the *Dream*.

Sarah was glad to plunge herself into the new season and forget the worries of the last week or so. She went several times to the scenery workshop to admire the Fentons' work. Acts II, III and IV of the *Dream* were set mainly at night and Frederick Fenton had half-painted a midnight-blue sky with wisps of clouds and stars. A large orange moon would slowly rise throughout the midsummer's night.

'I like the moon being larger than you expect,' said Sarah, smiling at Mr Charles Fenton, who was busily painting feathery trees with mottled trunks on one of the flats. 'It has a sort of magical effect. As if fairyland is just that bit nearer than you think.'

Charles Fenton nodded. 'That's what my brother is after. Something that's not quite real. Have you heard about his net?'

Sarah shook her head.

'He's ordered a large roll of blue net—in fact he's gone up to Glasgow to collect it. It will hang in front of the whole stage for Acts II, III and IV.'

'Blue, though,' said Sarah, doubtfully. 'Won't it look as though it's all underwater?'

Charles Fenton shook his head. 'The gas lights are yellowish, so the stage will be bathed in a green light. You will imagine, Miss Beale, that you are in fairyland.'

Sarah nodded. The costumes they were working on echoed this. Some of the fairies would be traditional spritely creatures, but others would have a touch of the grotesque. Puck, for example, would wear a large pantomime head and others outsize hands. Only that morning Sarah had been moulding papier mâché onto wire frames for the hands.

133

She peered at the tree he was painting on one of the flats.

'Why, it's like Puck's costume!'

Charles Fenton nodded. 'Miss Bailey and I co-ordinated our designs. When Puck steps out from behind the tree, it will look as though he is part of it. And he can disappear the same way.'

'Like a dryad,' observed Sarah.

'Just so.'

They smiled at each other. Sarah whisked herself back up the wooden stairs to the wardrobe room. The whole play would look wonderful. Already there was something magical about the Athenian wood, even half-painted, with the backdrop of that over-large moon.

There was not a lot of space backstage and the costumes were beginning to overflow the small wardrobe room where Sarah and Miss Bailey worked. For as well as the new *Dream* costumes, the theatre was currently performing *The Lady of Lyons*, followed by *Virginius* and the costumes had had to be cleaned, fitted and hung up somewhere. Mr Josephs, the assistant stage manager, had made a number of racks which were suspended from the ceiling in the large wardrobe room. The finished costumes were hung up on these out of the way, by means of a pulley.

Many of the *Dream* costumes were now

done, or needed only their trimmings after the final fittings. Miss Bailey and Sarah were now finishing off the fairies' costumes and lastly they would do Theseus's and Hippolyta's attendants.

'Miss Beale,' said Miss Bailey, looking up from her work. 'Mr Williams should have pinned up the final cast list for the fairies by now. Could you go and see? I think there are only four left. If they are not rehearsing, they should be in the Green Room. Send them up here, if you can.'

Sarah surveyed the hand she'd been moulding. Yes, that would do. She carefully placed it upright on its stick to dry and went to wash her hands. She took off her voluminous apron, liberally streaked with paint, hung it up, and went downstairs.

She could hear from the wings that the fairies were being rehearsed. Miss Mandlebert, the rather bossy first fairy, was poking Cobweb into standing properly and Puck, a self-contained little boy, was endeavouring to copy Mr Phelps's intonation and gestures. Sarah could hear his childish treble.

> *'Thou speak'st aright;*
> *I am that merry wanderer of the night*
> *I jest to Oberon, and make him smile . . .*

She peeped round one of the flats. He was rather good, she thought. Somehow, his serious imitations of Mr Phelps's rendition gave a freakish touch to his speech, as if Puck were only pretending to be human—but one couldn't tell what he might be like underneath. It gave his performance a slightly dangerous edge.

She stepped back and went to the Green Room. Mr Williams's cast list was up on the wall and she scanned it quickly. There were the last four names that Miss Bailey needed. Miss Batty; Miss F. Batty; Miss Goodwin; Miss Frampton. Sarah stared. Miss Frampton.

No, it couldn't be Rose, surely?

CHAPTER FIVE

At the same time as Sarah was admiring Mr Fenton's work, Lord Fulmar was having breakfast. He sat, as he always did, at the head of the dining-table. The room was imposing, decorated at the turn of the century in a sea-green brocade, with faded crimson swagged curtains, held back by dull gold cords. The butler, followed by a parlour-maid, came and went silently. The hot plate on the sideboard, heated by a small paraffin lamp, held his lordship's choice of kedgeree, eggs, bacon, ham and mushrooms.

He was alone, a state of affairs which didn't suit him. He preferred having somebody around whose day needed ordering, or at whom he could shout. Mrs Fulmar, who normally filled these roles, was paying her annual visit to her sister.

However, soon Miss Beale would be here. Doubtless she'd need schooling in manners. There would be gaucheries and vulgarities to be corrected. She would have to learn to be a lady. Fortunately, Midwinter reported that she was handsome enough, and it was a blessing that she was unmarried.

Mrs Charles Fulmar had extended her visit to Lady Rundell. Up to now Lord Fulmar hadn't cared one way or the other, but now he needed her to school Miss Beale into what he wanted. His daughter-in-law was a bore, but she was at least a lady. He would order her to return at once. She would come; she knew who held the purse strings.

He absent-mindedly sipped at his coffee and considered possible sons-in-law. Would her bastardy stand in the way of his ambitions? He thought not. If he adopted Miss Beale officially and changed her name, who would dare criticize a Miss Fulmar? Perhaps a second son of an earl or even a marquess? Somebody who would be happy to make Hoop Hall his home. Lord Fulmar didn't want his ancestral acres to become a mere addition to a larger estate.

The butler came in with the morning post on a silver salver and a freshly ironed copy of

137

The Times.

Lord Fulmar took up the ivory-handled paper knife and began to break the seals. There was a letter from his estate manager, which would have to be dealt with; several bills, which he tossed to one side; and a letter with a London postmark. He frowned and broke it open. The letter was a mere three lines.

Miss Beale has instructed me to say that she knows of no reason why she should come to Hoop Hall. She is no relation to Your Lordship and therefore owes you no duty. The cheque is herewith returned.
Yours etc
M. Wood

There was a pause while Lord Fulmar reread it and then a roar of rage. Moments later, the butler heard crashes as first the coffee pot and then the hot-water jug hit the wall, followed by the furious jangling of the bell.

'Oh my Gawd!' exclaimed the footman in the hall. 'Now what?'

The butler took a deep breath and went to answer it.

'You called, My Lord?' A swift glance round the room showed coffee dripping down the brocade on the wall and the silver coffee pot lying, badly dented, on the floor. The hot-water jug had hit one of the girandoles, which lay in pieces on the floor in a pool of steaming water. The jug had rolled under the table.

Lord Fulmar, scarcely able to contain himself, was striding up and down the room, his face contorted with anger. Great purple veins stood out on his temples.

'Clear this up! Tell Tolling to saddle Tamberlane. And send Jebb up to me.'

'At once, My Lord.' After one last look at the ruined wall, the butler retreated hastily. He jerked his head at the footman, who scurried away and moments later Lord Fulmar slammed out of the dining-room, shouting for his valet.

Twenty minutes later, Lord Fulmar, mounted on a heavy bay stallion, was galloping up the hill behind the house, thrashing at his horse.

'I hope he breaks his neck,' muttered the footman, as he closed the door. He turned to the valet, who had just handed his master his hat and riding crop, 'Any idea what caused this, Mr Jebb?'

'This by-blow of his won't play,' said Jebb sourly. 'She's refused to come.'

The footman whistled. 'There'll be trouble.'

*　　　*　　　*

Sarah tiptoed back towards the stage and peered round the wings. There, at the back, performing a graceful arabesque, was Rose. Sarah stared. What was she doing here? She was so thin and pale! What was the matter with her?

Sarah moved round and beckoned to Moth, who was standing nearby. 'Could you ask Miss Frampton to come for a fitting, please?'

The moment Rose appeared, Sarah grabbed her, almost ran into the Green Room, closed the door, flung her arms around Rose and hugged her. Rose, spoilt and devious, had exasperated Sarah over the years, and the whole household had known the ignominy of being pointed at when she had left with Lord Byland in that public way, but all that was now forgotten. Rose was her little sister once again. 'Oh, Rose! You don't look well.'

Rose's face crumpled for a moment. Sarah was so blessedly there, she thought. So real. She shed a few tears into Sarah's shoulder before straightening up and pushing her away gently. 'I've been ill, but I'm better now.'

'But why aren't you . . . ?' Sarah hardly knew how to go on. She stared at Rose's pale face, trying to read what had happened to her.

Rose shrugged. 'Byland got engaged to be married. And I didn't fancy the other offers I received.' She had no intention of confiding in Sarah.

Sarah didn't know what to say. It was a world so outside her comprehension that she wasn't sure how to begin. 'Where are you living?' she asked.

'I've taken a room in Penton Street. I'm lodging with my uncle.'

'Uncle? What uncle?'

'Mr Frampton. Surely you know him? He's in charge of the dancing here.'

'Is he really your uncle?' Sarah asked suspiciously. She knew Mr Frampton, of course, but she hadn't realized him to be Rose's uncle.

Rose gave a brittle laugh. 'Oh yes, it's quite true. He's my Uncle Alfred.' She saw that Sarah was still looking stunned. 'I know Aunt Hetty didn't like my father,' she said wearily, 'but Uncle Alfred was always very kind to me. He and Aunt Bessy take in theatrical people, so I am lodging with them. It was Uncle Alfred who got me the audition with Mr Phelps.'

'But how did you know he was your uncle?' asked Sarah, bewildered. 'You can't have seen him since you were five.'

'Don't be silly, Sarah,' said Rose. 'I used to go to dancing class on Wednesdays, remember? They were run by Uncle Alfred's wife, my Aunt Bessy—Miss Toller. I've always known Uncle Alfred.'

'But why did you never say?'

Rose shrugged. 'I was frightened that Aunt Hetty would stop me going if she knew.'

There was a pause whilst Sarah tried to take it in. Rose had been lying to them all for years, ever since she was a child? It seemed incredible. Had this uncle and aunt helped Rose to go off with her young lord, Sarah wondered. But she could not ask.

'Have you got enough money? I know you're not yet twenty-one, but I daresay I could persuade Mr Wood to let you have some of your income.'

'Thank you for offering, but I am all right. Lord Byland was very generous.' Rose gave a strained smile.

There were sounds outside. Mr Phelps had moved on to a new scene. Soon they would be interrupted.

'Come upstairs, Rose,' said Sarah. 'I need to measure you for your costume.'

'I think you'd better call me Miss Frampton,' said Rose, following her out of the room.

'But . . . but Rose. You are practically my sister.' Sarah felt hurt and bewildered.

'It wouldn't do,' said Rose, still in the same detached voice. 'I know very well that I've blotted my copybook. I passed Mrs Nutley in White Lion Street a day or so ago—do you remember her?—and she just stared straight through me. You can be sure that all of Myddleton Square will know of the prodigal's return by now.'

'Mrs Nutley is an evil-minded gossip,' said Sarah. She knew very well that Mrs Nutley referred to herself as "that Webster foundling".

'Perhaps.' Rose did not sound concerned.

Sarah kissed her. 'It shall be as you wish.' She gently ushered Rose upstairs and opened the wardrobe-room door. 'Miss Bailey, this is Miss Frampton. I'll go and see if I can find the others.'

* * *

Jack auditioned for Sadler's Wells almost by accident. After having been denied access to Sarah, he wandered round Myddleton Square, down Myddleton Passage, past the New River Head ponds and eventually reached Sadler's Wells Theatre. It was an unpretentious stuccoed building bordering the New River and on this warm September afternoon there was a group of children throwing bread to some ducks. Jack walked round until he came to the stage door and pushed it open.

Pepper Williams was not in his cubby hole just inside, which was fortunate, so there was nobody to stop him. Jack was curious as to what Miss Beale's job actually was. It was Monday and the theatre was preparing for a performance of Sheridan Knowles's *Virginius*. Men were swarming all over the stage with flats and props, but nobody took any notice of him.

Eventually Jack came across a small, taciturn man who was sweeping up sawdust and chippings. 'I'm enquiring about a Miss

143

Beale,' Jack began, reaching into his pocket and jingling the coins suggestively. 'Does she work here?'

The small man leant on his broom and considered him. 'In the wardrobe room with Miss Bailey.' He jerked his head towards a flight of wooden stairs.

'She doesn't act?' Jack was surprised. She'd look wonderful on stage, he thought.

'Not unless Mr Phelps pushes her,' the man grinned. 'She don't care for it. And I wish there was others who thought the same. Mostly, you can't keep them off the stage.'

'So there's nothing she's in at the moment?' He'd like to see her dressed up, he thought.

'Lawd no, sir. Miss Beale's been here all summer working on the costumes. They're very busy in wardrobe.'

'I see. Are there auditions for the new company, or does Mr Phelps employ the same people?'

'The principals are often the same, sir. The others, well, it depends on what's needed and who's available. But auditioning's finished. Was you wishful to audition yourself, sir?' A toff who was stage struck, he thought. He recognized the type. Useless, most of them were; always fancying themselves as Hamlet and unwilling to put in a stroke of work.

'I . . . possibly.'

'You'll be a Walking Gentleman, I daresay. I suppose you'll have evening dress, waistcoat, silk stockings and all, sir?'

'Yes.' Jack looked startled. 'Would I need them?'

'Lord love you, sir, a Walking Gentleman can hardly get by without them. An actor is expected to wear his own clothes for modern plays. In fact, I have known an actor get the part simply because of his clothes, though not in Mr Phelps's company, of course.'

'Do you think Mr Phelps would find space for me?'

The stage hand knew perfectly well that he wouldn't, but he wasn't one to discourage a tip, so he said, 'Mr Frost, one of our utility men, has broken a leg. He'll be off for several months, bad break it was. If you want to audition you'll find Mr Phelps in his office.' He jerked his head towards a door at the top of a small flight of steps.

Jack flicked him half a crown. 'I'm obliged to you.'

Was he mad, thought Jack. Did he really want to apply for a job which would no doubt be tedious and tiring and take up all of his time? Furthermore, he would have to pay for the privilege. And yet . . . there was something very attractive in the idea.

He had never had to work in his life; a substantial income had been his ever since his father had died when he was fourteen. It would be a challenge to hold down such a job for a couple of months. His grandfather had slaved in the cotton mill for twelve hours a day, Jack recalled: would his grandson show himself less of a man?

Nobody he knew would know, why should they? And he would be able to keep an eye on Miss Beale. If Lord Fulmar did try anything, though Jack didn't see what he could do apart from subjecting her to an unpleasant personal call, then he would be on hand to protect her. Legally, Lord Fulmar had no rights over Miss Beale, and she was over twenty-one. There was not a lot he could do. Jack wished he felt sure that that would stop him.

Mr Phelps was initially unhelpful. No, he was not taking on anybody else. Yes, Mr Frost had broken his leg and would be away a couple of months, but somebody else in the company would take over—and be glad of the money.

At Jack's insistence he allowed him to audition.

Mr Frost had been a reliable member of the company, putting in competent performances in a number of small roles. This season he would have been one of Theseus's attendants, as well as having a couple of other minor speaking parts. Phelps saw at once that, as far as looks went, Jack would do very well.

His acting was adequate, no more. But he had that indescribable something—stage presence. He took command of the space as though he were used to all eyes being on him. All the same, Phelps didn't want him.

Jack could see that Phelps was going to refuse.

'I'll pay five pounds a week to be in the company until Mr Frost returns,' he said. 'Providing that you allow me to take on his roles.'

Phelps raised an eyebrow. That was a lot of money, and expenses at the theatre had been heavy with the new gas pipes, not to mention the cost of mounting *A Midsummer Night's Dream*.

'You won't be popular in the company,' Phelps pointed out. Gentlemen actors who paid to perform were resented as taking work away from honest working-men.

Jack shrugged. 'I'll live.'

Phelps thought for a moment. The theatre could do with the money and the man in front of him looked as though he could cope with any unpleasantness.

'Five pounds a week it is. Now, Mr Midwinter, we keep strict hours here. Rehearsals from ten until two and I expect you to be word perfect in any speaking roles.' He eyed Jack shrewdly for a moment. He did not believe Jack's talk of always having wanted to be an actor. He thought it more likely that he was after some woman, or was doing it for a bet.

'This is a respectable company, Mr Midwinter. There will be no pursuit of actresses here. Any trouble and you will find yourself out of a job. You will excuse my plain speaking on the subject. I find it best to make these things clear at the outset.'

'Naturally,' said Jack, though how Mr Phelps hoped to stop human nature, he did not know. In his experience it was equally likely that actresses did the pursuing.

'Very well. I shall expect you—and the first five pounds—tomorrow at ten o'clock. You are one of Theseus's attendants in *A Midsummer Night's Dream*. You'd better tell Mr Williams at the stage door on your way out and make a note of your rehearsal timetable.'

Jack thanked him and turned to go. Then he turned back.

'This Mr Frost,' he said, 'how much did he earn?'

'Thirty shillings a week—but you're buying experience, Mr Midwinter, and that never comes cheap.'

*   *   *

Unaware of this new threat to her peace of mind, Sarah went downstairs the following morning for the read-through and blocking of *A Midsummer Night's Dream*. Mr Phelps wanted to ensure that Frederick Fenton's scenery and lighting would work with Phelps's own conception of the play. There would be a read-through of Act I, the end of Act IV when Theseus and Hippolyta go hunting in the

148

forest and find the sleeping lovers, and all of Act V. These scenes were in mortal time, as it were, and not subject to fairy enchantment. Sarah, as Hippolyta's attendant, was in all of them.

The basic blocking would be done and any problems noted. Mr Fenton was sitting in the stalls, notebook in hand. Miss Bailey was sitting next to him. None of the actors was costumed, but Sarah knew that Miss Bailey wanted to check that what she had in mind would work. Mr Frampton was there, too. As dance designer, he was doubtless concerned about the Mechanicals' bergomask at the end of Act V.

The moment Sarah walked onto the stage, she saw Jack. The shock was so great that she took a step back into the wings. Why was Mr Midwinter here of all places? How had he got into the company? Of course, he'd have paid to get in, despicable man. Did he not realize that because of him, other actors would be out of work? Could it be something to do with Lord Fulmar? What on earth should she do?

Mr Phelps caught sight of her. 'Miss Beale!'

There was no help for it. Sarah reluctantly stepped onto the stage. Her mind was still whirling. She could not bring herself to look at Jack.

'I want you to stand by Miss Portman. You are to be responsible for holding her train, so you will need to be slightly behind her at all

149

times. Is that clear?'

'Yes, Mr Phelps.' Sarah desperately tried to pull herself together and clumsily picked up Hippolyta's train, which was merely a long piece of material pinned to Miss Portman's shoulders.

Miss Portman turned to smile at Sarah and whispered, 'Good to see you again, Miss Beale. I trust you had a pleasant summer?'

Sarah managed to smile her thanks. She tried not to look in Jack's direction, though she could sense that he was looking at her. He was standing behind Mr Henry Marston, who was playing Theseus, and talking to Miss Warde, the prettiest of Hippolyta's ladies. Sarah saw at once that Mr Midwinter's attractions were not lost on Miss Warde. If the male members of the company resented him, this plainly did not extend to the female members.

Most of Act I concerned Lysander and Hermia's forbidden love. Hermia, small, dark and vivacious, was sweetly engaging and Lysander duly love-struck. Hermia's father wanted her to marry Demetrius, who strode around raging, just as he ought. Lastly Helena entered, tall and fair in contrast to Hermia. She had once been betrothed to Demetrius and was still in love with him.

There was very little for Sarah to do in the scene, apart from be attentive and, in her present state of mind, that was difficult

150

enough. Theseus pronounced the law; either Hermia married Demetrius, her father's choice, or else submitted herself *'To death, or to a vow of single life.'* Hermia's father, played with angry energy by Mr Lunt, forcibly reminded Sarah of Lord Fulmar in his obstinacy and unreasonableness.

The scene was nearly over. Hippolyta swept out, affronted. As Amazon Queen, she did not approve of Theseus's ordering about of Hermia, and Sarah had to be careful not to drop her train as Miss Portman, fine eyes flashing, swirled off stage. They were followed by Theseus and his attendants.

Sarah became aware that Jack was trying to get her attention. How dared he? She had made it very clear to him only a few days ago that she did not wish to talk to him. She was not going to change her mind. She turned to smile at Miss Warde, who was standing just behind her.

'Have you seen our new member?' whispered Miss Warde. 'He is taking over from Mr Frost. I declare I'm quite smitten.'

'Surely there are plenty of other utility men who could take Mr Frost's place?' said Sarah crossly.

'Oh, I daresay he paid to come,' said Miss Warde. 'I, for one, cannot be sorry.'

Sarah gave a swift glance round and saw Jack looking at them. Miss Warde raised her hand and waggled her fingers at him, coquettishly.

'He is a Mr Midwinter,' went on Miss Warde. 'He says his Christian name is Jack, so he must be Jack Frost while he has the chance!' She laughed.

Sarah was not amused. Doubtless Miss Warde would not be the only woman to succumb to Mr Midwinter's good looks, she thought waspishly. Well, she would not be one of them. Resolutely, she moved away.

They moved on to the end of Act IV. Theseus and Hippolyta were out hunting and came across the lovers, cast into an enchanted sleep by Puck whilst in the fairy wood. It was near the end of the play and time for the various plot entanglements to be unravelled. The difference of opinion between the fairy king and queen, Oberon and Titania, was resolved. Theseus's courtship of Hippolyta moved towards its consummation.

'Miss Beale!' called Mr Phelps. 'I want you and Mr Midwinter to stand together. You are both tall and will look very well.' He paired off the other attendants. 'Mr Midwinter, take Theseus's bow after, *"But soft, what nymphs are these?"* Miss Beale, you'd better take Hippolyta's.'

Rigid, Sarah moved towards Jack.

'*"Ill met by moonlight, proud Titania"*,' said Jack.

'Right play: wrong act,' snapped Sarah. 'What are you doing here?'

'Acting, the same as you.'

Sarah flung him an incredulous look.

'Come along,' cried Phelps. 'From Theseus and Hippolyta's entrance. Mr Williams, could you give us Titania's last two lines, please?' Pepper Williams was sitting in the prompt box.

The rehearsal continued. Sarah, acutely aware of Jack beside her, tried in vain to concentrate. She couldn't believe that Mr Midwinter was seriously wanting to act. It must be that he was Lord Fulmar's messenger. What else was possible?

'You are asking yourself whether my presence here has anything to do with you?' said Jack, helpfully.

'And does it?' Sarah stared firmly at Miss Portman's back.

'Could it not?' replied Jack, pressing one hand to his heart.

'Don't be silly,' Sarah dismissed the gesture. 'I presume you are here as Lord Fulmar's lackey?'

Jack straightened up. 'I have never been Lord Fulmar's lackey.'

'Lackeys do as their masters bid them, no matter how dishonourable,' said Sarah coldly. 'I confess I cannot see much difference.'

'My God, Miss Beale . . .' began Jack, furiously.

Sarah gave a small satisfied smile.

*   *   *

153

The moment Rose saw Jack she knew her luck had turned. She was not absolutely sure why he was at Sadler's Wells, but whichever way she looked at it, it must be flattering to herself. She knew that he knew that she was interested in taking Delia's place. He was reputedly a good lover and generous, too. This time Rose would make sure of a proper settlement before she committed herself. He must be keen, otherwise why come all this way to be near her? And he must have paid for the privilege, too!

It was a pity that he was one of Theseus's attendants, whilst she was one of Titania's. It meant that they never met on stage. But that might be no bad thing. Rose was still not feeling quite herself, and a situation which took a bit longer to resolve suited her better.

She crept into the back of the pit and watched the rehearsal. She was amused to see Sarah standing next to Jack and very starchy she looked. Had he said something to her she disapproved of? What would Sarah say if she knew the truth? Rose was fond of Sarah, but she could be uncompromising in her notions, and Rose doubted whether she'd be happy to have a man of Mr Midwinter's reputation next to her, if she knew of it. Rose toyed with the idea of teasing Sarah with it.

She switched her attention to Miss Warde, who was flirting outrageously with Mr

154

Midwinter, giving him coquettish glances over her shoulder at every opportunity. Why, thought Rose, Miss Warde must be twenty-five, if a day, and it was well-known that Mr Midwinter only went for girls of her own age. All his mistresses that Rose knew of were blonde, like herself, so Miss Warde, who was dark, was wasting her time. All the same, Miss Warde's presence worried her.

She pondered on how best to tackle the situation. Should she wait for Jack to approach her? Or should she take the first step?

*　　*　　*

Sarah and Jack were on stage for almost all of Act V, though they had very little to do for most of it. This would be a night scene. The blue net was gone and they were back in Athens, in mortal time. She had seen Mr Fenton's designs for Act V, with elegant Corinthian pillars inside Theseus's palace, and hanging candelabra. There were curtains at the back, which would open at the end of the play to reveal a terraced garden overlooking Athens, down which the fairies would dance. It would look splendid.

The quarrel between Oberon and Titania was now resolved, the lovers united and Theseus and Hippolyta must be shown as ruling justly. Order in the world was restored.

Theseus and Hippolyta sat side by side on

two rickety chairs, which did duty for thrones; on Theseus's right sat Hermia and Lysander, and on Hippolyta's left were Demetrius and Helena. Behind them, eventually on painted marble seats, but at the moment on wooden benches, were their attendants. They were all going to watch the Mechanicals' play.

Sarah and Jack, to Sarah's discomfort, were directed to sit together. Others were paired off to the best advantage. They had to wait while Phelps discussed the staging with Frederick Fenton. The mechanics of the play, together with the lighting effects, were complicated. Mr Fenton needed to know that his ideas would work before details were finalized.

'All right, Fenton?' asked Phelps. 'Anything else you need?'

'The final exits, please, Mr Phelps. And Mr Frampton wants a word about the bergomask.'

'What's a bergomask?' Jack whispered to Sarah. He could see that she was still set against him. She needed her ruffled feathers soothing, he thought. She reminded him of Charlie, who often needed cajoling. Jack was very good at soothing women's ruffled feathers.

'A dance.'

'Do we have to do it?' Jack was alarmed. It was one thing, he thought, to stand about looking decorative, but quite another to make a fool of himself dancing.

'No, just the Mechanicals. All we have to do

156

is laugh at their play.'

'Oh God,' said Jack.

Sarah looked at him.

'From what I remember of Shakespeare's humour,' Jack continued, 'some ass comes on stage and says something like, *"Nay, and thou cans't not smile as the wind sits thou'lt catch cold shortly"*, and we all collapse with laughter.'

'*King Lear*,' said Sarah at once. She was still angered at Jack's being there, but she couldn't help smiling. 'I know what you mean but I think you'll be proved wrong. Mr Phelps is playing Bottom and the Mechanicals' play will be very funny. You'll see.'

Jack looked at her with approval. Once she'd relaxed in his company, she was a most attractive woman. Not his usual style, of course, but she had an indefinable charm. She was dressed in a deep crimson, which suited her admirably. Jack was well-versed in ladies' couture and he recognized that her dress was simply, but beautifully, cut and made of excellent material. Sarah wore very little trimming—only a couple of rows of braid round the edge—unlike Miss Warde whose dress was so loaded with flounces and fringe, that she looked like an over-trimmed lampshade.

Miss Beale was indisputably a lady. Odd that he should think this. Jack was well aware any female who worked for money, unless it be

157

as a governess, instantly lost all pretensions to the title. As an actress, a dressmaker and an artist of sorts, Miss Beale was damned on all three counts. He knew well enough that that was what his mother would say.

Jack had spent his adult life dividing women into categories. Unless he was fulfilling some social obligation, he ignored young marriageable ladies. He acknowledged available married ones, providing they were discreet. The others, like Amy Rush, or Delia, were there for his convenience. Mrs Midwinter, though she might deplore her son's morals, would not have argued with his definitions.

Miss Beale, however, seemed to confound any such categorization.

Mr Frampton and Mr Fenton sorted out the bergomask to their satisfaction. The Mechanicals would exit stage right after their dance. Theseus, Hippolyta, the lovers and their train must exit stage left. Jack and Sarah were instructed to bow and curtsey as Theseus and Hippolyta passed.

'Mr Midwinter,' called Phelps. 'Will you and Miss Beale follow immediately after Lysander and Hermia? Offer Miss Beale your arm. Miss Beale, just the tips of your fingers on his arm. Keep your distance. Yes, very good. The rest do likewise.'

Their exit ended the rehearsal and Sarah dropped her fingers from Jack's arm as though it were hot. As soon as she could she fled up to the wardrobe room and tried to cool her flushed cheeks. She found being next to him embarrassing and it was not a feeling she was used to. She wasn't sure what to do or how to behave. Somehow, he agitated her thoughts. It was a relief to get upstairs and sit down with her needle. At least in the wardrobe room she'd have time to think.

It was just after two o'clock. She should be able to put in a good five hours' sewing while the light lasted. She went into the large wardrobe room and let down the pulley. There were hems to be sewn and she must finish Hermia's and Helena's belts. Their dresses owed more to the mediaeval than to ancient Greece, thought Sarah. The belts reminded her of one she'd seen in Pugin's Mediaeval Court at the Crystal Palace a couple of years before. They had two tapering ends down the front of the dress and a criss-cross pattern of ribbons sewn down the length. She unhooked the belts and went to fetch her pincushion. The ribbons had to be tacked on carefully; firm enough not to come undone, but removable if the belts had to be washed.

By the time she'd finished it was past seven o'clock and the light was going. She put the finished belts back with their dresses, pulled up the rack and secured it. Then she went downstairs.

Pepper Williams was in his cubby hole with Spot at his feet. Spot wagged his tail furiously and Sarah bent to pat him. Mr Williams was going over the script of *Hamlet*, which would be coming on soon.

'A naughty play, Sarah,' he said. 'Some of it is very coarse. Mr Phelps has had to cut bits that you just couldn't say nowadays. I hope you're not thinking of seeing it?'

'Oh dear,' Sarah smiled. 'Is it that bad?'

'I wouldn't want my daughter to see it,' said Mr Williams gloomily.

'I am twenty-eight,' Sarah reminded him.

'A babe-in-arms,' snorted Mr Williams. 'By the way, there's been a feller enquiring after you. Mr Midwinter.'

'What did he want?' snapped Sarah. Not him again, she thought.

'To know when you'd be going home.'

'I hope you didn't tell him,' cried Sarah, alarmed.

'I said it was none of his business.' Pepper Williams spoke with some satisfaction. He was fond of Sarah and didn't want to see her being pestered. 'Miss Beale is a respectable lady, I told him. There might be others—naming no names, who'd welcome his attentions, but he don't deceive me. He's a gentleman—anybody can see that. If he ain't up to mischief, my name's not Williams.'

'We shall be much together in the *Dream*,' said Sarah worriedly. 'I don't want any trouble.' She did not think that he had any personal intentions against her virtue, she was not nearly pretty enough, but he might importune her about Lord Fulmar, and she wanted to avoid that.

'You slip home now, pet,' said Williams. 'He's gone to help Mr Fenton with some flats. One thing I will say for him, he's not afraid of work.'

Sarah tied her bonnet strings firmly, thanked him and left.

There was a quick way back to Myddleton Square by Myddleton Passage, which cut past the New River Head. During the day it was safe enough, but it was to be avoided after dark, for there were no street lights and footpads sometimes lurked there in winter. Sarah preferred to go the long way round up St John Street, but tonight she thought there was still enough light to see by. It was not so very late, and it wasn't as if she had any money on her, only a shilling or two.

There was a gang of young boys kicking a ball about on the grass on the other side of the ponds, but they looked absorbed in their game. The pieman who came down every day from the baker's shop in Amwell Street was trudging homewards not twenty yards in front of her. Feeling safer, Sarah walked on briskly and set her face for home.

CHAPTER SIX

Jack swiftly became fascinated by the behind the scenes work at Sadler's Wells. Frederick Fenton had made a to-scale representation of the set for *A Midsummer Night's Dream* and demonstrated to Jack how the scenery would work.

'It's a diorama,' he said. 'Two sets of scenery moving together. See, Mr Midwinter, if you turn that little handle there, whilst I turn this one, you'll get some idea.'

The back set of the diorama was painted dark blue with star and cloud effects, while the front one represented the Athenian wood, with various cutouts and shapings for glades and spaces between the trees. When the two parts were moved slowly it looked as though the night sky was floating past in the background as you moved to different parts of the wood. As the diorama moved, the large orange moon rose and arched over the clouded night sky.

'Of course, that's not all,' said Fenton, with modest pleasure at Jack's admiration. 'There are various cut-out trees in grooves on the stage for the fairies to hide behind. And then we have the silhouettes.' He saw Jack's look of enquiry and added, 'When Puck has to fly off, young Artis will step behind one of the cut-out trees and seem to disappear. His costume will make him blend in. His silhouette will then fly up into the sky.'

'The timing will have to be impeccable,' observed Jack thoughtfully.

'Oh yes. Much of the play's atmosphere will lie in the scenery and the special effects. There will be at least a dozen people working on the scenery alone. Then there will be the lighting to do as well.'

'I should like to help, if I can,' said Jack.

'Your part is to strut about the stage,' said Fenton, grinning. 'I've heard a number of tributes to your magnificent legs. You'd better watch it. Miss Warde has her eye on you!'

Jack laughed. 'I think I prefer Miss Beale.'

'You'll have a job there,' returned Fenton. 'Our Sarah's not for flirting. A very serious young woman. Good at her job, mind.'

'She doesn't like being on stage,' said Jack. 'Strange, I'd have thought she'd look wonderful.'

'She does,' said Fenton, looking at him curiously. 'But she gets very self-conscious. When she first came she used to cower at the back.' He had noticed that Miss Beale wasn't at her ease with Mr Midwinter and he wondered why. 'Mr Thorpe is trying to fix his interest with her,' he added.

'Thorpe!' echoed Jack, displeased.

Fenton smiled to himself.

Jack had promised to help Mr Harvey in the

carpentry room, so he left Fenton and went back downstairs. As he passed the stage a crowd of fairies trooped out, chattering and laughing. Most of the fairies were children and several had harassed mothers in tow. But there were some older ones, too. One of them looked surprisingly familiar.

She stopped in front of him with an artless little start of surprise.

'Why!' cried Jack. 'It's pretty Rose.'

Behind him, Miss Goodwin, her sharp face alive with curiosity, peered at them both and moved quietly behind a wing flat.

'Gracious! Mr Midwinter!' Rose coloured modestly. She was glad she'd washed her hair yesterday. It clung about her face in a cloud of silvery-gold.

'What are you doing here, pretty Rose?'

'I've always liked the theatre,' replied Rose, looking up at him from under her eyelashes. 'I trained as a dancer.'

Jack didn't believe a word of it. 'Byland a skinflint? I think the worse of him for it.'

Rose put her chin up. 'He was very generous. So I can please myself for a while. I like the Wells and I have family working here. My uncle designs the dances.' She wouldn't mention Sarah. At least, not just yet.

'I see.' Jack surveyed her for a moment. 'So you're not looking for a replacement for Byland?'

Rose pointed her toe and drew a small arc

164

on the floor. 'I might be,' she said. 'If it were made worth my while.' She allowed a small pause. Jack was looking down at her and smiling, but he did not pick up her hint. Rose knew better than to wait. 'In the meantime, I'm very happy where I am. Gracious, I promised Miss Gilbert I'd help her with her routine. I must fly.' She laughed, blew him a kiss and darted away.

Jack turned and went towards the carpenter's room. Miss Goodwin stepped out from behind the wing flat. What a nerve, she thought. Why, Miss Frampton was no better than she should be, offering herself to Mr Midwinter in that brazen way. She wondered whether she should tell Mr Phelps.

Miss Goodwin was due for a costume fitting so, full of her discovery, she made her way up to the small wardrobe room, where Sarah was waiting for her.

Sarah had had a number of problems with Miss Goodwin's costume, mainly because of the inadequacies of that lady's figure, though she was too kind to say so. Miss Goodwin was a thin girl with a waspish expression. She was an excellent dancer, but would never move higher than the chorus because of her lack of figure and charm. Her shoulders were angular and bony and her knees and ankles knobbly. Her feet were far too large for her height. It was a great pity, thought Sarah, as she looked critically at Miss Goodwin's costume on its

165

stand, but Miss Goodwin would undoubtedly have more success if she stopped wanting to be a fairy or *coryphée* and settled instead for a comic character actress.

She had done her best for her, however. A tulle frill around the shoulders disguised Miss Goodwin's angularity and extra silk flowers over the bust and round the hips helped to give her a figure she did not naturally possess.

'It's not fair, Miss Beale,' burst out Miss Goodwin, as she stepped out of her petticoat and allowed Sarah to help her into her costume. 'That Miss Frampton! Who does she think she is?'

'Miss Frampton?' echoed Sarah warily. 'Why, what has she done?' She knew Miss Goodwin was inclined to take offence easily and decided it must be some small imagined slight.

'I heard her with my own ears! She as good as propositioned Mr Midwinter. It is plain that they are very well acquainted. Ouch!' For Sarah had inadvertently stuck a pin in her.

'How do you know?'

'Would he call her "pretty Rose" without an acquaintance?' Miss Goodwin's thin face was all screwed up. 'And they were talking about some lord who has been keeping Miss Frampton. I heard it all. I was standing behind one of the flats not two yards away. Oh, she's no better than she should be, Miss Beale, you mark my words.'

Sarah found that the ribbon she was trying to pin onto Miss Goodwin's skirt kept slipping as her hands clumsily lost their skill. Rose knew Mr Midwinter? Was that why he was here? Nothing to do with herself at all?

'I've a good mind to tell Mr Phelps,' went on Miss Goodwin. 'That Miss Frampton only got the job because of her uncle, I'm sure. And she's got her eye out for another gentleman to keep her.'

'Did Mr Midwinter seem interested?' Sarah couldn't help asking.

'He asked her if she were looking for a replacement for her protector, though he did not offer himself, I notice,' spat out Miss Goodwin. 'Serve her right.' She paused and then added, 'Do you think I should tell Mr Phelps?'

'It might be awkward,' said Sarah. 'Mr Phelps would be bound to ask you how you know.' She didn't think he'd be pleased to learn that Miss Goodwin had been eavesdropping on what was obviously a private conversation. Miss Goodwin was a good worker, but she was not well-liked. She could easily end up as the one dismissed.

Miss Goodwin must have realized it too, for she said, 'I shall say nothing for now. Far be it from me to spread such sordid gossip. But I shall keep my ears open, Miss Beale, you may be sure of that.'

When she'd gone Sarah sat down with the

discarded costume and tried to concentrate on where the trimmings should go. But her mind kept coming back to this new, most unwelcome, piece of news. She knew nothing about Mr Midwinter, after all, except that he had been a friend of Charlie Fulmar's and was willing to do Lord Fulmar's dirty work for him.

What sort of life did he lead in town? Did he, like Lord Byland, keep mistresses? Sarah was well aware that he was an attractive man. Wealthy too. Why should she doubt that he led as dissipated a life as his contemporaries? If she found the thought unpleasant, then she should learn to be less naïve.

Mr Midwinter was nothing to her, she told herself. Why should she care what he did? He had, she now realized, been making small overtures of friendship to herself. That must stop. She had no intention of allowing herself to be beguiled by a libertine.

This noble stance was to suffer a shaking that evening. As she was leaving the theatre, Mr Williams called her.

'Sarah, pet!'

'Yes, Mr Williams.' He was one of the few people Sarah allowed to use her Christian name.

'Could you drop in on the Frosts, Sarah? It's not out of your way.'

'Of course.' Sarah bent to stroke Spot. Mr Frost had been on her mind for some time. He had a wife and child and times would be hard

168

until he could get back to work.

Mr Williams handed her a basket which contained a purse from a quick whip-round among the company—Sarah herself had contributed a shilling—a shoulder of lamb and a bottle of brandy.

The Frosts had rooms above a grocer's in Arlington Way and it was only a few steps from the theatre. Sarah knocked at the door. A head in a becomingly frilled mob cap poked out of the window.

'Why! It's Miss Beale.'

A moment later Mrs Frost, clutching her baby, opened the door. Sarah searched for signs of malnourishment and was relieved to see that both she and the baby looked healthy. She followed them upstairs.

Dick Frost was sitting reading the paper in a Windsor armchair by the window, his plastered leg up on a footstool. He greeted Sarah warmly and thanked her for the goods.

'We're not doing too badly, Miss Beale,' he said in answer to her enquiries. 'Thanks to Mr Midwinter.'

'Mr Midwinter!' cried Sarah astonished.

'He's been ever so good, Miss Beale,' put in Mrs Frost, disentangling the baby's fingers from her hair. 'He's sent Mr Frost his thirty shillings a week, without fail. He said that, as he'd usurped Mr Frost's place, it was only right that he should pay him for it.'

'That's very good of him,' said Sarah, slowly.

He had been tactful, too, she noted. He had taken care not to make Dick Frost feel as if it were charity.

'Not everybody would think to do it,' said Dick. 'I take it very kindly of him. He comes to ask me tips, you know. Says he don't want to show his ignorance in front of the others.' Thirty shillings a week was not a lot for an actor, who often had to provide his own costumes, and it left very little for doctor's bills. But now they could just about manage.

Sarah left with a curious lightening of the spirit. Mr Midwinter's morals might be in doubt, but he also had a kind heart. He had undertaken this charitable action and never said a word about it to anybody. 'Doesn't want it known,' Dick Frost had said.

Sarah couldn't help feeling more kindly towards him.

*   *   *

Sarah had forgotten all about Lord Fulmar. After Jack's first visit, Sarah had confided in Miss Valloton, who wailed when she heard of Sarah's refusal of Lord Fulmar's offer. Sarah tried to explain, but Miss Valloton could not take it in, so she said nothing more and dismissed the whole thing from her mind.

She had enough on her plate with worrying about Rose and the problem of Jack Midwinter. She did not want to think of Jack mounting Rose as his latest mistress. With regard to herself, she supposed that, at some point, he would try to persuade her to accept Lord Fulmar's offer, and doubtless there would be some unpleasantness when she refused, but she hadn't thought much further than that. Mr Dick Frost would return when his leg was mended and Mr Midwinter would leave. Naturally, she would be relieved.

It had never seriously crossed her mind that Lord Fulmar might pursue her personally.

It was, therefore, a considerable shock when, after church that Sunday, there was a knock at the door and Polly came up with a card, which read uncompromisingly, *The Lord Fulmar*.

'Oh my God,' said Sarah. She went to the drawing-room window and peeped out. There, outside the house, to the obvious interest of the neighbours, was an elegant gentleman's carriage with a crest on the door. A bewigged footman stood on the perch behind the coach and another stood by the carriage door. Lord Fulmar, for it could be nobody else, was standing by the front door, tapping his cane impatiently.

Sarah pulled her thoughts together. 'Polly, ask Miss Valloton to come down immediately, please. And then show up Lord Fulmar.'

Miss Valloton, greatly flustered and in a state of some excitement, almost ran in. 'Oh my dear Sarah! Fancy him coming personally!

Such condescension. But, there it is, your real aristocracy will always behave well.'

'He has not behaved well at all,' said Sarah tartly. 'You forget how he treated Miss Webster. I have asked you down both as a witness and a chaperon.'

Miss Valloton stared. Sarah had told her of her earlier refusal, but she could scarcely believe it. Refuse so magnificent an offer? It was not credible. Whyever would she do such a thing? And surely a woman did not need a chaperon with her own father? But she was naturally curious so she said, 'Very well, dear Sarah,' and sat down obediently and folded her mittened hands in her lap.

Polly could be heard escorting a puffing Lord Fulmar up the stairs. The door opened. Sarah and Miss Valloton rose to their feet.

'Lord Fulmar, Miss Sarah,' Polly managed. She dropped a curtsey at Lord Fulmar's unresponsive back and sped back down to the kitchen to tell Leah.

Sarah curtseyed. 'Lord Fulmar. May I introduce Miss Valloton who resides with me?'

Lord Fulmar stared at Miss Valloton for a few seconds. 'Get rid of her.'

Flustered, Miss Valloton moved towards the door. Sarah motioned her back.

'Miss Valloton stays. Otherwise we both go.'

Lord Fulmar's colour began to rise. Sarah sat herself down and smiled reassuringly at Miss Valloton, who nervously followed suit.

What could he do? If she and Miss Valloton went, then he would be in the ridiculous position of being left alone in the room. She waited.

Something of this must have crossed Lord Fulmar's mind, for his colour subsided and he said, 'Do you really want to discuss your private affairs with this female listening?'

'Miss Valloton has known me since I was a baby,' returned Sarah. Unlike His Lordship, she thought. She had won the first round and she allowed herself to relax slightly and look at him. He had changed, though it was undoubtedly the same man. At Hoop Hall all those years ago, he had been a vigorous man, with grey hair. Now he was corpulent and red-faced. His gnarled hands clutched the top of his cane.

He was her father.

For a moment Sarah wanted to burst into tears, for somewhere inside her she recognized him and was both appalled and upset. There was something about the eyes and the set of the lips which echoed her own, but there was no softness in Lord Fulmar's stare as he surveyed her. She was a strayed piece of property, no more. She swallowed, and breathed deeply to calm her nerves as Mr Fenton had taught her.

'Very well,' said Lord Fulmar. 'I shall be brief. You will come with me to Hoop Hall and assume your rightful place as my daughter and

173

heiress to the estate. You will be schooled in all the manners of a lady and my daughter-in-law, Mrs Fulmar, will prepare you for your come-out next spring.

'As Miss Fulmar, with my name and a substantial dowry, you will take your place in society and I shall find a suitable husband for you.'

Miss Valloton clasped her hands together. Why it was just like a fairy-tale. She opened her mouth to congratulate Sarah, when Sarah spoke.

'No, thank you.' Nothing else was possible, she realized. There could be no compromises with this man. His nature would not allow it.

Lord Fulmar went puce with rage. With surprising force, he banged his fist down on a small table near him. 'I will brook no refusal, miss! This is not a request. This is an order. You are coming with me now.'

'No,' said Sarah again. She spoke quietly, almost sadly, but she was definite.

'How dare you? How dare you, I say! Do you know to whom you are speaking?'

Sarah raised her head. 'I know only this, Lord Fulmar, that I would rather die than accept anything from the hands of the man who is directly responsible for my mother's death.'

'I was tired of the wench. She became a bore.'

Sarah's knuckles grew white. Miss Valloton

put her hand up to her mouth. All at once she became afraid for Sarah. This was a house full of women, apart from Mr Johnstone, who was getting on in years. Could Lord Fulmar force Sarah to go with him?

'I am your father!'

'You cannot prove it.'

'Prove it! What the devil to you mean? I have a letter here from Miss Webster informing me of your birth.'

Sarah's lip curled. It must have been Mr Midwinter who suggested this meeting to Lord Fulmar. He probably thought that her previous refusal was mere pique. She had been right in her original assessment of him: he was nothing but Lord Fulmar's lackey.

'I also have a letter—from Mr Foxton, Your Lordship's lawyer, threatening action if Miss Webster attempted to lay the child to your charge.' There was no doubt at all which letter the courts would believe. Checkmate, thought Sarah.

Lord Fulmar glared at her for a moment and then, to her surprise, laughed. 'You have bottom,' he said. 'You remind me of my younger son, Arthur. You even look like him, too. Nothing of Maria Beale in you. You're all Fulmar.'

Sarah's knuckles grew white as she clasped her hands together. With an effort, she remained silent.

'Come, girl, what's the point of wrangling? I

175

gain an heir for the estate. You gain a fortune and a husband. A fair exchange, eh?'

Sarah shook her head. She felt sad suddenly, all her rage gone. Lord Fulmar would get everything he wanted, but she would pay the price. She would lose her home and her job, her friends, all the little things that made her life worth living. She was under no illusions. She would be bullied and browbeaten into becoming what Lord Fulmar wanted. There would be no escape.

'What do you want, girl? To be a lodging-house keeper all your life? On the edge of poverty. Unmarried. You're all about your head.'

'My Lord, let us be clear,' said Sarah earnestly. She felt immensely tired, as though she were pushing some huge boulder up a hill. 'Legally, I am fatherless. You have no rights over me at all. Why don't you adopt a Fulmar cousin—surely there are some? I daresay you can find a far more suitable heir than I am, somewhere on the family tree.'

Lord Fulmar rose. 'Ten thousand pounds a year in due course, think of that, miss. I have been patient long enough. Beware lest you never see a penny of it.'

Sarah rose to her feet and opened the door.

'Goodbye, My Lord.'

The heavy footsteps thumped downstairs and Sarah could hear him growling at Polly in the hall. The front door closed behind him and

Miss Valloton and Sarah watched from the window as the footmen sprang to attention. His Lordship clambered in and the carriage rumbled off in the direction of St James's.

Sarah said, 'Ten thousand a year. And he would give my mother nothing. He is a monster!'

Miss Valloton sat down suddenly, her head in a whirl. Secretly, she had always thought of Lord Fulmar as a sort of possible fairy-godmother for Sarah. Now, it seemed, he was an ogre.

'I should like a cup of tea,' she said at last, in a quavery voice.

*　　　*　　　*

That night, Sarah slept badly. Lord Fulmar's visit kept running through her mind over and over again. In the end, she rose, lit a candle, put on her dressing-gown and crept down to the basement. The kitchen range had been damped down for the night, but there was enough heat for her to do herself some warm milk with a little honey. It was a drink Aunt Hetty used to give her when she was a little girl and had had nightmares, and Sarah found it comforting.

She sat in the Windsor armchair with her feet on the fender and tried to come to terms with the events of the day. She was, she realized, more upset than she wanted to admit.

177

She had thought a lot over the years about her mother. As a child she liked to be taken to St James's Church in Clerkenwell, where Miss Webster had found her. She had seen the very spot where her mother had fallen; the very place where Aunt Hetty had found the rush basket. In her mind, the story of her arrival in Myddleton Square had assumed almost the status of legend.

Knowledge about her father was another thing entirely. The day at Hoop Hall was one to which Aunt Hetty never referred. It was forbidden territory. All Sarah had were her own memories, and these were frightening and made her feel unsafe. The memory of Lord Fulmar behind the desk in his library had gradually turned into a huge ogreish figure, whose rage filled the whole room and where small defenceless creatures, like the butterfly, were crushed under his heel.

It was a shock to see him as a real person, in her own home. It was worse to have to accept that they were indeed kin. There were differences; Lord Fulmar's face and figure spoke of years of self-indulgence, but his eyes were like her own, as were the eyebrows, even the way he laughed. Part of her wanted to scream out a denial; part of her wanted to weep.

He had fathered her, but he was not a father. He had neither sheltered her childhood, nor offered her affection, nor given

178

her his time as, say, Mr Copperstone had done. Even now, he was not interested in her for herself, only in securing, through her, the continuation of the family line.

What should she do now? Sarah realized that her old feeling of the home in Myddleton Square as a place of safety was gone. The house had been invaded by Lord Fulmar, and might be so again. Had he finally accepted her refusal of his offer? Where could she hide, if he were determined that she should come to Hoop Hall?

There were no answers to any of these questions.

*   *   *

The following day Sarah, still pale from a sleepless night, went back to work. Jack was talking to Pepper Williams in his cubby hole when she entered the stage door. He took one look at the black rings under her eyes and exclaimed, 'Good God, Miss Beale, what is the matter?'

Sarah's head jerked up. 'Why pretend you don't know?' she said angrily. 'Lord Fulmar called yesterday. I suppose it was too much to expect you to inform me of the impending visit?'

'The old brute!' said Jack. 'I had nothing to do with it. You'd better tell me about it. We'll go to one of the boxes, it'll be quiet there.' He turned to Mr Williams, who was looking from one to the other, as if a new idea had just entered his head. 'Please tell Miss Bailey that Miss Beale is delayed.' His tone brooked no argument.

The boxes were quiet at this time of day. Jack opened a door and ushered Sarah in. A little dim light came from the windows in the corridor outside. Jack left the door ajar Sarah noticed—some care for her reputation perhaps? She began to feel a little safer. They sat down in the shadow at the back.

'Fulmar turned up, then?' said Jack, without preamble. 'I feared he might.'

'Yesterday afternoon.' Sarah found her voice was trembling.

Jack possessed himself of her hands and held them comfortingly. 'Tell me everything.'

Sarah did so. 'I'd never been that frightened before,' she whispered. 'I don't know how I had the strength to defy him. Last night I couldn't stop worrying about the consequences. He is a powerful man, Mr Midwinter. What will he do?'

'Hard to say.' Jack stared thoughtfully out into the pit. 'Legally, he can do nothing, but I wouldn't like to say . . .'

'Is he violent?' Sarah shivered.

'He has violent rages certainly. He used to beat Charlie and Arthur. But he's not murderous. I have wondered whether I should have told him that you had died . . .'

Sarah stared at him.

'He wouldn't then be pursuing you now,' Jack pointed out. He looked down at her hands, which he was still holding and turned them over. Strong, capable hands, he thought. She kept her nails short, probably so as not to snag her work. There were a couple of rough spots at the tops of her fingers. He placed them gently back in her lap and then said, 'Miss Beale, I know very well that I mishandled the entire thing when I came to see you that day. I'm sorry. I assumed, wrongly, that you'd accept his offer. And when you didn't I thought you'd probably change your mind.'

'It's true I was cross,' admitted Sarah, 'but it was a reasonable assumption to make, after all.'

'If I'd had any sense I'd have discussed it with you,' returned Jack. 'However, what's done is done. I came to Sadler's Wells in expiation.'

Sarah looked at him warily. What about Rose, she thought.

'I wanted to make sure that you were safe and see you home at night. Unfortunately, you keep giving me the slip and our friend Mr Williams, I'm sure, suspects me of the worst.'

'I thought you wanted to urge Lord Fulmar's part.'

Jack shook his head. 'I never liked the man. He has much to answer for. I blame him myself for poor Charlie's downfall.' He noted, with some amusement, that his reference to Pepper Williams's suspicions passed unnoticed. For so striking a woman, she was remarkably modest about her attractions.

'What do you think I should do?' asked Sarah.

'Difficult,' said Jack. 'Let me escort you home of an evening, for one thing. I don't think he'd try to abduct you, but I cannot be sure.'

'I shall visit Mr Wood, Miss Webster's lawyer,' said Sarah after a moment's thought. 'He may be able to suggest something. And thank you, Mr Midwinter, for your offer to see me home. I accept. I daresay Lord Fulmar will soon grow tired of pursuing me, so it won't be for long.'

The notion of having his exclusive escort was evidently not Miss Beale's idea of a high treat, thought Jack, half-amused, half-annoyed. Nor was she making excuses to prolong the conversation, for she rose and said worriedly that Miss Bailey must be wondering what had happened to her. She thanked Jack again for his help and left the box.

Jack went to find Mr Harvey in the carpentry room. They had been having a problem with Starveling's dog, and Jack had been giving it some thought. Usually, in productions of *A Midsummer Night's Dream*, Starveling, the tailor, had a real dog.

182

Mr Phelps had other ideas. He had asked for a little wooden dog, on wheels. It was the wheels that were causing the problem. The dog (looking uncannily like Spot) that Mr Harvey had made, kept falling over. The joke soon went round that they should use the real Spot because nobody would notice the difference.

Mr Williams was not amused and the appropriately named Mr Meagreson, who was playing Starveling, refused to act with it. Jack offered to help. He thought about it over the weekend and decided that the dog's centre of gravity was too high.

It would have to have shorter legs. He was also pondering the idea of a tail made of a small spring with a wooden ball at the end, which could move. Possibly the head could do the same. The dog he designed did not look much like any known breed, but it was undoubtedly a dog. Jack didn't see that Mr Phelps would object—surely it would be in keeping with his conception of the play? In the Athenian wood, where nothing was what it seemed, it would be quite in order for Starveling to have a strange, but definitely doggy, dog.

Mr Harvey was busy with *Hamlet* and told Jack to go ahead. He didn't actually believe that Jack would do anything, but as *Hamlet* opened that evening and the *Dream* was still a couple of weeks away, the problem of the dog

183

was not pressing.

Jack had always enjoyed carpentry as a small boy, and had been quite good at it. He found that his old skill had not deserted him. The result was not as finished a product as Mr Harvey himself would have produced, but Jack's dog, with its wagging tail and gently nodding head, undoubtedly had charm. What was more, it stayed upright, even when jerked around the stage.

Mr Harvey was surprised, but reluctantly declared himself satisfied, and Mr Meagreson was delighted.

*   *   *

On Tuesday, Miss Bailey decided that they were ready to try on the costumes for Theseus's attendants. They had already taken the measurements and the garments, lightly tacked, were ready for fitting. Miss Bailey then went off with Mr Thorpe to the large wardrobe room, with his costume over her arm.

Sarah had chosen the peacock green for Jack. It comprised a Grecian tunic, decorated with dull gold acanthus leaves, a gold belt and a large barbaric brooch, which secured a draped cloak on one shoulder. His legs would be bare, but he would have green and gold greaves and gold boots.

When Jack appeared, Sarah sent him into

184

the small changing-room next door, and busied herself with tidying up the loose scraps of material.

'Well, Miss Beale, what do you think?' Jack opened the door and came in.

Sarah gave a smile of pure pleasure and almost clapped her hands. He looked magnificent. His eyes were hazel, rather like Rose's, but with far more green in them, and this was brought out triumphantly in the green and gold tunic he was wearing.

Sarah just stared. For suddenly, the Jack of her childhood dreams was back. His bare arms and legs were brown and muscular and, as he walked over to the cheval-glass, he looked as though he had stepped out of the pages of the sketch book.

Jack put one hand on his hip and looked at himself in the glass. Behind him stood Sarah and he smiled at her reflection and reached out a hand.

'Come,' he said, pulling her towards him. 'What are you wearing, Miss Beale? We shall be together at the end. I hope we match.'

Sarah was still staring at his reflection.

'Me? Oh, I shall be wearing red and gold. Mostly red so as not to outshine Hippolyta. I, too, have acanthus leaves so, yes, we shall match.' She seemed not to notice that he was holding her hand. 'I thought you'd look good in this,' she added, with artistic satisfaction.

Jack laughed. 'You designed it?'

Sarah nodded.

'Clever girl.' He dropped a kiss on the top of her head.

Sarah coloured and tried to move away, but Jack was still holding her hand.

'No, come on.' He pulled her gently back towards him. 'Surely a man may express his appreciation?'

Sarah swallowed. 'You just have.'

'No, my sweet, not yet.' Jack put one brown hand underneath her chin, tilted her face up to him, and kissed her.

There was silence for a moment then Jack slowly released her and stepped back. He ran his hands through his hair as if embarrassed.

Sarah turned away so that he should not see her face and said, in as disengaged a voice as she could manage, 'If you are happy with the fit, you should take the costume off now.' Her mouth still tingled and she could feel the colour surging up over her face and neck.

Jack came across and turned her round. 'Sarah,' he said softly. 'Did I embarrass you?' He could see her heightened colour.

'I'm not . . . I've never . . .' stammered Sarah.

'Are you saying that no man has ever stolen a kiss from you before?' Jack was smiling.

Sarah shook her head.

'What a set of slow-tops they must be!'

She put her hands up to her cheeks. 'No. Well, I'm not pretty and too large, so, of course . . .'

'My dear . . .' He saw that she was serious and said, 'Have you never looked at yourself in the glass?' He turned her round to face the mirror. 'Sarah, you're beautiful.'

'Don't mock me.' Her voice was trembling.

'Indeed, I am not. You are tall and shapely and you have the loveliest eyes I've ever seen. There, will that do?'

'Th—thank you.'

Creaks were heard on the stairs and Miss Bailey, panting slightly from the exertion, was heard coming up. Jack released Sarah and moved away from her. Miss Bailey came in, took one look at Sarah's heightened colour and came to a reasonably accurate conclusion.

'Very nice, Mr Midwinter,' she said, though to what she was referring was unclear.

'I have just been expressing my admiration of Miss Beale's talents,' said Jack.

'Humph!' said Miss Bailey.

CHAPTER SEVEN

Lord Fulmar returned from London in a thoughtful mood. When the coachman and footmen recounted what had happened at Myddleton Square, Jebb, His Lordship's valet, fully expected outbursts of rage. He answered His Lordship's bell in some trepidation. But

Lord Fulmar's mood was surprisingly affable.

'Ah, there you are, Jebb. Put out my evening things, would you? Can't keep Mrs Fulmar waiting.'

'Yes, My Lord.' Jebb's mind was seething with conjecture. Had Miss Beale agreed to come after all? Was that why Lord Fulmar was in so benevolent a mood?

Lord Fulmar saw his look and laughed. 'No,' he said, to Jebb's unspoken question, 'she saw me off the premises all right. But, damme, if I don't like her the better for it.'

'Miss Beale is a young lady of spirit?' ventured Jebb.

'Reminds me of Master Arthur,' said Lord Fulmar and sighed. He missed Arthur. Whilst he was alive Lord Fulmar's fondness for his second son hadn't stopped him from beating him for insubordination but, all the same, he was his father's favourite. His reckless spirit had appealed to Lord Fulmar and he never bore a grudge to anybody who stood up to him.

'She'd do well here,' said Lord Fulmar. 'She has a mind of her own. She could cope with the estate.'

'But if she won't come, My Lord?' He hoped Lord Fulmar was not thinking of abducting her. He frequently overrode people to suit his own convenience, but abduction was another matter. Jebb had no wish to find himself in a court of law charged with aiding and abetting.

'Miss Beale does not hold all the cards,' said Lord Fulmar. If she wouldn't come voluntarily, she would have to be brought to Hoop Hall.

'No, My Lord,' said Jebb anxiously.

'I'm not thinking of abducting the wench,' said Lord Fulmar. 'You may be easy.' Jebb had some damned inconvenient notions of morality sometimes, he thought. No point in stirring up a rumpus. Usually, Lord Fulmar found it easier to bludgeon other people into doing what he wanted, but he was perfectly capable of keeping his own counsel, if the occasion required it. Lord Fulmar rarely went up to London nowadays, but he still had enough contacts there to make it possible for Miss Beale to be removed from her home without fuss and with no questions asked. For a man with enough money nothing was impossible.

He needed to find out more about her and her movements.

But Jebb was still looking worried.

'She's very loyal to the memory of her mother,' said Lord Fulmar, thoughtfully. 'Perhaps it is time she met some of her mother's relations. Whether she will like them when she knows them is another matter, but it may reconcile her to coming here; what do you think, Jebb?'

'Bound to, My Lord,' said Jebb.

'I'll have a word with Foxton.'

In the wardrobe rooms things were frantically busy. Between the opening and the Christmas production of *Harlequin Tom Thumb*, they would be doing fifteen separate plays, each with their own costumes and elaborate scenery, to say nothing of the farces which rounded off the evenings' entertainment.

Jack's own personal debut would be as a Bravo in Colley Cibber's *Love Makes a Man* on 22 September, when he, Mr Brown, Mr Scholey and Mr Hands had to rush on, armed to the teeth, and abduct the hero and his uncle, or threaten to strangle the heroine. He enjoyed it tremendously. Miss Warde, who had been watching the rehearsal, waspishly told Sarah that Miss Cooper as the heroine, Angelina, looked perfectly prepared to be strangled by Mr Midwinter and kept inching backwards into his arms.

When he wasn't rehearsing *Love Makes a Man*, Jack found his way up to the flies and helped with the special effects for the lighting at the end of *A Midsummer Night's Dream*. The scenery for Act V was of a columned hall with closed curtains in the background. The fluted columns were partly made of waxed linen with lowered gas jets inside them. The lighting came from Greek candelabra, hanging down from the flies. When the Mechanicals' play was over and Theseus and his retinue had left the stage, the servants came in and put out the lights and, simultaneously the back curtains opened. The gas jets were now turned up and the columns suddenly looked as if they were illuminated by moonlight.

The opened curtains showed a terraced garden overlooking Athens, and Fenton explained that the fairy train with Oberon and Titania, all carrying glittering lights, would dance along the steps and down the terrace to bless the house and the newly wedded couples.

The effect, said Fenton, would be magical.

Jack was really impressed and said so.

'Illusion, Mr Midwinter,' said Fenton. 'It never fails. People see what they are expecting to see. You can trick the eye.'

'Have you alway wanted to work in the theatre?' asked Jack. 'Is it not rather narrow for a man of your talents?'

'Not the way I see it,' returned Fenton. He rubbed his chin thoughtfully, and looked at Jack for a moment, summing him up. Then he said, 'We are all given talents, Mr Midwinter, and to my mind, we are here to use them. Who am I to judge its worth? What should I compare it with? A business man? A politician? A man is a man wherever he is and whatever job he does.'

'You are right, of course,' said Jack, thoughtfully. 'You are a philosopher, too, Mr Fenton.'

'I do a lot of my work inside my head,' said Fenton, smiling. 'I have time to think.'

If Jack was busy and enjoying himself, Rose was getting bored.

She didn't like to say anything to her Uncle Alfred, whose kind offices had helped her to get her job, nor to Aunt Bessy, who assumed that Rose must be thrilled to be working in the theatre, but it was all too much like hard work.

From the moment the *Dream* rehearsals started, Rose was expected to be in the theatre every day, from ten until two, and then, as often as not, there were extra dance rehearsals. Then, she was often pushed into looking after the little ones, some of whom were only seven or eight years old. Rose was one of the older fairies. In fact, as she well knew, Mr Phelps thought she was only fifteen, otherwise she probably wouldn't have been employed.

She resented being an extra nursemaid.

When she was on stage, she had to be attentive towards Miss Wyatt, who played Titania. Miss Wyatt was far too big for her boots, thought Rose, and was always asking someone, often Rose, to fetch her a drink of water or to get her shawl from the dressing-room. Miss Wyatt might be a good actress, but Rose knew that she was ten times prettier and she resented having to act as her maid.

Worst of all, she had just learnt about Mr Fenton's blue net which, Miss Goodwin gleefully informed her, would hang in front of the stage throughout Acts II, III and IV. The new gas lights gave a yellowish glow. Blue and yellow made green. They would all be bathed in a green light.

'Your hair is so fair, Miss Frampton, it will look far greener than mine. Your skin, too.'

'Green!' echoed Rose, horrified.

'Won't Miss Frampton's hair look green, Mr Fenton?' asked Miss Goodwin, innocently.

Fenton glanced at Rose's silver-gilt hair and said, 'Yes. That's the whole idea. You will look wonderfully insubstantial, Miss Frampton.'

Rose hunched her shoulders furiously, and didn't speak to Miss Goodwin for the rest of the rehearsal. Any hopes of rich male admirers leaving bouquets for her were gone. Who would wish to pursue a green-haired and green-skinned fairy?

And Mr Midwinter was proving evasive. Where was he all day? She knew he had rehearsals, just as she had, and sometimes she glimpsed him waiting in the Green Room, but he never came over and made himself agreeable. She had several offers to escort her home, but none from Mr Midwinter.

Once she'd recovered her health, Rose realized that she missed the excitements of her former life, the ordering of new clothes from the dressmaker; Lord Byland bringing her presents; the fun of an evening at Cremorne or the theatre. Lord Byland was not the most exciting of lovers, but she had enjoyed several skirmishes with some of his friends. Not that she was unfaithful to Byland, but she liked to get men into a state, teasing them with snatched kisses.

Now she was chaste and oh-so-dull. The most exciting thing in the week was Aunt Bessy's and Uncle Alfred's friends coming over on a Sunday evening, and them all playing parlour games.

They had even invited Mr Brown from the theatre for her. As if she could possibly be interested in Mr Brown, who was tall and gangly and always seemed to have a fresh crop of spots on his chin. But Mr Brown was also one of Theseus's attendants, and it was from him that Rose learnt a piece of news that she could hardly believe.

'I suppose you have lots of admirers, Miss Frampton,' said Mr Brown, gloomily, when they were having supper. He had managed to extract a kiss from her as a forfeit, when they were playing Frincy-Francy, but he could not deceive himself that it had been a success.

'Perhaps I do,' said Rose.

'Most of the ladies admire Mr Midwinter,' continued Mr Brown, stabbing at his ham with his fork. 'He's handsome, I admit, but he must be nearly forty.' Mr Brown felt that Mr Midwinter's presence meant that younger men didn't get much of a chance. 'I know Miss Warde's after him. But he's taken to escorting

194

Miss Beale home. Does it every evening. I can tell you that Mr Thorpe doesn't like it.'

Jack escorting Sarah home every evening? It was not possible! Sarah! Why, when she was at school she was called 'the maypole' because she was so tall.

Rose thought over this conversation for several days. Could it possibly be true? In the end, instead of leaving the theatre as soon as she could, she hung around in the Green Room and sewed the trimming on her costume, which she should have done days ago.

Jack had disappeared into the carpenter's room with Mr Harvey and it wasn't until nearly six o'clock that she heard him come downstairs. Already the stage hands were preparing the set for the evening's performance. She had left the Green Room door ajar, and she could hear him quite plainly—and he was talking to Sarah.

'How are things progressing, Miss Beale?'

'We're having fun with Lion's tail,' said Sarah. Snug, the joiner, acted Lion in the Mechanicals' play. The costume was designed by Miss Bailey to have a home-made look— the sort of garment that Mrs Snug might have run up, It was in a yellow knitted string, with a thick orange fringe of wool for the mane. Its chief glory was its tail.

'Mr Phelps wants the tail to have a life of its own,' continued Sarah. 'It's causing some problems.'

'A spring?' suggested Jack, whose springy dog's tail for Starveling had been much admired.

Sarah shook her head. 'Lion's tail is too long, about six feet. No, Mr Cawdery says that it will have be worked from off stage.'

'How?'

'I'm not sure,' said Sarah. 'But he seems confident that he can do it.'

They had reached the stage door.

'Good-night Sarah, Mr Midwinter,' said Pepper Williams. 'Go carefully now.'

A few moments later Rose followed them.

'You're late tonight, Miss Frampton,' said Williams in some surprise. He had marked her down as a lazy little puss.

'Some sewing.' Rose made a face. 'Was that Mr Midwinter and Miss Beale I heard?'

'Might have been.'

'Do they usually leave together?' She shooed away Spot, who was showing signs of wanting to jump up at her.

'That's their business,' said Williams, beckoning Spot to him and giving him a consolatory pat. Miss Frampton wasn't the first woman to express an interest in who Mr Midwinter might be escorting home. At that moment, Mr Brown ran up, panting.

'Miss Frampton! What a lucky chance. Pray, allow me to see you home.'

Rose gave him a tight smile and agreed. She

ignored Pepper Williams. Rude old man, she thought. As they turned down Myddleton Passage, she could just see Jack and Sarah. They were still talking animatedly though, she was pleased to notice, Sarah had not taken his arm.

She listened to Mr Brown with half an ear and kept an eye on the couple in front. After a few moments Rose and Mr Brown entered the square. Their path was up past the church and on to Claremont Square, but Rose managed to glance to the right and see Jack and Sarah standing on the steps of her house. Polly had just opened the door and Sarah stepped inside. Jack bowed, the door shut, and he retraced his steps.

Rose's mind was full of conjecture. At the very least there was an opportunity for a quick kiss on the doorstep, but Mr Midwinter had not even taken Sarah's hand. Why on earth was he bothering, then?

Perhaps he was sorry for her? That must be it. Poor thing, she'd never had any fun. No man had ever come calling at Myddleton Square for Sarah. It was sad, really.

All the same, Rose didn't like it. Supposing she told Sarah of Jack's reputation with women? Surely that would put an end to her allowing him to escort her home? And Rose would make sure that Mr Midwinter would find her a much pleasanter substitute.

The following morning Sarah was surprised to see Rose come into the large wardrobe room, which was full of people, for they had taken on several extra seamstresses to cope with the work. Sarah was busy making a tassel for Lion's tail. Miss Bailey looked up as Rose entered and raised her eyebrows. It was unlikely that Miss Frampton had come to help, she thought.

'Yes, Miss Frampton?' Miss Bailey's bright blue eyes looked quizzically over the top of her spectacles.

'May I speak to Miss Beale for a moment, please?' Rose threw Sarah a beseeching look.

Sarah left her tassel. 'Of course, Miss Frampton. Come into the other room.'

They went into the small wardrobe room and Sarah motioned Rose to a chair.

Rose fiddled with a button on her cuffs for a moment before saying, 'I understand that Mr Midwinter is escorting you home.'

'Yes.' Sarah suddenly remembered Miss Goodwin's assertion that Rose had as good as propositioned him. Was she now come to announce some sort of liaison? Sarah felt a surprisingly violent revulsion to this idea.

'I think you ought to know more about him, Sarah,' said Rose earnestly. 'He really is not a proper person for you to know.'

Sarah stared at her. Rose, of all people, to

198

be preaching propriety? 'What on earth do you mean?'

'Oh come on, Sarah,' said Rose impatiently. 'He keeps mistresses. Scores of them. He takes apartments for them, they have their own maids, visits to Paris, their barouche in the park, he denies them nothing. Then there are the married ones. Society ladies. His reputation among women is notorious. It is generally agreed that he may have any woman he asks for.'

'He has not propositioned me,' said Sarah. She felt horribly uncomfortable and slightly sick. Mr Midwinter so much of a libertine? Could it be true?

'Oh, I don't believe for a moment that he'd be after you,' said Rose. 'He likes girls about nineteen or twenty. Older than that, he's not interested.'

'Like you?' suggested Sarah. Miss Goodwin was right, she thought. This must be what Rose was after.

'Oh, you do take one up so!' cried Rose crossly. She was disconcerted that Sarah had put two and two together so quickly.

'I'm curious as to why you have brought up this conversation.'

Rose's eyes filled with tears. 'I'm concerned for you.'

Rose in tears had always made Sarah feel guilty. But this time she held her tongue. What could she say? Mr Midwinter was escorting her home out of concern for her safety, but Sarah was certainly not going to confide in Rose about Lord Fulmar. It would be all round the theatre in days.

'Thank you for telling me,' she said at last. 'I have no intention of allowing myself to be seduced by Mr Midwinter. I hope that makes you feel easier in your mind.'

'Several people have already noticed that he takes you home,' said Rose, resentfully. The conversation was not going as she expected. She had enjoyed imagining Sarah's horror. She wasn't sure what to do with Sarah's disconcerting lack of sensibility.

'I can't see that it matters,' said Sarah. 'There is nothing clandestine about it. Anybody going our way is welcome to join us.'

'Oh, you're impossible!' Rose stamped her foot pettishly. 'Don't blame me if your reputation suffers!' She flounced off and was heard running down the stairs.

Sarah went back to her tassel. She realized that she had pretended a lack of interest in Rose's information that she did not feel.

She had supposed Jack to have had some amorous adventures—most gentlemen had, but she had not thought him a positive Casanova, if what Rose had said were true. And it probably was. Half the females in the company were sighing over him and Sarah herself had to admit that she found him far more attractive than she liked. Moreover, he had taken a kiss from herself with not even a token protest on her part. It was true that she had been taken unawares, but had she slapped his face? Fainted? No, she had done neither of these things.

The shocking truth was that she had not disliked it. She supposed, in the light of this new information, that an experienced seducer must necessarily be adept at making himself agreeable to women. She found the knowledge surprisingly unwelcome.

On the other hand, he had had the delicacy not to pursue her further, once he knew her inexperience. Nor had he made her feel awkward or ashamed. In fact, he had behaved (if the kiss be excepted) like a gentleman.

All the same, Sarah could not help worrying what Jack's intentions were towards Rose.

* * *

It was half past eight in the morning and Jack was drinking coffee and had just eaten several slices of toast. Archie was expressing his disapproval of having to be up at so ungodly an hour by being very correct and saying nothing.

Jack ignored him and picked up his morning's post. There were surprisingly few bills nowadays, for he had had very little time to go out and buy anything. There was a letter from Tessiers, discreetly advertising some

201

choice new pieces of jewellery just arrived, which Jack threw straight into the waste-paper basket.

There was, however, a letter in answer to his, from his uncle, Josiah Pinks.

If you want to work with Midwinter and Pinks then you must come up and discuss it with me. I should expect you to take it seriously, mind. But there is plenty for you to do. In the longer term, a family business link in London could be an advantage, so you would not have to live up here, if you didn't want to.

Your Aunt Agnes sends her love.

Your affectionate uncle,
Josiah Pinks.

'If you've finished with your plate, sir, I'll take it away,' said Archie.

'Come on, you old curmudgeon,' said Jack. 'What is it?'

'How long's this start going on for?' growled Archie. 'It don't suit me, these hours you keep nowadays. I'm a night owl, always have been. You being up all night, like a gentleman, don't worry me. But I expect to have my morning lie-in.'

Jack laughed. He knew, as well as Archie, that his valet would never leave him, however much he grumbled.

'Want to be pensioned off, then?'

'It may come to that,' said Archie, gloomily.

'I'm committed to the theatre until Mr Frost returns, probably at the end of October. But I have also to see that Miss Beale is all right. You know that.'

'Do you really think Lord Fulmar would abduct her?'

'No, I don't. But I cannot be sure.'

'Just you watch it,' growled Archie. 'You seem to find this Miss Beale pretty taking. You'll find yourself in parson's mousetrap afore you know it.'

'Nonsense,' laughed Jack.

*   *   *

That Sunday, Rose took one of the Angel omnibuses down to the West End. She was going to tea, once again, with Amy Rush. Amy, she thought enviously, had just spent an expensive couple of weeks in Paris with her new lover, Lord Penning. Doubtless she'd want to show off all her purchases and Rose would have to grit her teeth and put up with it. But she would get all the current gossip.

She needed Amy's advice. It was Amy who had given her the necessary push which got her out of Myddleton Square. 'What are you waiting for, girl?' she'd said. 'Byland won't offer you marriage, but he'll see you're all right. If this is the life you want, you take it. Chances don't come along every day.'

And Rose had done so. On the whole she hadn't regretted it. She'd had a good couple of years and the boredom of Byland's company, after the first excitement had worn off, had swiftly faded from her memory. What remained was the fun, her own rooms and the pretty clothes.

When they parted Byland had given her £200 and she still had her wardrobe of clothes and the jewellery he had given her. That was better any day than the dull respectability of Myddleton Square and marriage to some spotty youth like Mr Brown.

Amy's new rooms were in New Bond Street and looked very similar to the old: the same riot of gilt and crimson.

To Rose it all looked familiar—and she had lost it.

'Oh, it's wonderful!' cried Rose, when she had kissed Amy, and had time to look around. 'It's just like your old rooms—only better,' she added hastily. 'Heavens! Look at those prints!' She burst into a fit of giggles. 'You've never tried to do it like that?'

Amy giggled too. 'We did try one of them. It was terribly uncomfortable. I fell over.'

'What a beautiful gown!' Rose reached out to finger it.

Amy sank down onto the *chaise-longue*. 'We're just back from Paris. Penning was most generous. The clothes are simply divine. Everything is named after the new empress.

They say she's very beautiful—it's "Eugénie" this and "Eugénie" that, everywhere.'

'Oh, you are lucky!'

Amy could not help but be gratified by Rose's admiration and willingly showed off her new clothes, and even gave Rose a silk scarf that she found was the wrong colour for herself.

Later, over tea, Rose told her about Jack Midwinter. 'Why is he working at the theatre, Amy? That's what I want to know. Surely, he's come to be near me? But he makes no opportunities to see me—and when we do meet, he doesn't take advantage of it, and you know how unlike him that is. Yet, why else could he possibly be there?'

'I haven't seen him around,' said Amy thoughtfully. 'Normally, I'd expect to see him at Cremorne or the opera. I'll ask Penning. He used to know him quite well.'

'What should I do?'

Amy shrugged 'Find another man, my dear. What else? Was everything all right with . . . ?' She paused delicately.

'It was a false alarm, thank God,' said Rose. 'Lizzie was very kind. How is she doing?'

'Very well. And she's not so pretty that you need to worry about her making moves on her own account when you're out of the room. She certainly seems to have seen the way the wind was blowing with Byland.'

Rose didn't like to be reminded. 'He'll be

getting married soon, I daresay?'

'November, Penning told me.'

Later, Rose said, 'Keep your eye open for me please, Amy. I can't stand being good for too long.'

Amy laughed and promised.

* * *

Mrs Fanshawe, a pleasant, somewhat highly-strung widow in her early fifties, sat at her breakfast-table in her house in Portman Square, and opened her post. Her daughter, Louisa, sitting opposite, toyed with her toast.

Suddenly, there was a shriek from Mrs Fanshawe. The letter she had just opened fell unheeded to the floor, and she burst into tears.

'Oh, my poor Maria!' she wailed. Her face had crumpled up and tears were running down her cheeks so fast that they splashed onto the dining-table.

Louisa was horrified. She rang the bell and ran round to her mother. The moment the butler came in she said, 'Call Mrs Fanshawe's maid at once, please. My mother is not well.' Who was Maria? Whatever could have happened?

Mrs Fanshawe, still sobbing, bent down, picked up the letter and clutched it to her bosom.

As soon as Mrs Fanshawe had been helped up to her room, Louisa wrote an agitated note

206

to her uncle, Sir George Cranborne, who lived in Seymour Street, begging him to come round without delay. She then paced the dining-room carpet, every now and then going to the window and peering out anxiously.

As soon as his footsteps were heard in the hall, she ran out, almost dragged him into the dining-room and poured out the whole story.

'Maria, eh?' said George thoughtfully.

'Who is Maria?'

'Can't be sure. I suspect it's Maria Beale, a distant cousin.'

'I've never heard of her.'

'Before your time. It's an unsavoury story, not fit for your ears.' He went back into the hall and crooked a finger at the butler, 'Ask if Mrs Fanshawe is well enough to see me, would you?'

He was shown up almost at once, leaving Louisa unenlightened and indignant in the dining-room.

'Oh, my dear George,' cried Mrs Fanshawe, as soon as they were alone. 'Read that!' she sat up and mopped at her eyes.

Mr Foxton, he read, had been instructed by Lord Fulmar to inform Mrs Fanshawe that Sarah, the daughter of Maria Beale and His Lordship had been born on 22 May, 1825 and christened at St Matthew's in Bethnal Green. Maria Beale had died sometime in January 1826 and was buried at St James's, Clerkenwell. The said Sarah Beale was now residing in Myddleton Square, Islington, and was wishful to meet her mother's relations.

That was all. There was no explanation of how Lord Fulmar came by this information. Nothing.

'Sounds like a hum to me,' observed Sir George.

'What do you mean?'

'Why should this Beale girl turn up now, after all these years? What does she want? Long lost relations tend to want something other than the pleasure of one's acquaintance. Like money. No, this will have to be thoroughly checked.'

'Lord Fulmar is acknowledging her, George,' protested Mrs Fanshawe. 'But poor Maria, to die so young. How I missed her! I know she wasn't steady, but she was such fun.'

'She caused our poor mother a great deal of anguish,' said Sir George austerely. 'Remember that business with young Turner?'

Mrs Fanshawe shuddered. 'Don't!'

'Mama had a damned difficult time hushing that up. Maria's reputation was saved by the skin of her pretty teeth.'

'What shall we do?'

'Leave it to me. I'll check it.'

*　　　*　　　*

It was the second night of *Hamlet*. Neither Jack nor Sarah was needed at the theatre that

208

evening, so Sarah was able to get home early and Jack did what he hadn't done for weeks, went to his club.

It was strange to be dressing as befitted a gentleman on a night out and the clothes seemed unfamiliar. As he walked into the elegant Italianate hall at the Reform Club he found he was noticing things he normally passed by; the porters who jumped up from a quiet game of cards in the cloakroom as he entered; the young messenger boy, who hastily stuffed a penny dreadful into his back pocket and stood to attention. Presumably they had always shown evidence of other things in their lives than being correct servants in a gentleman's club? He nodded at the porters and handed over his frock coat and top hat. He realized that he didn't even know their names.

There were a number of gentlemen in the smoking-room, most of whom looked up as Jack entered, nodded and resumed their conversations or their newspapers; it was considered bad form to hail a man unless he had indicated that he wished to converse.

Still feeling slightly out of place, Jack picked up a copy of *The Times* and sat down on one of the leather sofas. His neighbour looked up.

'Good God!' he exclaimed. 'Midwinter, as I live! I understand that you are treading the boards now. When's your first night, old chap? Or are we not to know?'

'How do you know?' Jack demanded. Lord Penning, as he well knew, was something of a rattle. 'I, certainly, haven't told anybody where I am.'

Penning saw that Jack was seriously put out and said, 'Amy told me. Strange start, eh, Midwinter? What the devil are you doing there?'

'My own business,' said Jack curtly. 'Amy Rush, you mean? Are you with Amy now?'

'Been out of circulation, old boy.'

'I'd like a word with her.'

Penning rose and tossed his paper onto the table. 'We'll be at Drury Lane tonight. Box eighteen. Join us.'

'Thank you.' Jack thought he could guess who had given Amy the information.

Archie was not surprised at the news. He put out Jack's shaving water and laid out the black dress coat and trousers, embroidered waistcoat and silk stockings, which were the correct evening wear for a gentleman going out to the theatre.

'Of course, it's going to get around,' he said. 'People talk.'

Jack entered Penning's box during the first interval of *The Betrothal*. He kissed Amy's cheek, told her she was looking ravishing and said, 'I gather you've been talking to Rose Frampton.'

'Oh dear, was it meant to be a secret?' Amy was intrigued.

'Just private.'

'But Mr Midwinter,' Amy teased, 'if you want Rose, why bother to go through such a charade? She's eager enough.'

'Oh, a whim,' said Jack. So that's it, he thought. Rose thinks I'm after her. Foolish girl. Yet, in the past, he had done things quite as stupid to get some woman into his bed.

As he watched the play he found, to his amusement, that he was criticizing the lighting effects and thinking how much better a job of it Fenton would have made. The play itself was boring and predictable and probably only chosen as a vehicle for G.V. Brooke, who was playing Marsio. Amy, he remembered, was an admirer of Brooke's acting, though he ranted too much for Jack's taste.

He turned his attention to the audience, using his opera glasses to see who else was in the boxes. The *demi-monde* was out in force. There were plenty of enticing white shoulders and plunging *décolletages*. He could tell that his name was being whispered behind open fans, and several ladies smiled in his direction.

Amy turned to him and whispered, 'The word's going round. Mr Midwinter is back. Who will it be this time?'

Jack smiled, but it was an effort. He knew all the moves; the flirtation, the capitulation, the inevitable week in Paris, the equally predictable set of rooms, and then the quarrels and making-up and the final parting. Then the whole merry-go-round would start again.

He was done with it, he now realized. He wanted no more of its tawdry glamour.

He left Penning's box after the second interval and went home.

The following morning saw Jack at Sadler's Wells, feeling strangely relieved to be back at work. The rehearsal schedule was pinned up by the stage door and he scanned it. There was a dance rehearsal of the fairies until twelve. He would talk to Rose when it finished. Later, there would be a technical rehearsal of *Love Makes a Man*, which opened the following evening. In the meantime, he would go and see if Mr Harvey needed any help.

Rose had worked hard during the rehearsal. Underneath her spoilt exterior, she was fond of her Uncle Alfred, who, as dance designer, was taking the rehearsal, and realized that she must do him credit. It wouldn't do to let him down.

When she saw Jack, as she entered the Green Room, it seemed like virtue's true reward for her efforts that morning. He was smiling, and Rose enjoyed seeing Miss Goodwin's sour face as he came over to her. At last, perhaps something would be sorted out. Ten minutes later she found herself sitting with him outside the theatre on one of the benches overlooking the river and enjoying the late summer sunshine. Jack bought them both a pie.

But his first words were far from loverlike.

'You must learn to mind your own business, pretty Rose.'

'What do you mean?'

'I saw Amy Rush last night. I gather you told her I was here.'

Rose glanced up at him from under her lashes. 'What if I did?'

'You are under a misapprehension. I am here entirely for private reasons. Nothing to do with your pretty self.'

Not here about her? It didn't make sense. Rose felt a sudden chill. If Jack wasn't going to take her away, then what would become of her? She'd have to stay for ever. Or be prepared to put up with Lord Walmsley's meanness and braying laugh.

She didn't believe him. So what could have made him change his mind? He was wondrous great with Sarah nowadays. It must be her. Rose didn't stop to think that Sarah could have told Jack nothing that he didn't already know about her.

'You've been talking to my preachy stepsister,' she said accusingly.

'Stepsister?' Jack was puzzled at the sudden change of subject.

'Sarah Beale. She always—'

'Miss Beale is your stepsister?' Jack was astounded. 'How can that be?'

'Miss Maypole is nothing better than a foundling, a gutter child, picked up by my

213

great-aunt and raised for charity.' Why should Sarah always be held up as a model of good conduct, she thought?

'But you are not related, surely?'

'No. I came to live with my great-aunt when I was five, after my mother died. Sarah and I were brought up as sisters, though she is twenty-eight now. Much older than I am.'

'She has said nothing about this,' said Jack thoughtfully.

'No. I asked her not to.' Rose tossed her head. 'I don't want unkind rumours going round about me.'

'Rose,' said Jack gently, 'don't you think it's you who is being unkind, telling me all this about Miss Beale?'

In a sudden pet, Rose threw the rest of her pie into the water. 'Sarah's so superior sometimes,' she complained. 'She's never liked me. Just because I'm prettier than she is.'

'Is she unkind to you? I find that hard to believe.'

'No, not exactly. But I don't understand why you keep taking her home.'

'You mean, rather than escorting you?'

Rose pouted.

'Miss Beale has been the subject of some unpleasantness,' said Jack, after a moment's thought as to what he might say with safety. 'I see that she gets home safely, that is all. But really, Rose, I don't think you should say such things about your stepsister.'

By now Rose was feeling thoroughly ashamed of herself, a state she never found at all comfortable. 'Oh, you're like all the rest,' she flared up. 'Preach, preach, preach.'

'Is that what you think?'

'You used to be different. I thought you'd understand.' Tears filled her eyes.

'If you're after the bright lights again, you should go for somebody more your own age. I'm far too old for you.'

'Since when?'

'Since I realized that I should stop playing about with girls half my age.'

'I like older men,' suggested Rose.

'Maybe. But you're not getting this one.'

'You'll have no chance with Sarah. I'll tell you that!'

'I wouldn't dream of asking Miss Beale to be my mistress.'

'Oh!' Two spots of angry colour flew on Rose's cheeks. 'She's too good for it, is she?'

'Rose, stop talking like a spoilt child,' said Jack wearily.

There was a swirl of skirts and Rose flounced off, leaving Jack ruefully aware that, for the first time in his life, he had behaved as any sensible man of thirty-eight ought to do with an overwrought nineteen year old. It might have been a sobering reflection, but instead he felt only amusement. Why on earth had he put up with such silliness all these years?

He sat for a while contemplating the ducks and idly throwing them bits of pie crust. The knowledge that Rose had been brought up with Sarah worried him. Was that why Sarah was wary of him? How much had Rose told her? His past life looked sordid, when seen through Sarah's eyes. He would much rather that she didn't know.

What could he ever say to excuse himself? To put his side? To his shame, Jack couldn't think of a single occasion when he had ever done anything remotely useful. He had never worked, always evaded any responsibilities and tolerated his mistresses only as long as they amused him. The most that could be said was that he didn't think he had harmed anybody and, though it was a negative virtue, he had not run into debt nor mortgaged his estate.

That evening, as he saw Sarah home, he found himself broaching the subject. He had not meant to, but somehow he couldn't keep off it.

'I was talking to Rose Frampton today,' he began.

'Oh?' Sarah looked at him.

'I hadn't realized, until she told me, that you were brought up together.'

'Poor Rose,' Sarah sighed. 'She was always so pretty and she longed so for riches and the easy life. I've sometimes thought that she should have been Lord Fulmar's daughter. How much she'd love it.'

216

'Surely you had to cast her off when she . . . er . . . ran away?'

'I'd never want to do to Rose what was done to my mother,' said Sarah indignantly. 'She has always known that.'

Not quite the story he had from Rose, thought Jack. Sarah's generosity encouraged him in his next question. 'Did . . . did she tell you that she was acquainted with me?'

'Yes,' said Sarah shortly. Her colour had risen.

'You must be wondering—'

'Mr Midwinter, your private life is no concern of mine.'

For some reason, thought Jack, that was not true. 'I did not come to Sadler's Wells in pursuit of Rose, as she seems to think.'

Sarah was unaccountably relieved but said, 'She won't be pleased.'

'She wasn't.'

'She's like a lily of the field; she toils not neither does she spin. She has no application. Still, most gentlemen don't mind that. And she is very pretty, of course.'

'You don't have a very high opinion of men,' observed Jack.

'Nonsense!' Sarah was startled.

'But we are led astray by our liking for feminine beauty?'

Sarah smiled. 'I daresay that is just sour grapes on my part.'

'I thought I had made my views clear with

regard to your own attractions,' said Jack.

'Your behaviour was disgraceful.' Sarah turned her face away, but he could see the colour in her cheek.

'But very pleasant.'

Sarah had no answer.

CHAPTER EIGHT

Rehearsals for the *Dream* were now in full swing and Sarah began cautiously to enjoy them. Whenever she had previously been on stage, she had felt huge, gawky and out of place. She always tried to hide away at the back, where she felt useless and self-conscious. Rationally, she knew that nobody was looking at her, but she was always relieved when the performance came to an end and she could escape.

Mr Phelps had decided that Jack and Sarah were to be the chief attendants. Both were tall and good-looking and they must be together, certainly in the last act. He noticed, with some amusement, that if some of the men still resented Mr Midwinter being able to buy his way into the company, the ladies had quite forgiven him. Even Miss Beale, who could be prickly, appeared to have succumbed to his charm.

Sarah found herself infected with Jack's

self-confidence.

'Come along, Miss Beale,' he said, as they exited at the end of Act IV. 'You are twice as beautiful as Miss Portman. Hold up your head!' He offered her his arm.

Such was his authority that Sarah drew herself up, placed her hand lightly on Jack's arm, and swept off the stage. Pepper Williams, from his position in the prompt box, winked at her. Sarah made a face at him.

Jack, she saw, whilst perfectly conscious of his good looks and the effect they had, wore them lightly.

She had begun to realize this a day or so earlier, when he had been trying on his Bravo costume for *Love Makes a Man*. The costume was vaguely Portuguese, which was where most of the play was set. Jack had black knee breeches, white stockings and black shoes. His shirt was white with loose sleeves banded at the wrist, and he wore a flame coloured sash. He looked outstandingly handsome. He swept them both a low bow.

'What do you think?'

'You must be so well aware that you look magnificent, that you don't need me to add to your swollen head,' said Sarah tartly. She dragged her eyes away from him with an effort.

'Ouch!' said Jack and laughed. He turned to Miss Bailey and added, 'Miss Beale has claws I see.'

'So it appears,' said Miss Bailey composedly.

'Shall you come and see me act, Miss Beale? Miss Bailey? It opens on Thursday. It will be my début, you know.'

'Your début!' echoed Sarah mockingly. 'Hark at him! You'd think he was the star of the show.'

'I'll see you home safely afterwards.'

Sarah looked at Miss Bailey, who smiled and nodded.

'Oh, very well.' She spoke grudgingly out of embarrassment, but she was not displeased at the idea.

When Jack had gone, Sarah said reflectively, 'Considering how good-looking he is, he's not really vain. He enjoys his looks, but he doesn't mind being teased.'

'I like him,' said Miss Bailey. 'I admit I didn't at first. Gentlemen who pay to be on stage can be such a bother and you can never rely on them, but Mr Midwinter is certainly pulling his weight.'

She had once or twice been to the back of the pit when a rehearsal of the *Dream* was in progress and could see how much more confident Sarah had become. Much of this was due to Mr Midwinter's encouragement. He was certainly the only man who dared to flirt with her without being frozen out.

Sarah, too, realized that something in herself had changed. She no longer felt such an outcast. Mr Midwinter knew her history and it plainly made no difference to him; perhaps she had allowed herself to be over-sensitive about her bastardy.

Even Sarah could see that Jack enjoyed her company. She saw him every day and usually walked home with him of an evening. They always seemed to have plenty to talk about and he appeared interested in what she had to say.

One evening she told him about the puppet theatre that Mr Copperstone had made for her when she was a child.

'I'm sure that is what started off my interest in costume design,' she said. She didn't tell him that ever since she had seen him at Hoop Hall, he had been her secret model of a proper man.

'I should like to see this theatre,' said Jack. He was intrigued, as always, by models, and had already told Sarah about the millwheel he'd made as a boy.

'It got broken,' said Sarah sadly. 'At least, some of the little puppets did. Rose broke them. She was very young, so I don't blame her, but I was very upset at the time.'

'If you bring them in, I may be able to mend them,' said Jack. 'I'd like to try.'

'Would you?' Sarah's eyes lit up. 'I'd be so grateful.'

'I'll have a look, at any rate.'

Sarah touched his arm lightly in thanks. Jack looked down at her and smiled.

It was Thursday and Jack's début in *Love Makes a Man*. Sarah and Miss Beale got two pit seats from a grumpy Mr Williams and took the evening off to enjoy themselves. The play, one of Colley Cibber's from the eighteenth century, had a perfectly preposterous plot involving rival brothers, a beautiful heiress, a shipwreck, an adventuress, plenty of skulduggery and, of course the bravos. Jack was kept busy being villainous and dragging various characters on and off stage and generally behaving like a reckless desperado.

'I must say,' said Miss Bailey, as they applauded at the end, 'he's perfect for the part.'

'I know. He can't really act, but he puts an immense amount of energy into it.'

'You don't need to act in that sort of play,' said Miss Bailey. 'The characters are just stock types. Still, it's very entertaining.' She did not often take the opportunity to see the plays and she enjoyed seeing her costumes in action.

Miss Bailey went home with Mr Brown, who lived near her, and Sarah waited for Jack at the stage door.

'We enjoyed your performance,' she said at once. 'We particularly liked the way you were about to strangle Angelina. Most effective.'

Jack laughed. 'For two pins I *would* have strangled her,' he said cheerfully. 'Miss

222

Cooper would keep trying to shrink artistically towards me.'

Sarah remembered Miss Warde's remarks on Miss Cooper's behaviour, but decided not to comment. Instead she said, 'It's very kind of you to see me home, Mr Midwinter.'

'I enjoy it,' said Jack simply. 'Don't you?'

'Ye . . . s,' said Sarah. She did, but it had begun to dawn on her that when Jack left, it was going to leave a blank in her life.

'But?' queried Jack. 'So doubtful a yes always carries a "but".'

'You cannot stay at the theatre for ever, Mr Midwinter. In six weeks or so Mr Frost will be back. Don't you miss your old life?' The thought of him once more taking mistresses and leading the life of a wealthy gentleman of fashion with nothing to do but indulge his whims, was most unpleasant.

'Go back to my old life? No,' said Jack decidedly. 'I shall be thirty-nine at the end of November, Miss Beale. I do not want the second half of my life to be as wasted as the first.'

Sarah knew a real lightening of heart. 'What shall you do then?'

'Probably go into business with my uncle in Manchester. Cotton.'

'In Manchester. That's a long way away.' Sarah looked out over the New River ponds, which looked suddenly desolate in the moonlight.

223

'Not so far now there are trains. A day's journey. No more.'

'I suppose so.' Sarah's voice sounded hollow. In an effort to disguise her dismay she added brightly, 'Is it a pleasant city?'

'Not very. There are some appalling slums. But it has a raw vitality and energy that I like.'

They had reached her house in Myddleton Square. Sarah reached into her pocket and said, 'Oh, I nearly forgot.' She held out the two broken puppets, each about three inches high. 'See, the Green Knight's arm is broken and Princess Eglantine has lost her wand.'

Jack moved under a gas light and looked at them, turning then over carefully. 'What was the Green Knight doing?'

'He held a sword. That's gone too. And his arm could move up and down.'

'And Princess Eglantine's wand?'

'Just a wand. I made a little star for the end of it. You can see how it slotted into her hand.'

Jack tucked them carefully into his coat pocket and Sarah tapped on the lion's head door-knocker. Polly could be heard puffing up from the basement.

Sarah turned to Jack. 'Thank you,' she said. 'You are very kind.' She gave him an uncertain smile and vanished into the house.

Jack walked thoughtfully back to the theatre.

Polly had saved some supper for Sarah, but she waved it away. 'Thank you, Polly, but I'm

224

not hungry.'

She took the candle Polly offered and went through to her bedroom where she undressed slowly, as if the process were too much for her and all her garments unaccountably heavy. Then she slipped on her cotton nightdress and began to brush her hair and tie it in two plaits for the night. She sat at her dressing-table, her fingers working swiftly and automatically, but her mind was elsewhere.

Mr Midwinter would be going to Manchester and, once there, it was unlikely that she would ever see him again. She didn't know why, but Manchester seemed infinitely further away than it was in reality—almost at the end of the earth. She would be just as unlikely to see him again even if he stayed in London, their worlds were so different, but it didn't feel that way.

The awful realization that his going would leave a hole somewhere in the region of her heart must be stamped out. Their lives lay apart. She would not allow herself to be affected. Their acquaintance would stay in her memory as a pleasant interlude, that was all.

She had lived without him before and must do so again. Emotion in the theatre, she knew, could be very intense. It was a genuine intimacy, made of shared endeavour and proximity but, like Mr Fenton's lighting effects, largely an illusion. Powerful, but not real. It had no existence outside the theatre world, she must remember that.

All the same, she was shocked to realize that, were Mr Midwinter to ask her to become his mistress, she would have some difficulty in refusing. Refuse she would, she did not think she could bear the transitory nature of such a relationship, but part of her would want it very much indeed.

Had this been how her mother had felt? Had she ignored the warning signs and allowed herself to believe that Lord Fulmar would be willing to offer her marriage? Her mother had at least been more of Lord Fulmar's social equal; it would have been a talked-about, but not impossible, match.

Mr Midwinter had made his future plans very clear. And they did not include herself. His feelings were quite platonic. She had Rose's confirmation for that.

'He said he'd never ask you to be his mistress,' Rose had reported. 'He just doesn't think of you in that way at all.'

Sarah sighed, finishing plaiting her hair—tightly, as if confining any unruly thoughts—and went to bed.

*　　　*　　　*

The following morning Sarah woke up later than usual and had to scramble into her clothes and rush through her breakfast cup of coffee. She wanted to be at the theatre early to mend one of the *School for Scandal* costumes, where a seam had split. Then there was a *Dream* rehearsal at ten o'clock, and after that things would be busy.

Usually, Leah accompanied her to the theatre on her way to do the morning's shopping. It was slightly out of Leah's way, but she enjoyed the walk and it was a time when she and Sarah could discuss any household matters in comparative peace.

Today, Sarah was in a rush. She called down the kitchen stairs, 'Leah! I must dash. I'll talk to you about those tiles under the sink this evening.'

'Yes, Miss Sarah.'

Sarah did not notice the carriage at the corner of Myddleton Square and River Street. She turned quickly down Myddleton Passage towards the theatre.

She never reached it.

She was in so much of a hurry that she didn't see the two men blocking her path until it was too late. She bumped straight into them. Suddenly, a hand with a chloroformed handkerchief was clamped over her nose. She choked, clawed the air and collapsed.

Seconds later the carriage had moved up. A muffled sagging figure was pushed into it. The two men climbed in and they were gone. The whole thing had taken less than two minutes.

Sarah had confused impressions of somebody making her drink something, of

227

cold, of darkness, of movement and then nothing.

When she came to she was lying along the seats on one side of a railway carriage. The window blind was down, but she could see edges of light around the blind. Her head felt thick and heavy. She lay with her eyes closed.

A voice spoke, 'She awake yet?' It was a rough male voice. Sarah didn't recognize it.

'No, not a peep.'

'Best that way. She won't make no fuss when we arrive.'

'Who'd believe her?' said the second man. 'She's His Lordship's mad niece. That's the word.'

Sarah's brain took another lurch into reality. She opened her mouth to speak but her tongue wouldn't obey. She could hear the rhythmic noise of the wheels, *ra-ta-ta-ta-tat, ra-ta-ta-ta-tat*. Gradually, her mind swam back into focus.

She had been kidnapped by Lord Fulmar and she must now be on her way to Hoop Hall. Nothing else was possible. Her mind still felt too fuzzy for clear thought, but escape didn't seem likely. She drifted back to sleep.

The next she knew was the cold of the station platform as she was lifted out of the railway carriage and carried to His Lordship's chaise. There was a chink of coins, a door shut, and they were off again.

She opened her eyes a fraction and saw a

228

gnarled hand with a signet ring, gold with a bloodstone, on the little finger. It must be Lord Fulmar.

'So you're awake.'

Sarah didn't reply. She desperately wanted a drink.

'Well, miss?'

'I need some water.' Sarah spoke in a faint voice. She struggled to raise herself into a sitting position.

'You'll have to wait until we get to Hoop Hall.' A hand rested with surprising gentleness on her forehead for a moment and a cushion was pushed behind her head.

Sarah tried to focus on the scene outside. She vaguely recognized the gingerbread house by the gates of the Hoop Hall estate. Then they were bowling up the avenue and there was the house, smaller than she remembered, with the stone lions at the bottom of the steps. The chaise pulled up and the coachman climbed down and opened the door.

A frightened-looking lady came down the steps. 'Oh My Lord,' she cried, 'what have you done?'

Sarah attempted to climb out, missed her footing and fell onto the gravel.

'Quiet, woman. Help Miss Fulmar up. Take her to the blue room.'

Sarah was struggling to rise. 'No!' she cried. 'I am not Miss Fulmar. Nor will I ever be.'

She was jerked to her feet. 'You will do as I

say!' he shouted. 'Or I shall shut you up until you do.'

'Shut me up then,' said Sarah. She simply didn't care. The world was going round and round again and she had to clutch at the chaise to stop herself from falling.

'What have you done to her?' cried the lady, even more agitated. She was wringing her hands.

'Laudanum. She's shamming it. Jebb!'

The valet appeared. He took one look at Sarah and paled.

'Take Miss Fulmar up to the attic floor. Carry her if necessary.' He turned to the agitated lady. 'As for you, go back to your drawing-room. And I don't want a word of this to get out. Do you hear?'

The lady turned and fled.

Sarah was half-hauled, half-carried up three flights of stairs. Jebb had his arm around her waist and Lord Fulmar, leaning heavily on his ebony cane, was panting behind. At the top was the attic floor: maids' rooms and storage rooms mostly.

'Go away, Jebb,' ordered Lord Fulmar.

Jebb disappeared. Lord Fulmar opened the door to a small room with an old linen press in one corner, and closed it behind them. Sarah sank down onto a stool.

'It's high time I took control of your life,' he informed her. 'A daughter of mine to be working in the theatre! A drab of a seamstress and, I'm told, you are sometimes on stage as well, like the veriest slut. You are a disgrace to the name of Fulmar. Either you're sensible and behave like a lady, or else I'll put you somewhere until you do.'

Sarah said nothing. She was beyond thought. All she knew was that she would never give in to the man in front of her. She would as soon sign away her soul.

Lord Fulmar waited a few moments and then said, 'So be it.' He bent down, touched a bead on the panelling and a small panel opened. 'Kneel,' he said. 'Get in.'

Sarah shook her head. Lord Fulmar picked up his cane and swished it. 'Get in,' he said again.

Sarah did so. The panel closed behind her with a final click and she was alone.

Inside there was an old straw pallet and a couple of saddle blankets, a flagon of water and a bucket with a cover. Sarah crawled to the flagon and drank deeply, then she fell back on the pallet and closed her eyes.

*　　　*　　　*

It was not until that evening that it finally dawned on the company at Sadler's Wells that Sarah was missing. Miss Bailey assumed that she had gone to the rehearsal, and Phelps assumed that she was held up with the costumes.

231

Jack himself realized only when he went up to the small wardrobe room at six o'clock and found that she wasn't there. Nor had she been the entire day. He ran down the stairs to the stage door. Mr Williams had not seen her either.

He went straight to Phelps's dressing-room, where Phelps was getting ready to play Sir Peter Teazle in *School for Scandal*. Mrs Phelps was always there to help her husband dress, and she smiled at Jack when he knocked at the door and poked his head round.

'I'm sorry to disturb you, Mr Phelps,' he said, 'but Miss Beale is missing.'

Phelps raised an eyebrow. 'Surely not?' What was the matter with this excitable young man?

Jack opened his mouth to explain and then shut it again. It would all take too long. And time was what he didn't have.

'I shall have to go,' he said. 'If it is merely some domestic problem that has kept her, then I'll be back tomorrow. If, as I fear, it is more serious, I'll be back when I've found her.' He shut the door and was heard running down the stairs.

'He's serious,' said Mrs Phelps. 'I always did think that his being here had something to do with Miss Beale.'

'That's your romantic heart, my love,' said Phelps. 'All the same, there is something going on. It's not like Mr Midwinter to be so

232

agitated.' But there was a performance in less than an hour. He had other things to concentrate on. He would worry about Miss Beale, if necessary, in the morning.

Jack's arrival alone at Myddleton Square caused horror and alarm and for a while he was unable to get anything out of Leah, who felt it her duty to her mistress to go into hysterics. Finally, Polly slapped her. But there was little to tell. Miss Sarah had left the house at about half past eight that morning. That was all they knew.

She had been gone for ten hours.

'Oh my poor Sarah,' wailed Miss Valloton. 'It must be that nasty Lord Fulmar. Who else could it be?'

'So I think,' said Jack. He was pacing up and down Miss Webster's drawing-room. Finally, he stopped. 'I think you should keep this quiet for the moment.'

'You don't think we should inform the police?' asked Miss Valloton hesitantly. The idea of the whole square knowing that police officers had been calling was shameful, but if it were the right thing to do?

'No, I think not,' said Jack decidedly. 'I believe her to be at Hoop Hall. There is nothing the police can do at this stage. You'd better leave it to me.' He was well aware that the police would hesitate to accuse a peer of the realm of abduction.

He left the house and was fortunate to get a

cab in Amwell Street. Half an hour later he was back in his rooms in Half Moon Street.

Archie was shocked but unsurprised.

'I thought Lord Fulmar wouldn't give up that easily,' he said. 'What are you going to do?'

'Go home first thing tomorrow morning. See what I can find out. Ulthorne may know something. If I'm to get to Hoop Hall without Lord Fulmar's knowledge, I shall need inside help. I'll ask Salter; he was always good to me as a boy.'

'It's one thing to let you raid the garden for strawberries and quite another to allow you to housebreak,' said Archie sourly.

'We'll see,' said Jack. 'Salter won't want to be mixed up in an abduction. A guinea or two may help him make up his mind.'

Jack spent a wretched evening going over everything in his head. He ordered a meal from the chop house, but scarcely touched it when it came. The thought of Sarah, alone and terrified, shut up in that priest's hole, for he was pretty sure that's where she was, nearly sent him out of his mind. Would she know that he would come for her? He hoped so. But even if she did, how could she know that he knew about her prison?

He slept fitfully and was relieved when dawn broke and he could be up and doing.

Archie had packed and, as soon as breakfast was over, they set out for King's Cross and the

Great Northern Railway. When they arrived at St Alban's, Archie hailed a cab to take them to Holly Park and Jack questioned the porters. Yes, he was told, Lord Fulmar's chaise was seen yesterday, late morning it was. No, no young lady, so far as they knew, but it had been very busy.

Jack climbed into the cab and they set out for Holly Park. Mrs Midwinter was surprised to see them and horrified when she learned the reason.

'Lord Fulmar abduct Miss Beale!' she cried. 'Why, it's scarcely credible.'

'Where else can she be, Mama?'

'How do I know where the wretched girl is? She seems to be nothing but a pack of trouble. And you certainly cannot go interfering in other people's business.' Ever since Miss Beale had appeared on the scene, she thought, Jack had been quite unlike himself. She wanted her son to take an interest in some nice girl, not in a woman from a lodging-house who might, or might not, be the daughter of Lord Fulmar. It was too provoking.

'I want you to see that a room is prepared for Miss Beale, Mama.'

'Prepare a room! Are you out of your mind? And what, pray, do you think Lord Fulmar would have to say to that? Our name in the county would be mud.'

'Mama,' said Jack, in a voice she had never heard from him before, 'am I master in my

235

own house, or am I not?' He rang the bell and Mrs Harding, the housekeeper, appeared. 'Prepare the pink room at once, please. We may be having a guest.'

Mrs Harding curtseyed, looking from Mrs Midwinter's set face to Jack's, and left hurriedly.

'I'm going out to see Ulthorne. I shall probably be in for luncheon, but don't wait for me.' He left the room.

Mrs Midwinter sank down onto a chair. She found she was trembling. She had spent much of her time bewailing her son's bachelor state to her friends but the truth was, it did not entirely displease her. She was mistress of a large estate and able to order things exactly as she chose. When he did eventually marry, she wanted it to be to some pliant young lady, who would allow her mama-in-law to continue organizing things as she thought best. Not that she suspected that Jack would be so foolish as to become serious about this Beale woman, but the fact that he was turning the house upside-down for her sake struck her as being an ominous portent of things to come.

The last thing Mrs Midwinter wanted was to find herself moving out to a small dower house and some other female taking over at Holly Park.

Jack came in late for luncheon and Mrs Midwinter preserved a frosty silence on the topic of Miss Beale's whereabouts. Jack scarcely noticed. As soon as he'd finished his cold lamb and salad, he left again, calling for Archie.

They went to the library and Jack told him what he knew so far.

'Ulthorne reports that she arrived yesterday lunch-time. She was in a bad way, he said. Kept falling over.'

'Drugged probably,' said Archie.

'Yes, damn him. Apparently she refused the room Lord Fulmar had made ready for her. She was dragged upstairs and hasn't been seen since.'

'Sounds like your priest's hole,' observed Archie.

'Yes, it does, doesn't it? I've asked Salter to come and see me. I'll make plans when I've heard what he has to say.'

One of the maids scratched at the door and entered. 'Please sir, Mr Salter's here to see you.'

'Thank you, Mary. Show him in. You'd better stay, Archie.'

A moment later Salter came in, awkwardly twisting his cap in his hands. He looked white with anxiety and Jack at once motioned him to a chair. Salter sat down gratefully.

'It's a bad business, sir,' he began. 'None of the servants like it and there's such a to-do in the house, you wouldn't credit it. Mrs Fulmar a-weeping and a-wailing, the housekeeper ready to hand in her notice and poor Mr Jebb near out of his mind with worry.

'I can't let you into the house, sir. Lord Fulmar has had all the doors bolted and locked and keeps the keys.'

'I don't need to get inside the house,' said Jack.

'Lord, sir,' exclaimed Salter. 'You ain't a-going to fly?'

Jack smiled. 'Not quite. There's an old priest's hole, which has an external exit. I need to get to the outside of the house, somewhere near the window of the butler's pantry, so far as I can recall. What time does Lord Fulmar retire for the night?'

'Usually about half-past ten, sir. But last night he was up late, about midnight. I saw the light in the library from my cottage window. I fear he's not in his right mind just now.'

'Never has been,' growled Archie.

'I want to come up to Hoop Hall by Hoop Wood about half-past midnight, maybe later. I shall need the back gates unlocked. I don't want to have to climb over them, particularly if I have the lady with me. I shall also need to put the horses somewhere. Archie, you'd better take Clover and I'll have the big bay. I'll need the old pillion saddle.' He turned back to Salter. 'Is there somewhere Archie can stay with the horses? What about that old hut at the end of the wood?'

'That was burnt down, sir. Would the old byre in Upalong field do?'

'Is that by the dew pond?'

'Yes, sir.'

'That'll do.' It was a bit further than he wanted, but there was no help for it.

'Y—you're not thinking of bringing a gun, sir?'

Jack laughed. 'No, there'll be no violence from me, I can promise you that. I cannot speak for His Lordship,' he added dryly. He reached into his pocket and handed Salter a guinea. 'When the lady is safely out, there'll be another one of those.'

Salter touched his cap and left.

The evening passed quietly. Mrs Midwinter was still in a touchy mood, but allowed herself to be mollified when Jack set himself to please, and asked after her garden and her efforts at the village school. He said nothing of any rescue attempt and Mrs Midwinter hoped that he had thought better of it. She, too, had heard rumours during the course of the day, brought to her by her maid, who had a sweetheart up at Hoop Hall. It was quite absurd to think that Miss Beale would refuse a fortune. She would capitulate and the whole fuss would die down.

Mrs Midwinter hoped, doubtfully, that the new heiress would not prove to be a very vulgar woman. It was a thousand pities that her son had ever become involved with her.

Tea was called for at ten o'clock and by half-past ten the house was, to all intents and purposes, asleep.

Jack and Archie sat quietly in the library and listened as the housekeeper shooed the maids up to bed and locked the back door.

'Do you mean to tell me what your plans are, sir?' asked Archie. He spoke respectfully for once. He had been impressed by Jack's confidence.

'Of course. I think it is very probable that Miss Beale is being kept in the old priest's hole. If she were taken up to the attics and then vanished, where else could she be?'

'And you know how to get her out?'

'There's a secret staircase down the main chimney stack. I never told anybody about it, not even Charlie.'

Archie rubbed his chin in a worried way. It was all a long time ago. 'Could you find it again?'

'I hope so. In fact, I still have the key. I took it when I discovered the stairs and I've kept it ever since. I just hope it works after all these years.'

'Best take a bottle of oil and a feather,' said Archie. 'And a sharp knife for the ivy. And a chisel in case the key doesn't work. And a dark lantern.' With each item his face grew longer and more pessimistic.

'I know, I know,' said Jack. 'But what else can I do?'

Shortly after half-past twelve Archie and Jack, both dressed in dark clothes, led the two horses out of the stables and up the back paddock. Once out of the yard, they mounted and cantered quietly up the hill and in a loop to reach the back of Hoop Wood. Most of the journey was over the Midwinter estate and it was only when they reached the field with the byre and the dew pond that they were on Fulmar land.

The byre door was unlocked and fresh straw had been laid. There was water for the horses and hay in the manger. Salter had done his work well. Archie would stay here with the horses.

'Good luck, sir,' said Archie, as Jack checked his pockets for everything he needed and took the dark lantern, which was blacked out on three sides.

'I don't know what time I'll be back,' said Jack. 'It could be as little as an hour. More likely two or three. I'll take no chances.'

'I'll be here,' said Archie grimly. He watched Jack cross the field and enter Hoop Wood and then turned to loosen the horses' girths. He wouldn't risk unsaddling them, but he did remove the heavy pillion carried by the bay. He then sat down within sight of the wood and waited.

The wood, when Jack entered, was full of strange noises. A badger grunted and trotted off into the distance, a mouse rustled in the undergrowth. Jack moved slowly. There might be man traps and he had no wish to disturb the colony of rooks. An owl hooted, and floated feather-light across his path. It took Jack twenty minutes to reach the end of the wood and be in sight of the house.

The house was dark. To his left, he could just make out Salter's cottage. That, too, was dark, but doubtless Salter would be awake. He stood for some minutes by the gate, listening to the night.

Eventually Jack felt it safe to move. The wooden wicket gate had been oiled by an efficient Salter and made no noise. Jack moved stealthily down towards the house and the back wrought-iron gate let into the estate wall. Once through, he'd be on enemy territory. He'd have to pass by the stableyard and he hoped that the dogs would be quiet. Lastly, there was the gravel and ten yards of back lawn to cross. That would be the most dangerous, for he'd be in full view of the house.

The dogs were mercifully quiet. Perhaps Salter had doped them, or at least shut them away. He stopped by a small bush just on the edge of the gravel and looked towards the house, trying to make out where he needed to be. There was the butler's pantry window. He and Charlie used to sneak in there sometimes and steal sugar plums. The hidden door he wanted was to the left, about two arms' width along. He must remember that it was a nine-year-old boy's arms' width. The door was low down, possibly only a yard off the ground. Any priest would have had to crawl to get in or out.

He was just about to move, when he heard the crack of a twig behind him. Jack froze. Then a voice, low, said, 'It's only me, sir.'

'Go back to your cottage, Salter,' said Jack. 'This is no place for you.'

'His Lordship's restless tonight,' said Salter. 'Came out once, early on. He also went up again to the priest's hole. 'Bout ten o'clock it was. I saw the light high up by the chimney as you said, sir.'

'Damn him,' said Jack. He'd expected something of the sort. Fulmar had a nose for trouble.

'You go ahead, sir. If he comes out again, I'll speak to him. You'll hear me on the gravel, I'll say I was checking.'

Jack nodded and crept over the lawn. He hung the lantern on a protruding piece of ivy and set to work. It was not as difficult as he feared to locate the door, and within a few moments he had found it. The question was, how difficult would it be to open? He got out the knife and began to cut through the ivy. Then he took out the feather and oil and anointed the hinges and then the lock. Ancient rust had clogged it up. It was far rustier than he remembered.

Then he tried the key. Nothing. He gave it more oil. Still nothing. He tried harder, it creaked, half-turned and the key snapped in his hand.

Cursing under his breath, he reached into his pocket for the chisel, pushed it in as far as it would go and put pressure on. There was a loud crack and the lock gave way.

From the side of the house a window opened. Jack could see Salter looking at him and gesticulating towards the library. Jack nodded. He unhooked the lantern, made sure his tools were in his pocket, knelt down, pulled the door open and crawled inside. It would not close behind him. There was an inch or so of faint moonlight showing. If Lord Fulmar knew of the door's existence and came to examine it, all would be lost.

There was nothing Jack could do.

He turned his attention to the stairs. They were in far worse a condition than when he had last seen them. Damp had got in and some of the treads had rotted. It looked wildly unsafe. Would Sarah be able to come down them? Would he be able to get up?

*   *   *

Sarah had woken late that morning. Thin dusty air was coming in from the little window when she sat up in sudden terror and looked around. She was shut in. Locked away, possibly for ever. The room was bare, though once it had been whitewashed, for flakes of it still clung here and there. She crawled over to

244

the flagon of water and drank. She was desperately hungry but there was no good thinking of that.

It seemed so impossible a situation to be in that, at first, she could hardly take it in. It was as if she had been imprisoned in one of Colley Cibber's melodramas. She could imagine Angelina, the heroine of *Love Makes a Man*, revelling in the situation. She would doubtless have a speech, preferably in blank verse, all ready for when her dastardly captor appeared. The thought made Sarah giggle and she at once felt better; she had been dangerously near losing heart.

Supposing she agreed to the comfortable room she had been offered? What then? Would it really be quite impossible to get out of the house? She remembered Mr Midwinter telling her that his estate was nearby. Surely she could claim sanctuary there? She must not despair. What she needed to do was rethink her situation—Lord Fulmar in particular. Before, she had always put him out of her mind, but this was now impossible. Her tactics of defiance had not been successful. Capitulation was not an option she wished to take. Was there any other way?

It was a very long day. Nobody came near her. Occasionally she could hear faint sounds from a distant attic room but, though she shouted, nobody came. It wasn't until that evening, when the light had gone, that Lord

Fulmar reappeared.

There was the tread of heavy feet and the creak as the panel opened and the wavering light of a lamp.

Sarah crawled out, back into the small attic room with the linen press. Lord Fulmar was looking haggard, she noticed, as though he had slept badly. His eyes were bloodshot and he seemed to be in pain, for he sank down heavily on a broken-backed chair and winced.

'Well, miss? I trust you have come to your senses?'

Sarah looked at him steadily for a moment and then said, 'May we talk, My Lord?'

He seemed disconcerted. 'Talk? What is there to talk about?'

'I should like to know about my mother.'

'Why? She's dead.'

'When Miss Webster found me,' Sarah went on, 'it was a bitterly cold January. My mother was in the last stages of starvation but I was in quite good shape. I was eight months old, and she had plainly fed me better than she had fed herself.' Lord Fulmar said nothing and after a moment or two, Sarah continued, 'I need to know what she was like. She is half of myself.' She was all too aware what the Fulmar side was like, she thought.

'Still harping on Maria. I tell you she was not worth it.'

'Why not?'

Lord Fulmar sighed. 'Very well then. But

you won't like it. She was a very pretty girl, a poor relation of the Cranbornes and brought up by Lady Cranborne with her own daughter, Susan. They were educated together. Maria was always—how shall I put it?—on the qui vive. She threw herself at me and made no bones about clandestine meetings. I don't know what she had got up to at the Cranbornes—she must have been quite a handful—but she was no virgin when she came to me.'

'What! Are you saying . . .? But she was scarcely eighteen!'

Lord Fulmar laughed. 'You are naïve, my dear. Do you really think that all young girls are virtuous?'

Sarah thought of Rose and flushed painfully. 'But she was a guest in your house,' she protested. 'Surely, however coming she was, that should have given her some protection. You were far older than she was.'

Lord Fulmar shrugged. 'I wanted her.'

'I have your letters to her,' said Sarah. 'You promised her marriage. At least, that's how it read to me.'

'A man will promise anything to get a girl into bed.'

Sarah looked sadly down at her hands. Would Jack do that, she wondered? It was a painful thought. 'Poor, poor girl,' she said. 'It's all such a waste.'

'Yes,' said Lord Fulmar unexpectedly.

'Maybe it is. Perhaps I should have married her. I don't know. Frankly, when she wrote to me that she was with child, I didn't believe her. She had become very hysterical.'

'I see,' said Sarah.

'I thought, if it were true, she would write to the Cranbornes.'

'There was nothing from anybody of that name among her belongings,' said Sarah.

'You really haven't forgiven me for all this, have you?'

'You cannot know what it is like to be a foundling,' Sarah burst out suddenly. 'I had love and attention from Miss Webster, but nobody of my own. To lose a mother is very hard. Especially when so very little would have saved her. And she was so young. How can I forget that?'

'You know, there is something of your mother in you,' said Lord Fulmar thoughtfully. 'You are not just like my son Arthur. There is something in the passionate way you speak. I had quite forgotten.'

A silence fell. Neither seemed to know how to continue. Then Lord Fulmar spoke.

'I have instructed Foxton to get in touch with Maria's people. You may be happier about being here if you have some acquaintance with your mother's family.'

'Why, thank you, My Lord.' Sarah couldn't help being touched. All the same, she noted that her presence at Hoop Hall was taken for granted. 'You have given me much to think about. If you could add to your goodness by getting me something to eat, I should be grateful.'

'Not so fast, miss,' said Lord Fulmar, standing up. 'You'll get fed when you come to heel. Tomorrow morning you will apologize to Mrs Fulmar for your rudeness and I shall then consider allowing you down to the dining-room.'

The change from understanding to bullying was so abrupt that, for a moment, Sarah was too upset to speak. Then she said, 'In that case, I shall wish you good-night, My Lord.' She crawled back into the priest's hole and pushed the door shut.

CHAPTER NINE

Sarah had just dozed off when she heard the noises. She sat up, heart pounding. It was coming from behind her, by the chimney breast. Rats! She hated rats, but this noise sounded different; there was no squeaking. Then, as she strained her ears in the darkness, came a quiet knock. Cautiously, Sarah crawled over and knocked back. There was another creak, the sound of a panel opening and then the wavering light of a lantern.

'Sarah?'

Sarah gave a gasp of relief. 'Mr Midwinter!'

Jack crawled in. He was filthy and covered in cobwebs, but to Sarah he looked like the archangel Gabriel. She reached out to him and started to cry. Jack put his arms round her.

'I'm sorry, I'm sorry,' she kept sobbing.

Jack kissed the top of her head. 'There, there.' He gently let her go. 'Sarah, we must get you out of here.'

Sarah straightened up and blew her nose firmly. 'You don't by any chance have something to eat, do you?' she asked plaintively.

'What! Has he been starving you?'

Sarah nodded.

'I'm sorry, I didn't think of it. Are you strong enough to come with me? The stairs are not at all safe.'

'Anything.'

Going down was a nightmare. The stairs went from the top of the house right down to the bottom and they were steep and narrow. Several times Sarah nearly tripped. Once she grazed her knee and then she put her foot through a rotten tread, but at last they reached the bottom.

'That was the easy bit,' said Jack. He, too, had various cuts and grazes.

The bottom few treads were still complete and Sarah sat down on the third one. There were cobwebs clinging to her hair, but she took no notice. She must be filthy anyway, she thought. She probably still had smuts from the train. Was it only yesterday? No, the day before.

Jack dropped to his knees and carefully inched open the door. He could hear that the wind had got up outside. Just as well, he thought, it would mask any sound. He was about to push open the door when he suddenly saw the stocky legs of Lord Fulmar not three yards in front of him. And he was carrying a gun. He was turning this way and that.

'There's someone out there, I know it!' he shouted. 'Salter! Where is the damned fellow? Salter, I say!'

'Here, My Lord.'

'Go round the front. I'll stay here. Leave me the lantern.'

Jack could hear the gravel crunch as Salter disappeared. He turned round to see if Sarah had heard. He had turned his own lantern to the wall, and only the faintest glimmer showed. He could just see her white face.

'We'll be here some time,' he whispered.

Sarah nodded her understanding. She knew Lord Fulmar's obstinacy as well as he did. Jack came and sat down next to her. They could be in for a long wait. He wouldn't put it past Fulmar to stay there all night. If he hadn't had a gun, Jack might have risked it: in a struggle between the two of them, he would undoubtedly win. But with Fulmar armed, they had no option but to stay where they were.

'Do you think he knows about the stairway?' Sarah whispered in his ear.

'I doubt it. Otherwise he'd have come looking. I found it quite by chance as a boy. I never told anybody, not even Charlie.'

'What happened to Charlie?'

It seemed to be a night for confidences. Jack told her, speaking very quietly, so that they had to move closer to hear each other. Sarah recounted the events of the last couple of days. Every now and then Jack went to the door, opened it a fraction, and peered out. Lord Fulmar had moved further off, but he was still prowling around.

Then, without quite knowing how it came about, they were exchanging kisses as well as confidences.

'Your hair is tickling me,' whispered Sarah.

'Sorry.' Jack put a hand up to smooth back his hair and found her cheek instead. He began to stroke it with his forefinger.

'I'm sure I'm covered in smuts from the train,' whispered Sarah.

'I can't see, so it doesn't matter.' Jack kissed her cheek gently.

'You're bristly.'

Jack moved and found her mouth instead. 'Mm.'

This new activity was so engrossing that some considerable time passed. Jack had moved on from her lips to her eyelids and was just exploring the soft skin underneath an earlobe, when there was the sudden report of a gun.

They jumped apart.

'Got it! Damned fox. After the hens, no doubt.'

There were running footsteps and then Salter's voice. 'Clean through the head, My Lord.' He had obviously picked up the dead fox.

'Good shot, eh?'

'Indeed, My Lord. But then you always was one of the best in the county.'

A satisfied chuckle, then Lord Fulmar said, 'That's it, I daresay. If there were any other poachers about, this'll have scared them off.'

Footsteps retreated and a moment or two later they heard the closing of the door by the library. There were, however, other noises; windows being pushed up, voices asking each other what had happened. They waited.

Eventually, Jack said, 'I think we might risk it.'

He opened the door cautiously. Silence had surged back. He dropped to his knees and crawled out. Sarah followed. It was a clear night and, although there was only a sickle moon, the starlight was enough to see by. Jack put out his lantern, took Sarah's hand and ran with her towards the stableyard. Once they were safely behind the stable wall, he stopped and peered round. All was still silent.

The back gate, when they reached it, was

mercifully still unlocked. They stepped through and shortly were in the wood again. Once more Jack looked back.

'Oh my God!'

'What is it?'

'He's up in the priest's hole!' He pointed to where a tiny flickering light, high up by the chimneys, waved to and fro.

He relit the lantern from his tinder box and said, 'We've no time to lose. Now we walk as fast as we can.'

'I could probably run.'

'No,' said Jack. 'We try not to disturb the rooks. They would give our position away at once.'

The next twenty minutes were agonizing for Sarah. She was feeling weak and faint and her legs didn't always do what she wanted them to. Several times Jack had to haul her to her feet. Her side began to ache.

Then, faintly on the air, came the sound of barking.

'Damn,' said Jack. 'It must be that old pointer of his.'

'Can it find us?'

'Oh yes,' said Jack grimly. They were near the end of the wood now and quickened their pace. Once out, Jack could see the byre just under the brow of the hill. He put his hands to his mouth and made the sharp 'ke-wick' of the tawny owl.

A figure came out of the barn. Jack waved.

'Archie,' panted Jack to Sarah. 'He'll saddle the horses.'

They were out of cover now and began to run up the slope, Jack half-carrying, half-pulling Sarah.

They could hear crashes behind them, then a shout, 'Shoot, Salter, shoot!'

A bullet whizzed by over their heads.

'Give it to me!'

Inside the barn, Archie was frantically tightening girths and struggling to get the heavy pillion back onto the bay, who was shifting uneasily as the weight dropped onto his back.

'Easy, boy.' Archie worked fast.

He led out the bay just as Jack and Sarah ran up.

'Here!' cried Jack. He picked Sarah up and put her on the pillion. 'Can you ride?'

'No!'

'Sit astride, you'll find it safer.'

Somehow Sarah bundled up her skirts.

Jack swung himself into the saddle and found the stirrups. 'Put your feet into my stirrup leathers.' He showed her.

Archie brought Clover out and leapt up.

Suddenly there was another shot and Jack gave a cry. The horse whinneyed in terror and reared. Sarah clutched on for all she was worth.

'Winged, damn it! No matter. We'll have to go on. Sarah, hold tight.' He clapped his heels into the horse's sides.

Sarah, looking down, saw the ground speeding past and the shadow of the horse with their two figures strangely blue and flattened on the grass in the starlight. Her heart was in her mouth; the speed was so great and it seemed so far to fall, that she felt she would almost certainly be killed if she lost her balance. It was terrifying, but that flight in the starlight was strangely exhilarating as well.

Another bullet whizzed past, but they were now out of range. The shots died away.

*   *   *

At about three in the morning, Mrs Midwinter was woken by a clatter of hooves in the stableyard of Holly Park. There were shouts and voices as a sleepy stableboy came down from his room over one of the loose boxes.

She got up, lit her bedside lamp, put on her dressing-gown and went downstairs. Her housekeeper, Mrs Harding, was bustling down on a similar errand. They both reached the back door as Jack, Sarah and Archie came in. Archie was supporting his master. Blood dripped everywhere.

Jack slumped down onto a kitchen chair.

'Sorry about the mess, Mama.'

'Jack! What on earth have you been doing?' She glanced at Sarah. The young woman was filthy. Her bonnet was in shreds, her face streaked with dirt and her petticoat was torn. What sort of female was she, thought Mrs Midwinter, to allow herself to get into such a condition?

Archie was cutting Jack out of his jacket.

'This is Miss Beale, Mama. She hasn't eaten for two days and I have been shot by Lord Fulmar.'

Sarah sank down onto a chair and closed her eyes. Everyone was rushing round Jack. She could hear the scissors cutting away at his clothes, bandages being ripped. She was feeling weak with reaction and hunger. Archie was trying to explain. It all began to go round and round in her head.

Jack turned to look at her. She was swaying.

'For God's sake, Mama,' he cried, 'never mind about me. See to Miss Beale.'

'I can wait,' said Sarah faintly.

'At least give her something to eat.'

'Mrs Harding,' said Mrs Midwinter, 'cut Miss Beale a slice of bread and butter, would you?' She turned back to Jack.

Two of the maids appeared and were hurried off by Mrs Harding to boil water. Things began to sort themselves out. Mrs Midwinter's personal maid came over to take care of Sarah. She had heard a garbled version of events from her young man up at Hoop Hall and was thrilled to meet Miss Beale. What a tale she'd have to tell!

'I'd give anything for a bath!' whispered

257

Sarah.

'You shall have it, miss. I'll take the hip bath up to your room. And Mrs Harding shall find you a nightdress. Would you like some soup?'

Sarah accepted gratefully and half an hour later, bathed, hair washed and with a slice of bread and a little soup inside her, she fell into bed.

Downstairs, Jack was still expostulating. He looked at the wound. 'Flesh wound only, thank God.' The thought of having the doctor in to extract a bullet was more than he could stand. Dr Abbott was not noted for his discretion. This way, his adventures could be kept to his own household.

'Some basilicum powder, Mama, and I'll do. Archie, organize a bath for me.'

'Yes, sir.'

'Is Miss Beale all right, Mama?'

'Never mind Miss Beale now,' said Mrs Midwinter. 'We can discuss what to do with her in the morning.'

Jack frowned, but he was in no condition to think clearly. He allowed himself to be helped upstairs.

*   *   *

Sarah had fallen asleep heavily, but was woken a few hours later by an appalling nightmare. She was back in the priest's hole. The water had run out and Lord Fulmar had gone away

258

and left her. She would slowly starve to death. The terror of being left to die in that room was so real that she cried out loud, but could not wake up.

There was the bustle of a dressing-gown and Mrs Harding came in, candle in hand.

'Don't lock me in!' Sarah was moaning.

Mrs Harding went over to her and shook her gently, 'Wake up, miss. Wake up.'

Sarah gave a jerk, sat up suddenly and looked around, wild-eyed.

'There, there, miss. Here, have a drink of water. It was just a nasty dream.' She patted and soothed Sarah into wakefulness. She could feel the fear, still thick in the room. Poor girl she thought, when Sarah had sobbed out her terror of the priest's hole, what a dreadful experience. And how brave she had been.

She sat with Sarah for twenty minutes or so, reassuring her and then said, 'You should try and sleep now, miss. I'll light the lamp for you, so that you have some light.'

'Thank you, Mrs Harding, I feel much better. I'm so sorry to have woken you up, especially when you have already had such a disturbed night.'

'That's all right, miss. You go to sleep now and if you should want anything, just ring your bell.'

Sarah awoke late. It was about noon when Mrs Harding came in with some hot chocolate, rolls and marmalade. There were some beurré pears on a pretty china dish. A maid followed her, carrying Sarah's clothes which had been washed, cleaned, brushed and ironed, her black buttoned boots were freshly polished.

Sarah sat up in bed and inhaled the aroma of the chocolate gratefully. It smelled wonderful.

'Delicious!' she said. 'I am sorry to have given you all that trouble last night, Mrs Harding.' She caught sight of her clothes. 'Good heavens! How did you do that?'

The maid smiled. 'We've been working all morning on them, miss. But I'm afraid your bonnet is beyond repair.'

Sarah expressed her gratitude and asked after Mr Midwinter.

'Nothing too serious, thank the Lord,' said Mrs Harding piously. 'It was only a flesh wound and he's bandaged up nicely. He had a quiet night and he'll be as right as rain in no time.

'If you'd like to ring the bell when you're ready, miss, one of the maids will escort you down to the drawing-room.'

Mrs Harding and the maid left. As they went downstairs Mrs Harding said, 'Miss Beale has pretty manners. She didn't forget to thank us, and there's plenty who would think it no more than their due.'

'Mrs Midwinter didn't seem too pleased to see her, though,' ventured the maid.

'It was three o'clock in the morning,' said

260

Mrs Harding repressively, for she did not wish to encourage gossip. 'Any lady might be forgiven for being put out at that hour. I've no doubt that Mrs Midwinter will do her duty by her guest.' All the same, she couldn't help agreeing that her mistress had been less than welcoming. She didn't say so to the maid but, in her opinion, it was Mrs Midwinter's place to comfort her guest if she had a nightmare, not hers. Not that she grudged Miss Beale her time, poor lady, but it would have been more fitting coming from Mrs Midwinter.

The maid sniffed. She had her own thoughts and they were that Mrs Midwinter didn't like her son being interested in Miss Beale, which anybody could see he was.

* * *

The moment Sarah walked into the drawing-room, Mrs Midwinter knew that she didn't like her. She had long decided in her mind that Miss Beale must be a brassier version of her mother and was therefore expecting a petite blonde, as Maria Beale had been, perhaps owing more to the bottle than nature. Her manners would be those of someone brought up in a lodging-house.

Then, there were those dreadful shrieks in the night. She had already been disturbed once because of that young woman, was she really expected to get up and minister to her again?

To be confronted by a tall, dark young woman of real elegance was a shock and not one she liked. Her uninvited guest, she could see, was not some drab. Her dress was in impeccable taste, she made the proper enquiries and offered the correct apologies and could not be faulted on her manners, and she was undoubtedly the daughter of Lord Fulmar.

She glanced at her son, who had risen to his feet as Sarah entered the room. He was doing nothing more than expressing the conventional hope that she had slept well. Had she recovered from her ordeal? But there was a warmth in his voice and in his eyes that made Mrs Midwinter feel uneasy.

'You are still looking pale, Miss Beale,' he said. 'You must stay a few days and rest.'

'Thank you,' replied Sarah, noting that this invitation was not seconded by his mother. 'But I must get home. Everybody will be so worried about me. Besides, I must get back to work.'

'Work!' echoed Mrs Midwinter. What female with any pretensions to gentility actually worked? 'Pray, what do you do, Miss Beale?'

'I work in the theatre, Mrs Midwinter.'

'The theatre!' Real shock sounded in her voice. 'Are you an actress?' How dared her son bring an actress into the house? He must be out of his mind.

'I design the costumes, and make them of course.'

'A dress-maker!' It was scarcely better than an actress, though marginally more respectable.

Sarah looked at Jack. It was obvious that he had not told his mother of his own involvement in the theatre. Whatever would she think if she knew that her own son was treading the boards? Not to mention helping in the carpenter's room and with the scenery. Her lips twitched. She could just imagine that lady's horror.

'I shall escort you home tomorrow, Miss Beale,' said Jack.

'Jack!' cried his mother. 'I am sure Miss Beale will forgive me if I say that you should travel nowhere with your arm like that. I shall send one of the maids with her, although there is not really the slightest need, she may be very comfortable in the ladies' carriage.'

'Pooh, a scratch, no more. And I shall take Miss Beale home. I could not think of allowing her to travel without a proper male escort after her experiences of the last couple of days.'

'I shall take Dr Abbott's advice,' said Mrs Midwinter, lips pursed.

Sarah listened, more and more embarrassed. It was plain that Mrs Midwinter had taken a strong dislike to her and was anxious to separate her from her son. What

263

should she do? Should she protest her willingness to travel alone? But she wasn't willing, she realized. She was still frightened. Whenever she thought of Lord Fulmar catching her, terror clutched her heart.

'You will do no such thing. Dr Abbott is over at Hoop Hall at the moment. Lord Fulmar had a mild seizure this morning—Archie had it from Ulthorne.'

Sarah went white. 'Will he live?' She remembered that curiously intimate conversation up in the attic room. She did not want him to die. His conduct was still despicable, but somehow her avowed hatred had vanished.

'I believe so. He is extremely tough. His right side is affected, so he won't be abducting, or shooting, people any more.'

'What brought it on?' asked Mrs Midwinter.

'Rage and a dislike of not getting his own way,' said Jack.

'I feel almost sorry for him,' said Sarah reflectively. 'I have a temper myself and can only be grateful that my dear Aunt Hetty taught me to control it.'

'You believe in controlling your emotions, do you, Miss Beale?' There was a warmth in Jack's voice that made his mother look from one to the other and for Sarah to colour up.

'Certainly,' said Sarah.

'Admirable,' said Jack, laughter in his eyes.

Sarah was relieved to be back once more in Myddleton Square. The afternoon at Hoop Hall had been something of a strain. Mrs Midwinter was determined not to leave her guest alone with her son for a moment. Whilst her hostess was perfectly polite, Sarah was well aware that her company was not welcome.

The conversation was stilted. There seemed to be no subject that Mrs Midwinter would agree to discuss without giving Sarah the impression that she was being encroaching. She was extremely relieved to retreat to bed as soon as courtesy allowed. She found that she was almost as exhausted by the strains of that afternoon and evening exchanging polite nothings with the Midwinters, as she had been by the traumatic events of the previous couple of days.

That evening, as she was undressing, she couldn't help hearing voices raised downstairs. Mrs Midwinter was making her displeasure plain and Sarah, with a sinking heart, realized that she was probably the cause of their disagreement.

Sarah, Archie and Jack caught an early train to London, on Sarah's side at least, with immense relief.

As soon as she was home and had been hugged, kissed and exclaimed over by everyone, she sat down at her writing desk.

She dropped a note to Mr Phelps saying that she would be back at work on Monday, and another to Miss Bailey, who she knew must have been worried about her, and she sent them at once round to the theatre by Leah. She then wrote a polite thank you letter to Mrs Midwinter.

She had scarcely finished this—and the letter to Mrs Midwinter was by far the hardest to write—when Miss Bailey appeared and was shown in by a still tearful Polly.

'Pray forgive me, dear Sarah, for coming uninvited, but I have been so anxious about you. I wanted to see that you were safe and sound with my own eyes.'

Sarah jumped up and embraced her. 'I am delighted to see you!' It was true. Miss Bailey represented all that was wholesome and real and important in her life. 'Please sit down. I daresay when you hear of my adventures it will all sound absurd and melodramatic.'

'My dear Sarah, life is melodramatic. Why, I came across an article in *The Times* only the other day, of a Miss D, aged fourteen if you please, who left the security of her parents' home and eloped with the footman!'

Sarah laughed. Then, in measured tones, she related her history and Lord Fulmar's part in it.

Miss Bailey listened carefully. It was not entirely new to her, for she had already heard the early part of Sarah's history from Miss

Valloton. 'Where money and property are concerned, people will do anything,' she said, when Sarah had finished. 'Though usually, not run away from it, as you have done!'

'You mistake me,' said Sarah slowly, for she had only just worked this out herself. 'It's not the Fulmar estate I'm escaping from, it's being in the power of Lord Fulmar.

'Did you ever read that absurd book, *Varney the Vampyre*?' Miss Bailey shook her head. 'Mr Copperstone used to like it and I borrowed it from him. The villain, Sir Francis Varney, attacks the heroine, Flora, by night and tries to suck her blood. I felt like Flora, as if Lord Fulmar were trying to turn me into his creature and take over my very soul.'

'We are in a fortunate position, you and I,' said Miss Bailey, after a reflective pause. 'We have some control over our own lives. So few women do.'

'Yes,' said Sarah listlessly. It was true, but the benefits, though very real, were limited. She had work she enjoyed, a secure home, but what of the demands of her heart?

Not everything would return to normal. Her relationship with Jack, for instance. It was only now, having visited Holly Park and seen how large it was, with its elegant Georgian frontage, the numerous servants, the stables and outbuildings, and this morning, as they drove away, the park with its deer and mature trees, that she fully recognized the gulf between them.

'I've tired you,' said Miss Bailey contritely, rising to her feet. 'Forgive me, my dear. Make sure you rest and I will see you on Monday.'

When she had gone, Sarah resumed her thoughts. Jack might talk of his lack of interest in his estate but, to Sarah, the reality seemed very different. Seeing him there, in his home surroundings, made her realize how much a part of it he was. He was only at Sadler's Wells because he had assumed responsibility for her safety. If Lord Fulmar's health should leave him permanently incapacitated, then any threat to her safety would be effectively over. Mr Midwinter could leave at once; there would be no reason to remain and any quarrel with his mother would be healed. In any case, Mr Frost's injuries were healing as they ought, and he would soon return.

She wiped away a stray tear.

Sarah had always believed that falling in love was an irrational indulgence not to be taken seriously by any right-minded female. She now discovered, painfully, that she was wrong. She had fallen in love with Jack against all reason and certainly against her own best interests.

For what could become of it? Nothing. She didn't think he would insult her by asking her to become his mistress and he would certainly never consider marrying her. Gentlemen did not marry women from her sort of background, even if she were Lord Fulmar's daughter.

Sarah had just been reading Mr Dickens's *Bleak House*, whose last episode had come out that very month. She had been particularly struck by the heroine, Esther Summerson, illegitimate like herself. In spite of being Lady Dedlock's daughter, Sarah noted that Mr Dickens only allowed Esther to marry a doctor, a man who, however talented, was of little social standing. The lesson was not lost on her.

*　　　*　　　*

Life at Hoop Hall began to relax. Everybody knew that Miss Beale had escaped, but from where and how was something of a mystery. The butler spoke of hearing voices outside. There had certainly been gunshots, but nobody knew what had happened for sure. Salter, with a couple of guineas from Jack, kept his mouth shut. A fox had been shot was all that he would say, and he nailed the brush to the potting-shed door in proof.

The doctor came and went, Mrs Fulmar hovered about with gruel and was told to go away and take that pap with her. Gradually things returned to normal. Lord Fulmar himself was quieter than before, much of the time he seemed lost in thought. His right side slowly improved, but he could no longer use his arm.

Salter had denied recognizing the man they had been pursuing, but Lord Fulmar was quite certain that it was Jack Midwinter who had helped Sarah escape, though how he had done it was a mystery. There was no point in going over to Holly Park, even if he were well enough to do so, for Mrs Midwinter would not welcome enquiry and Jack himself must have left. It never crossed Lord Fulmar's mind to worry about having shot Jack. The fellow was trespassing on his land—he must be prepared to take the consequences.

Instead, Lord Fulmar sent a note to Mrs Harding, Mrs Midwinter's housekeeper, asking her to call at the hall. One of the grooms would fetch her. He wished to ask her opinion on the relationship between Mrs Midwinter's maid and one of his footmen. He didn't of course. Frankly, he didn't care one way or the other, providing his comfort were not affected, but he needed an excuse.

Lord Fulmar saw Mrs Harding in his library, a room which seemed designed to intimidate. But, on this occasion, it failed in its effect. Mrs Harding was in fighting fettle. She knew that her own position at Holly Park was secure, whatever complaints Lord Fulmar might make of what she had every intention of saying. Even if Mrs Midwinter wished to dismiss her, Mr Midwinter would never permit it, especially if she were defending Miss Beale.

Mrs Harding had seen, quite as well as her mistress, that Jack had a considerable regard for the lady he had rescued.

No, she told Lord Fulmar, she had no idea how Mr Midwinter had rescued Miss Beale. 'All I know, My Lord, is that it was a wicked, cruel thing to do to shut her up in that nasty priest's hole. Why, the poor lady woke up in the night crying out with fear. I saw her with my own eyes. She had a nightmare that she would be left there to die. I can picture her now, she was clinging to me and sobbing, "What have I done that he should hate me so much?" And I had no answer to give her, My Lord.'

'The remedy was in her own hands,' replied Lord Fulmar.

'Begging Your Lordship's pardon, the remedy was in yours. You behaved like a Tartar and a barbarian. No wonder she wanted nothing to do with you. I tell you straight, My Lord, you don't deserve such a lovely daughter.'

'You seem very free with your opinions, Mrs Harding.' Lord Fulmar seemed more curious than angry. Possibly he was too tired for rage. 'Pray, what do you think I should do?'

'Apologize, My Lord, and think of what you can do to please her instead of how she may be of use to Your Lordship.' Mrs Harding folded her hands in her apron. He might throw her out now if he liked. She had had her say.

271

When she had gone, Lord Fulmar remained sunk in thought. The picture of Sarah, crying and frightened by her nightmare, touched him. Damn it, he had become fond of the wench.

*   *   *

It was Monday 3 October, and Sarah returned to Sadler's Wells. *A Midsummer Night's Dream* was to open on Saturday. Sarah realized that, with the wound to his arm, it was possible that Jack would decide not to return, and she was grateful that there was so much to be done at the theatre. It might not stop her heartache, but it would at least take her mind off things.

One thing, however, had changed. The old secrecy of her life was gone forever. Mr Phelps, having heard her story and questioned her closely, decided that, for her own safety, the truth must be known.

'It is not difficult for a stranger to get into the theatre,' he said. 'The stage door is not that secure. Delivery men call and so on.'

'I have always preferred to keep quiet about my background,' said Sarah. 'Nobody wishes to be known as a . . . a bastard.' She added, with an attempt at a smile, 'Look at them in Shakespeare: Edmund, Don John; villains, all of them.'

'My dear Miss Beale,' said Phelps, 'this is the nineteenth century. Whilst I admit there is prejudice, nevertheless you cannot be blamed for the condition of your birth.' He eyed her shrewdly and added, 'I think you will find openness a much more comfortable state to live with.'

So, indeed, it proved. If there were a few, like Miss Goodwin, who were inclined to be censorious, most people were sympathetic, not to say intrigued.

'My dear,' whispered Miss Portman at the rehearsal, 'it's too romantic for words!'

When Jack appeared, arm bandaged, a ragged cheer went up. Sarah's world suddenly righted itself.

'Trust him to play the hero,' said Mr Thorpe gloomily to Mr Brown. 'Much chance I'd have of rescuing Miss Beale.'

Sarah and Jack had to endure much good-humoured teasing, Miss Warde going so far as to say to Sarah that she didn't deserve to be rescued by Mr Midwinter—she had no sensibility at all. She was sure that she would have fainted into his arms.

'I'd have been a nuisance if I'd fainted,' protested Sarah.

'Ah, but then he'd have been able to press burning kisses on your pale lips,' cried Miss Warde, who had obviously seen a lot of melodramas.

Sarah thought that Jack was quite capable of that without her having to be unconscious first.

'I don't see that it would be much fun if you

had fainted,' observed Miss Cronin, another of Hippolyta's attendants, who was standing by.

Miss Warde gave a mock shriek of outraged virtue and moved away.

'I'll confess something to you, Miss Beale,' whispered Miss Cronin. 'My parents only married when I was about two months old. So you see, we are in the same boat.'

Sarah smiled gratefully at her.

Rose was highly put out by the revelation of Sarah's background. The daughter of a lord! The potential heiress to an estate. It was all most unfair. What had Sarah ever done to deserve such luck? She was resentful that Aunt Hetty had never mentioned a word of it to her. Miss Webster had been discreet and all Rose had been told was that Sarah was a foundling. Hetty didn't see that it was anybody's business other than hers and Sarah's.

Aunt Hetty, thought Sarah, had meant well but, to Sarah, it had felt like an injunction to secrecy. It was, she now realized, a blessed release for it to be out in the open.

*   *   *

Sarah was sitting at the back of the pit, watching the rehearsal of Act III of the *Dream*. She and Miss Bailey, together with Mr Cawdery, had been working on the ass's head that Bottom wore after he had been transformed by Puck. Mr Phelps wanted its

274

jaws and ears to move and be controllable by him. It had also to be comfortable to wear.

It had taken time and trouble to come up with something. Miss Bailey had designed a realistic-looking head, made out of rabbit skin stretched on a padded wire frame. The ears and jaws were worked by strings which were concealed inside Bottom's jacket and worked by Phelps's fingers.

A number of other people had crept in to watch, Sarah noticed, for word had got round that this performance was something special.

The keynote of Phelps's interpretation was Bottom's natural stupidity, coupled with a boundless conceit. When Puck gave him an ass's head, it was merely an outward mark of his inward asininity. To Bottom, it was quite natural that Titania should be in love with him, and Phelps made Bottom's ears twitch in ludicrous gallantry. Everybody recognized Bottom's posturings in people they had known; some perhaps, even in themselves. Sarah enjoyed it immensely. So, judging from the laughter around her, did the others. There was a rustle and Jack slid onto the bench next to her.

'You were right,' he said, after a while. 'The man is brilliant.'

'Only a very great actor could allow himself to be so foolish,' said Sarah, acutely aware all down her left side of Jack's proximity.

Titania was stroking Bottom's furry nose

275

and caressing his ears, which twitched appreciatively.

Mine ear is much enamour'd of thy note;
So is mine eye enthralled by thy shape;

Sarah thought, so am I enamoured and enthralled, God help me.

The rehearsal moved on to Act IV. Bottom was lying at his ease ordering the fairies about. Peaseblossom, Mustardseed and Cobweb were scurrying hither and thither and Bottom was fingering his ears as though he were immensely proud of them. Sarah had seen Jack run his hand through his hair in just such a self-satisfied way. She could hear him laughing ruefully beside her.

Finally, Bottom and Titania were alone on stage. Titania entwined herself around him.

Sleep thou, and I will wind thee in my arms.

Sarah became aware that Jack's hand was gently stroking the nape of her neck.

'Stop it,' she said crossly.

O how I love thee! How I dote on thee! sighed Titania.

Jack turned his head to kiss her cheek. 'Come on, Sarah,' he said. 'You welcomed my kisses before.'

'That was different. I was half-starved, exhausted and desperate.'

Jack grimaced. 'So much for my conceit. I begin to feel like bully Bottom. Am I really so unacceptable to you?'

'Use your common sense, Mr Midwinter,' Sarah snapped. 'I am no light o' love, to be toyed with. Why don't you try and put yourself in my position?'

'But, Sarah . . .'

She stood up and left. Mr Midwinter may have rescued her, she thought angrily, brushing away the tears that started in her eyes, but that did not give him permission to toy with her whenever he wanted. The working out of love in the play seemed so painfully at variance with her own experience that it began to feel like a nightmare. Oberon could wave a wand and sort out the mortal lovers on stage; her own situation was not so easy.

She began to think that, if Jack were going to leave, then it would be better if he did so quickly. She wasn't sure how much more of this she could take.

*   *   *

It was Wednesday and Sarah was beginning to feel nervous about the opening night of *A Midsummer Night's Dream*. She kept telling herself that nobody would be looking at her, but it made little difference. Her stomach knotted in anxiety whenever she thought about it.

There was only one letter for her that morning and she looked at the heavy paper with her heart sinking. Could it be another letter from Foxton? Her hands trembled slightly as she opened it. The writing was shaky and the letters ill-formed.

*　　*　　*

My dear Sarah
　　You have nothing further to fear from me. I shall make no further attempts either to see you or to force you to come to Hoop Hall. I was wrong to pursue you as I did and I am sorry for it.
　　I have not yet decided on the future of the estate. I do not want it to pass out of the family after three hundred years. I would like your thoughts on the matter.
　　　　　Your affectionate father,
　　　　　Fulmar.

Such a letter was not soon to be recovered from. Lord Fulmar apologizing? Could that be right? She re-read it. He must have written it with his left hand, she thought, that was why it was so shaky.

Her predominant feeling was one of relief, but then other feelings came crowding in. The danger was over—she must tell Jack. But would that mean that he would leave immediately? There would be no reason for him to stay. He must be longing to start his new life up in Manchester. She could not put it off. He must be told today. Mr Frost had already limped back to the theatre to see them all. In a week or so, he could probably be Theseus's attendant, even if he were not agile enough to be at the front as Jack had been.

She walked to the theatre with a heavy heart. Pepper Williams was at his usual place by the stage door.

'What is it, Sarah, pet? More bad news?'

Sarah sighed. 'Oh no.' She told him, then added, 'I must tell Mr Midwinter as soon as possible. Have you seen him this morning?'

Mr Williams looked at her kindly. Sarah had not confided in him, but he suspected that Mr Midwinter had touched her heart. 'He's with Mr Harvey. If you'll wait a minute, pet, I'll go and fetch him.'

'Oh, thank you.' She bent over to stroke Spot and hide her tears. The last thing she wanted was Mr Williams feeling sorry for her. She was grateful for his tact, too. She did not want to have to be seen looking for Mr Midwinter herself—the gossip that Miss Beale was pursuing Mr Midwinter would be all over the theatre within hours.

Five minutes later Sarah and Jack were once again sitting at the back of one of the boxes. Sarah showed him the letter. Jack read it slowly and then handed it back.

'For once he is behaving as a gentleman ought,' he commented. He looked at her downcast face and added, 'What is it, Sarah? Don't you believe him?'

'I believe he regrets his behaviour, yes. But I notice that he has still kept a few strings to pull, with this about the estate. It's like a lollipop to lure a child.'

'Do you really not want it?'

Sarah sighed. 'Aunt Hetty warned me never to allow myself to be blackmailed by half-promises of future wealth or goods. She said that her own father suffered dreadfully because of it. Her family lost a lot of money in the South Sea Bubble. They had a small estate in Norfolk. Her father grew up there, but it had to be sold when he was quite young and he never got over the loss. He always felt that life had done him down, was unfair, and was constantly pressing his attentions on elderly relations, who he hoped would leave him money.'

'Which they half-promised to do, but never did?'

'Exactly. They were quite happy to have his attentions, but left their wealth to others.'

'And this is what you fear Lord Fulmar means to do?'

'Why would he not?' asked Sarah. 'He has used everybody else.'

Jack could understand her scepticism. At

the moment, Lord Fulmar was sorry. He was ill and mortality was staring him in the face. But Jack could not see the selfish habits of a lifetime suddenly broken. Lord Fulmar might believe that he would never coerce Sarah again but, if she put herself in his power . . . ?

'Would you like to see him?'

'I don't know. It's so hard to explain. He is my father, Mr Midwinter, and once or twice there were times when I felt that we might come to understand each other.'

'Do you still feel that you owe it to your mother to repudiate him?'

Sarah shook her head. 'My mother appears to have been something of a light-skirt, not unlike Rose's mother. Isn't it ironic? She took such care of me, at the cost of her own life, and yet had little regard for her own virtue.' She still felt that Lord Fulmar had behaved very badly, but she could understand that a man wanted a wife whose virtue he could trust. She both condemned him and understood, at least in part.

'I shall write,' said Sarah after a pause. 'But I shall not see him.' Let him do what he would with the estate. Aunt Hetty was right, she must not allow herself to become involved. Deliberately, she turned her thoughts to the other question that, if truth were known, loomed far larger in her mind. 'So you will soon be leaving us. Shall you be going up to Manchester immediately?'

281

'Within a couple of months. I have had a difference of opinion with my mother.'

'I do hope it wasn't because of me,' cried Sarah. 'I couldn't help but realize that I was an unwelcome guest. I understand, of course. It must have been most disagreeable to have a ragamuffin female foisted on one. And one whose rescue had involved her son in getting shot!'

'I can't deny that you were part of it,' said Jack, 'but you were certainly not the cause. It did not seem fair that you were being vilified for working in the theatre, when I was doing the same. So I told her the truth about that. And then I told her that I was going to Manchester. Poor Mama, all her plans for me to crumble so abruptly.

'She used not to be like this,' continued Jack, after a pause. 'It was only after my father died that she became so difficult. I suppose she wanted me to take his place. I really do not like quarrelling with her.'

There was another silence. Mrs Midwinter would certainly never forgive her, thought Sarah. She must see it as all her fault. Sarah had found her extremely jealous of anything to do with her son. Had Sarah been at Holly Park on her own and nothing to do with Jack, Mrs Midwinter might well have been perfectly pleasant. No wonder Jack had never married. What man would want to play piggy-in-the-middle between his wife and his mother?

Perhaps, once he was in Manchester, he would look about him and find a suitable wife. The thought was extremely depressing.

CHAPTER TEN

The rest of the day passed somehow for Sarah. She felt restless and depressed and, for once, did not enjoy the rehearsal. She was glad to get home. Jack was staying late to help with the set changes for *Othello*, which was on that evening, and Mr Thorpe escorted Sarah back to Myddleton Square.

She arrived to find the house in a state of some excitement.

Oh God, thought Sarah, what now? It was not going to be Lord Fulmar this time, nor hired ruffians, so who was it?

'A gentleman and a lady have come to see you, Miss Sarah,' said Polly, offering her two cards from the tray in the hall. 'I said as you would be back shortly and they are up in Miss Webster's drawing-room. I offered them tea. I hope that was right?'

'Of course. Pray tell them I shall be with them in a moment.' She looked down at the cards. *Mrs Edward Fanshawe* read one. It meant nothing. *Sir George Cranborne* read the other. Cranborne? The name rang a bell, but she couldn't immediately place it.

She went to change her shoes and to brush her hair. Ten minutes later she entered the drawing-room. She thought wryly, that, of all the people who had entered that room in the last few months, by far the greater proportion had been completely unknown to her.

The gentleman who rose as she entered was a pleasant-looking man of some fifty years of age, with grizzled hair and blue eyes. He had a good, if somewhat portly, figure though, thought Sarah, he should not have worn checked trousers, which did nothing for his thickening waistline. Mrs Fanshawe looked very like him, with the same blue eyes and slightly tilted eyebrows. Could they be brother and sister?

The company introduced themselves. Sarah indicated that Sir George be seated and sat down herself.

'How may I help you, Sir George?'

Sir George and Mrs Fanshawe looked at each other. 'We were under the impression that you wished to see us,' he replied.

Sarah looked puzzled.

Mrs Fanshawe handed her Foxton's letter. Colour surged up in Sarah's cheeks. 'Are you . . . ? Can you be my . . . mother's cousins?'

'You mean you don't know?' Sir George was sceptical.

'Lord Fulmar mentioned the name Cranborne, Sir George. That was the first time I had heard of it. There is no mention of you

284

in the correspondence my mother left.'

Sir George and Mrs Fanshawe exchanged glances again.

'I should like to see something in your mother's writing, Miss Beale.'

Sarah rose. 'If you will wait one moment, I shall show you what I have. It is not much.' She left the room.

'Extraordinary,' said Mrs Fanshawe. 'I had expected that she would be all over us.'

'Her christening is valid, as is the register of Maria Beale's death,' said Sir George. 'I checked them myself. And she certainly looks like a Fulmar.'

Sarah returned bearing a rush basket containing the wooden box which held her mother's letters, the few clothes she had when she died and the rag doll she had made for Sarah.

'This is all I have of my mother,' she said. She took out the box reverently and opened it. 'Most of the letters are from Lord Fulmar to my mother. The last is hers.' She handed it to Mrs Fanshawe.

Mrs Fanshawe read it and burst into tears. Sir George went and sat down by his sister and patted her hand. He, too, read the letter. Sarah, tears in her own eyes, watched them.

'This is certainly poor Maria's hand,' sighed Sir George.

'Why did she not ask Mama for help?' wailed Mrs Fanshawe. 'Oh, Miss Beale, we never heard from her from the day she disappeared! Nothing. For years I hoped for a letter. If only we had known.'

Sir George coughed. 'Difficult, after the Turner affair.'

Mrs Fanshawe coloured.

'I gather,' said Sarah carefully, 'that my mother was . . . not as careful of her reputation as she might have been.'

'Oh, my dear Miss Beale,' cried Mrs Fanshawe, relieved that she might be open. 'I was prodigiously fond of Maria, she was such a lively, pretty girl, but she was not . . . steady. She always craved affection. It seemed she could never get enough.'

There was much to say: explanations to give and knowledge to be exchanged. For the first time Sarah heard of her mother's childhood; of a feckless wastrel father and a consumptive mother; of her coming to live with the Cranbornes, much as Rose had come to live with Aunt Hetty and herself. In fact, as they were talking, Sarah felt that she understood her mother for the first time, not so much through what Mrs Fanshawe was telling her, but because she could see echoes of Rose's life.

How strangely things turned out, she thought. Poor Maria was a very different creature to the noble martyr she had always thought her; more wayward and more human. And yet, that sacrifice of herself for her baby was part of her too. However badly she may have behaved before Sarah's birth, the last eight months of her mother's life had surely redeemed her?

Sir George and his sister were outraged by the treatment Sarah had received at Lord Fulmar's hands. If they couldn't quite credit her refusing to take up Lord Fulmar's offer, Mrs Fanshawe at least understood Sarah's reluctance to put herself in his power.

Sir George, whose instincts were for family and property, thought that, with a bit of care and attention, Miss Beale might persuade Lord Fulmar to settle the estate on herself. It was a prize worth catching—some £10,000 a year, if he were not mistaken. He would cultivate this new cousin. An heiress in the family must always be a good thing.

'But, my dear young cousin,' he said, 'you cannot go on working in the theatre! A young lady, in your position in life, why it is outrageous!'

Sarah laughed. 'I am very well employed here,' she said. 'I do not expect you to understand it, but I enjoy my work. I can assure you that it is all perfectly respectable.'

Sir George and Mrs Fanshawe looked at each other. Sarah reflected that much of her time recently seemed to be spent in asserting her right to live her own life.

'Why don't you come and see what I do?' she said mischievously. 'We are opening *A*

Midsummer Night's Dream on Saturday. It will be a very special production, and you may admire my costumes. The performance begins at seven o'clock.' She didn't dare add that they could admire her performance, too.

Again brother and sister looked at each other. Still, the play itself was unexceptionable, thought Sir George, if tedious. Shakespeare usually was. There could be no harm in it. Afterwards, they would have another word with Miss Beale. She must be made to accept a proper allowance from Lord Fulmar and live as befitted a lady.

Mrs Fanshawe was thinking along similar lines. Miss Beale could come and live with her. She would be a companion for Louisa and, with a handsome allowance from her father—which naturally would be managed by Mrs Fanshawe for her young cousin's benefit—she could be properly launched on the world. Later on, when Lord Fulmar died, Miss Beale would inherit Hoop Hall, and Mrs Fanshawe had no objection to being on visiting terms with the owner of a large estate.

They parted with mutual expressions of esteem and Sir George promised to take a box for Saturday's opening night.

The moment they had gone, Sarah sank back with a sigh of relief. The first twenty-seven years of her life had passed, apart from the visit to Hoop Hall when she was nine, in peace and tranquillity. Suddenly, over the last couple of months, far too much seemed to have been happening. She felt quite drained with the effort of trying to absorb it all.

She rang the bell for Polly to bring up her supper and, when Polly came with the tray, said, 'I have got tickets for you and Leah to come to the play on Saturday, Polly, as I promised. In fact, I think everyone in the house is coming.'

'Oh yes, Miss Sarah. Mr and Mrs Johnstone are coming, and Miss Valloton will be going with Miss Bailey and her mother. We're looking forward to it ever so, Leah and me.'

'Good. It's going to be something special.'

After supper, Sarah sat down at her writing desk and pencilled a draft letter to Lord Fulmar. She would see how it looked in the morning before doing a fair copy.

Dear Lord Fulmar

I accept your apology and assure you that I harbour no feelings of animosity towards you.

As to the estate, you must do as you think best.

Yours most sincerely,
S. Beale

She was hazy about how to finish off the letter. Should she say, 'Your most obedient servant'? In the circumstances that would surely be absurd. Nor was she going to write

'Dear Father', or worse, 'Papa'. There seemed to be no end to the shibboleths she might offend. She was so exhausted by all this that, as soon as she had drunk her evening chocolate, she went thankfully to bed, though it was scarcely nine o'clock.

*　　*　　*

The following morning, Sarah was alone in the small wardrobe room. She and Miss Bailey were now hard at work on the pantomime costumes for *Harlequin Tom Thumb*. They always had to look ahead and just now Sarah found it a relief to do so. She was not called for rehearsal until twelve o'clock, so she had plenty of time to get on with things. Unfortunately, that also meant far too much time to think.

She must have a plan for her life, she decided. There must be no harking back to what might have been. Aunt Hetty would certainly not have approved of that: it would be akin to sighing over an inheritance that would never materialize. No, she must embark on something new.

She would decorate her room, that would be a start. It had never been touched since she was a little girl and still had the now-faded wallpaper with its swags of roses. She would allow herself something more dramatic. She began to turn over various colour schemes in her mind.

Her reverie was interrupted by familiar footsteps and, before her heart could miss more than a couple of beats, Jack entered. He was carrying a small packet, which he placed on the table in front of her.

'I'm sorry,' he said. 'You must have been wondering what had become of them.' He saw her looking puzzled and added, 'The Green Knight and Princess Eglantine.'

Sarah put down her sewing. 'I had quite forgotten them. There has been so much else going on.' She opened the packet carefully. Not only had Jack mended them beautifully, but they had been repainted.

Sarah smiled down at them. 'They look wonderful!' she cried. 'Why, they are just like they used to be. Only better.'

Jack pulled up a chair and sat down. 'I'm pleased that you like them. I worried a bit about repainting them—you might have preferred them in their familiar state. But I decided that they would look wrong with a brand-new arm and wand and the rest of them with chipped paint.'

Sarah gently moved the Green Knight's arm up and down and admired the new sword. 'Thank you. It's lovely to see them again, just as they ought to be. I don't play with them now, of course, but I like to have them around.'

Jack reached his hand into his pocket and

took out another small packet. 'I thought you might like these, too,' he said. 'I didn't want to waste my newly acquired expertise in puppet making!'

Sarah opened the second packet. Inside were two more puppets, carefully made to the same pattern as the first, so that they would fit into the grooves on the floor of the theatre. One was of Jack as Theseus's attendant, and the other of Sarah as Hippolyta. They were wearing the costumes that Sarah had designed; Jack in peacock green and Sarah in red, both with the acanthus leaf decoration. They were so constructed they could hold hands.

Sarah looked down at the little figures and, for a moment, could say nothing. He could not have given her anything more precious than this memento of their shared experience but, at the same time, she was overcome by a feeling of desolation. For all that she would have of Jack, when he had gone, were these tiny memories.

She swallowed hard and managed to thank him. 'You must have taken a great deal of trouble, and I assure you that I shall treasure them.'

Jack looked closely at her. 'Have I upset you?'

'No, no!' Her fingers automatically moved to tidy some cotton reels. She was aware of Jack watching her. He must never guess. Pride gave her the courage to say, 'They are lovely and I couldn't be happier to have them.'

'Good.' He was still watching her.

'I was going to ask your advice,' Sarah went on brightly. She recounted the problem about the ending of her letter to Lord Fulmar.

'"Yours very sincerely" sounds about right to me. "I am Your Lordship's most humble and obedient servant" or whatever is for a formal letter addressed to "My Lord". Don't you worry about it.'

Then, because it had become natural to tell him things, Sarah told him about Mrs Fanshawe's and Sir George Cranborne's visit.

'Cranborne, eh?' said Jack. The last time he had seen that gentleman was at a party he had been to with Delia Sharpe. Cranborne had been enjoying himself with a very pretty little piece, he recalled.

'You know him?'

'Company acquaintance only.'

Sarah eyed him sceptically. 'You mean in company not fit for ladies, I take it?'

Jack smiled and said, 'Perhaps. But all that's over for me now. I swear it.'

He looked at her as he spoke and Sarah could see that he was serious. A thousand thoughts whirled through her head. Could he really have given up all that? All those mistresses, the luxurious apartments, the weeks in Paris that Rose had described in such detail? But why tell her?

'Won't you miss it?' Sarah knew perfectly

293

well that she should not be discussing these things with a gentleman. Indeed, a respectable female should have no knowledge of such goings-on whatsoever.

Jack shook his head. 'Tawdry,' he said. 'I don't miss it at all. In fact, I don't know how I stood it for so long.'

'Oh,' said Sarah. There were many questions she would have liked to have asked, but each one seemed more improper than the last. In the end she picked up her discarded sewing and began, with unsteady stitches, to tack two seams together.

Jack watched her for a moment and then rose.

'I must go,' he said. 'I promised to help Fenton with some scene shifting. I shall be helping with *School for Scandal* tonight, but Thorpe will see you home.'

'Yes,' said Sarah, staring down at her sewing.

'I understand that we may leave immediately after the technical rehearsal on Friday. I hope you will allow me to take you home then? There's something I wish to talk to you about.'

'Yes, of course,' said Sarah, puzzled.

She sat staring at nothing in particular for some moments after Jack had gone, and when Miss Bailey came into the room twenty minutes later, Sarah had still not finished her seam.

294

Jack rose early the following morning and called for Archie to bring his shaving water. His arm had healed well, but shaving was still tricky and Jack allowed Archie to shave him.

'All spruced up for the big day, then?' said Archie, sourly. It was only eight o'clock and Archie never felt at his best before noon.

'That's tomorrow,' said Jack. 'Today's the technical rehearsal. By the way, I've got you a ticket for tomorrow.'

'You want me to come and see you capering about on stage?'

'You'll enjoy it. It's going to be good. I don't mean me, I'm just an appendage. The play, Archie. It's something special, I swear it.'

It was too, thought Jack. The whole company was aware that this production was indeed something special. More and more people had been sneaking in to watch rehearsals. Word had got round and tickets were selling briskly. Apart from Madame Vestris's production of *A Midsummer Night's Dream* thirteen years ago, nobody had done Shakespeare's *Dream* for over 200 years. It was generally thought to be unstageable.

Jack had initially thought so himself. He had been forced to read it at school and found the idea of fairies who could creep into acorn cups, ludicrous. Phelps would never be able to stage it. But he had been wrong. This production would be a triumph.

Archie grunted, but he was not displeased. He had been curious about his master's work at the theatre and was eager to see the play, though nobody would have guessed this from his grumpiness.

The shaving done, Jack sat down to have his breakfast. There was a pile of letters by his plate, one of them in his mother's unmistakable hand. He sighed and picked it up. Another epistle of distress, he thought. He felt sorry for her, but what could he do? He was sure she would settle down once he was up in Manchester.

Archie brought him his bacon, egg and mushrooms.

Jack opened his mother's letter, read it and sighed. Archie looked sympathetically at him.

'My mother writes that she is sure that by this time my *playing with theatricals* will have palled, and we can discuss my future sensibly. The devil I will. She conveniently ignores my joining Midwinter and Pinks, apart from a reference to my behaviour distressing my father.'

He threw down the letter in disgust.

'Well, that ain't true, sir. Your pa was a great one for live and let live. He'd not have minded you going back to Manchester.'

'Yes, that's true,' said Jack, brightening up. He disliked being on bad terms with his mother but, on this, his mind was made up. 'I remember him being rather proud of the millwheel I'd made.'

'She'll come round,' said Archie, flicking at a crumb with a duster. 'Especially when she sees how her shares go up.'

'You really think that I'll make that much difference?' It was rare for Archie to express such faith in him.

'Bound to. Mr Pinks is getting on. They are getting a bit stick-in-the-mud, if you ask me. If those designs you have are anything to go by.'

Josiah Pinks had sent Jack the design samples from the previous year. These were the staples of the company, the designs that sold year in, year out. Good quality cottons but, as Archie said, boring.

'I'm not sure what time I'll be back today,' said Jack. 'Don't wait up for me. If I need a meal, I'll go to the chop house.'

He pushed his plate aside and rose. To Archie's interest Jack picked up the sample designs and put them carefully in their leather case and took them with him. Strange, thought Archie, whatever did he want with them at the theatre?

When Jack got to the theatre there was an almost palpable buzz of excitement. Fenton and his cohorts had been there since daybreak, getting the set into place and arranging the lights. Mr Harvey was rushing round shouting about the props. Sarah and Miss Bailey were busy checking last minute details of the costumes. Sarah wore a pincushion wristband and carried a small basket of cottons, needles and scissors.

Jack left his leather case with Pepper Williams for safe-keeping and went to get changed.

The technical rehearsal was the usual chaos of such occasions. Props went astray, lights were either too bright or not visible, the diorama got stuck, but gradually these things sorted themselves out.

For the first time Jack and Sarah were able to see the Mechanicals' play in Act V in its entirety and it was everything Sarah had hoped it would be. Starveling's wooden dog on wheels worked, Lion's tail—after a hiccup or two—seemed to have a life of its own and Mr Charles Fenton's Flute the bellows-mender, who was playing the heroine, Thisbe, made Jack laugh so much that he nearly fell off his seat.

Even Rose was happy. Several of the male members of the company had complimented her on her fairy grace and, whilst they scarcely counted in Rose's eyes, still it was pleasant to have their appreciation. She hadn't realized until the technical rehearsal, that at the very end of the play, when the fairies dance through Theseus's palace in the moonlight, they would be free of Mr Fenton's detestable net, which turned her and everybody else on stage, green.

If there were any gentlemen in the audience who might be interested in her, at least they'd be able to see her as she really was in the last act.

By five o'clock they were done. If there were a myriad of problems to be sorted out, they now had to stop, for *School for Scandal* would begin in a couple of hours. Jack and Sarah met at the stage door, Jack collected his leather case and they left the theatre.

Sarah remembered that Jack wished to talk to her about something. When to hand over to Mr Frost, probably. Just to think of him going made a leaden weight settle itself somewhere near her heart.

But Jack seemed to have forgotten that he wished to talk about anything in particular, for they spent the short walk discussing the rehearsal. Jack mentioned that Archie would be coming and that he was getting nervous about the performance. Sarah retorted that she was far more worried about Mrs Fanshawe and Sir George recognizing her. She must have been mad to suggest that they come.

'I didn't mention that I would be on stage, and now I'm terrified lest they recognize me.'

'I hope to God Cranborne doesn't recognize me,' said Jack with feeling. It would be all over Town in days. Yet, why should he care? He'd be up in Manchester. He suddenly began to laugh. 'Isn't it ridiculous? I cannot think of a more respectable place to work and yet both of us are made to feel like pariahs!'

'I know,' said Sarah smiling. 'Poor Aunt Hetty was horrified when I started to work here. But she came round, of course.'

They had now reached the house. Sarah was just about to turn and thank Jack for his escort when Jack spoke.

'May I come in for a moment?'

'Yes, of course.'

In silence she led the way to the drawing-room, offered him tea and said that she'd be with him shortly. For some reason she felt nervous and her hands were suddenly cold. She brushed her hair, washed her face and re-entered the drawing-room trying to quell a feeling of doom.

Jack gestured to the sofa, where he was sitting. 'Please come and sit here.'

Sarah did so. She took a deep breath and faced him resolutely. Whatever he was going to say, even if he were to announce his imminent departure, she must not give herself away.

'Being at Sadler's Wells has changed my life,' began Jack. 'It has given me the impetus to make a fresh start in a number of directions.'

'I hope they will prove productive ones,' said Sarah formally.

'Yes,' said Jack, with a sudden laugh, 'and in more ways than one. I am determined, Miss Beale, that by the time I am forty, say by

Christmas next year, I shall have a nice baby to bounce on my knee.'

Sarah was completely thrown. 'But, Mr Midwinter,' she exclaimed, 'you cannot have thought! Babies take some time to arrange. How shall you go about it?'

'Oh, in the traditional way!'

Sarah blushed. 'I—I mean, you weren't thinking of adopting a foundling?'

'No, I was thinking of getting married.'

'Oh. Yes. Of course.' Sarah did not seem to know how to continue. 'I mean, you wouldn't want a bastard, of course. And I'm sure your mother wouldn't want . . . And then . . .' Her voice tailed away miserably.

Jack took hold of her hand.

'Sarah,' he said, 'could we start this conversation again? It seems to be going off course. I daresay it's my fault. I've never proposed before and I can see I'm making a mull of it.'

'Propose?' said Sarah, her eyes huge with anxiety.

'Sarah, listen to me carefully. I love you very much and I hope that you will consent to be my wife.'

'You love me?' echoed Sarah.

'I do.'

'You want to marry me?'

'Yes, my darling,' said Jack patiently.

'Oh.' Sarah gulped twice and tried to take it in. She held his hand tightly and stared down

301

at the carpet.

'Sarah,' pleaded Jack, after some moments of silence, 'could you please say something? I find this uncertainty most unnerving.'

'Do you mean it?'

'Sarah! Will you marry me or will you not?'

Sarah nodded.

'Really, truly, yes?'

'Yes.' It came out as little more than a whisper.

'You love me?'

'Oh, yes!'

Jack pulled her into his arms and hugged her. Sarah clung to him half crying, half laughing. Then they were kissing as though they did not know how to stop and Jack was murmuring words of love in her ear and Sarah was trying to tell him how much she loved him and how it had all begun. Eventually, some shreds of reason returned.

'My darling, shall you mind moving to Manchester?' Jack asked.

Sarah sat up. Reality returned like a deluge of icy water. 'Oh God!' she said. Suddenly a host of objections rushed into her mind. What would she do about the house? She could not desert Polly and Leah after all these years; they had been part of her life ever since she had arrived as a baby. Where would they go? And Miss Valloton, too? She was well over seventy now. She couldn't throw her out.

And what about her work? She knew that

women always gave up paid work on their marriages. They were expected to look after husband and home and, in due course, children. Much as she loved Jack, could she really bear never to work again? She loved designing costumes, it gave her a real pleasure and satisfied some creative need that she didn't think would be filled otherwise. Going to Manchester would leave a great, jagged hole in her life.

But how could she deny the experience of love? Manchester would prove a challenge, too. How could she turn all that down without breaking her heart?

How much of this could he possibly understand?

'I'm worried about leaving my work,' she whispered. 'It means so much to me.'

'I've thought of that,' said Jack. He reached down to the leather case, opened it, took out the book of samples and showed them to her. 'The bread and butter of the firm,' he said. 'Good quality. Washes well. Won't shrink and so on.'

'But dull,' said Sarah. She turned them over thoughtfully. She could design better than that. She looked up. 'Jack, are you thinking that I could work for your uncle, too?' Her eyes had lit up again.

'Not directly,' said Jack. 'I'm sorry, my darling. Uncle Jos would never employ a woman as a designer. But you could work freelance, if you were interested. You could have a studio at home.'

As they talked Sarah saw that things would not be the same, but she need not lose everything that was precious to her. She would have to learn all about cotton production and dyeing techniques, and she could then put her talents to a new use. If one door closed, another opened.

The house, too, need not be an insuperable problem. Polly and Leah might like to come with them, for example. Miss Valloton had once or twice talked of moving to share a house with Miss Bailey and her mother, where she could have a room on the ground floor. The Johnstones might be interested in taking over the lease. There were a number of different possibilities. Life would go on.

The colour came back into her cheeks. For the first time since he had met her as a child and she had made her joke about Belisarius, Jack saw a look of mischief in her eyes.

'Your mother's not going to like this,' she said, with a saucy look.

'Nor is your father,' retorted Jack. 'Parvenu, he thinks me.'

*   *   *

The atmosphere in the theatre on Saturday evening was one of cheerful expectancy. The Wells was popular and Phelps himself had many admirers. There was a contingent for whom Miss Cooper (who was playing Helena) could do no wrong. There was a group of young lawyers who came up for every new production. There were the usual lively Islingtonians who mustered in the gallery and enjoyed a good night out.

The new gas lights dimmed, silence descended and then the curtains rose on Theseus's palace and the play began. The thwarted lovers, Hermia and Lysander, fled to the wood outside Athens and freedom. Hermia's old father ranted about filial obedience. Demetrius, crossed in love, followed Hermia, and Helena, spurned by Demetrius, followed him.

The magic began in the Athenian wood. The stage was bathed in a green light, through which could be seen trees and distant glades. Fairies appeared and disappeared as if by magic. Strange flowers materialized and vanished. Puck stepped behind a tree and the next moment his silhouette floated up into the sky. The scenes glided into one another and clouds continuously moved across the star-sprinkled sky, the vistas of the wood altered; now you were in one part of the wood, now another.

An enchantment settled down on the theatre. Nothing seemed improbable.

The star-crossed lovers were bewitched by Puck; quarrelled, changed partners, chased each other and finally, exhausted, fell asleep in the greenwood. The mortals' disarray was echoed in fairyland. Oberon quarrelled with Titania. The Mechanicals, practising their play in secret in the wood, were caught up in it. Bottom, the conceited weaver, was transformed into an ass—and became the darling of the fairy queen.

When daybreak came the lighting changed. The green mist faded away and reality returned. The bemused lovers awoke. Oberon's love potion had transferred Demetrius's affections to Helena. Theseus, coming on stage with Hippolyta and their attendants, blessed the two pairs of lovers. Order in fairyland and on earth was restored.

The last act was in Theseus's columned hall, splendid with lustrous candelabra and swagged curtains. The lovers united and the Mechanicals' play over, the mortals left the stage. The lights dimmed, moonlight streamed in, and the columns became standing moonbeams. A stream of fairies, each holding a glimmering light, danced down the stairs and along the terraces, blessing the palace as they went. When Puck gave his epilogue, the benediction spread over the whole audience.

There was silence in the theatre. Everyone remained half-enchanted. Then they stirred and sat up, some rubbing their eyes as if they were still seeing visions. Then the applause came, roll on roll of it.

Jack and Sarah taking their bows at the back of the stage, turned to each other and smiled.

*   *   *

The Grand Refreshment Saloon, which catered for the gentry in the boxes or the dress circle, was full. There was an animated buzz of conversation and glasses clicked and waiters scurried round. Sarah entered some fifteen minutes later, after she had changed out of her costume.

Sir George was delighted to see her. He shook her hand warmly and introduced her to Louisa Fanshawe 'my niece, y'know.' He had seen the most delightful girl among the fairies and was wondering who she was. She looked tantalizingly familiar, like a very pretty piece of cherry-pie he used to meet with Byland some months ago. Rumour had it that he'd treated her shabbily. Sir George wondered what had become of her.

Mrs Fanshawe, who had recognized Sarah among Hippolyta's attendants but decided not to comment, congratulated her on the success of the play. 'Beautiful,' she said. 'I had no idea that Shakespeare was performable nowadays. I had thought him to be very coarse and unrefined.'

'I believe some lines were cut,' said Sarah. 'I am pleased that you enjoyed it. What about you, Miss Fanshawe, how did you find it?'

Louisa gave an ecstatic sigh. 'Oh, Miss Beale, it was wonderful!'

Sarah smiled. 'There is something very magical about being able to create an illusion.'

'Miss Beale,' broke in Sir George. 'I could swear I saw Midwinter on stage. Ridiculous, of course. You don't have an actor of that name here, do you?'

'Mr Midwinter is here temporarily,' acknowledged Sarah, recognizing that fate had stepped in. 'He has been taking over the part normally played by Mr Frost, who broke his leg. It is Mr Midwinter who saw that I came to no harm in that trouble I told you of with Lord Fulmar.'

'Mr Midwinter!' echoed Mrs Fanshawe. 'Why, you may see him everywhere in society.' Indeed, she had once had hopes of him for Louisa.

'You must meet him,' said Sarah. 'I see he has just come in.' Jack was looking round for her and Sarah raised an arm and waved.

Introductions were made.

'Didn't expect to see you treading the boards, Midwinter,' said Sir George, eyeing him quizzically. What was he after? Some light skirt? 'Enjoying yourself, eh?'

'Yes,' said Jack cheerfully. 'As Mr Frost has broken his leg, I am taking over his part. I confess that I enjoy it immensely. I also help backstage wherever I can be useful.'

'What on earth does a gentleman know of

things backstage?' asked Mrs Fanshawe. The play had certainly been excellent, but for a gentleman to become involved . . .'

'I learned. I am proud to say that I made Starveling's dog.'

'I think it was very clever of you,' cried Louisa. 'I loved the dog.' She gazed at him, her cheeks flushed.

'Why, thank you, Miss Fanshawe.'

'Mr Midwinter may do as he pleases,' said Mrs Fanshawe. 'But you, Miss Beale, you really cannot remain at the theatre. A lady! It's unheard of.'

Jack took hold of Sarah's hand. 'She is not staying at the theatre,' he said. 'She has agreed to marry me and we shall be going up to Manchester.'

For a few moments there was the usual hubbub of congratulations and questions. Louisa looked stricken, but she was a good-natured girl and she added her good wishes very creditably.

'But . . . have you asked Lord Fulmar's permission?' asked Mrs Fanshawe. From what Miss Beale had told her, she couldn't see His Lordship agreeing.

'Permission be damned,' said Jack. 'Miss Beale and I are getting married by special licence in about six weeks' time and nobody, but nobody, is going to stop me. I shall tell him once I have my wife safe.'

Sir George frowned. What effect would this

match have on Miss Beale's chances of inheriting Hoop Hall? On the other hand, Fulmar was unpredictable and might change his mind any number of times. Midwinter had a good estate of his own—£7,000 a year was not to be sneezed at. If Miss Beale produced a son or two, the chances were that Fulmar would be reconciled.

'My dear Miss Beale,' said Sir George. 'Pray, allow me the pleasure of giving you away. A member of your family, you know.'

'Why, Sir George,' exclaimed Sarah. 'That is kind.' She had thought of asking Mr Phelps. The theatre was her real family.

Mrs Fanshawe saw the advantages at once. The marriage was practically an elopement. Anything which gave it respectability was to be encouraged.

'You must have Sir George, my dear,' she said. 'And Louisa and I will come and see you wed. Now, what are you going to wear?' In a moment Sarah, Mrs Fanshawe and Louisa were deep in conversation about materials and styles.

The Refreshment Saloon door opened and Mr and Mrs Frampton entered with Rose. Mr Frampton was pleased with the performance and had promised his wife and niece wine and oysters to celebrate. Rose was looking particularly pretty. Her hair had been newly washed and hung about her head in a silvery-gold cloud.

Sir George nudged Jack. 'I say, Midwinter, is that the little Frampton, by any chance?'

'Yes,' said Jack. 'Would you like to meet her?' He could see that Rose had spotted Sir George and was eyeing him speculatively. He crossed the room with Sir George in tow. 'Miss Frampton!'

Rose gave her artless start and coloured prettily.

'May I introduce Sir George Cranborne, who has been admiring your performance this evening.'

Sir George bent over her hand. Jack caught Rose's eye and winked.

When Jack got back to the ladies, Sarah raised an eyebrow and glanced in the direction of Sir George and Rose. Jack grinned at her but said nothing.

'Mr Midwinter,' said Mrs Fanshawe firmly. 'You must invite your mother to the wedding.'

Jack looked sceptical. 'She won't like it and I won't have Sarah upset.'

'Miss Beale is stronger than you give her credit for. Your mother will never forgive you, or Miss Beale either, if you do not. Write to her today, and Louisa and I will look after her. I shall write and invite her to stay with us.'

Mrs Fanshawe remembered Mrs Midwinter. A pleasant woman, but over-sensitive about her social position. She probably feared that her son was making a *mésalliance*. She would reassure her. Point out the advantages:

grandchildren, reconciliation with Lord Fulmar and so on.

Mrs Midwinter was a sensible woman. She might not be overjoyed about the match, but she would put a good face on it.

'I understand that you are planning to go straight up to Manchester.'

'Yes. We hope to marry on 24 November. It's Mr Greenwood's benefit night at the theatre, so we won't be interrupting things too much there. If we marry early, say about half-past nine, then any friends from the theatre who wish to come, will be able to do so. And we can catch the midday train to Manchester.'

Louisa's eyes lit up. A theatre wedding! She had lived a very respectable life, and much enjoyed this glimpse into Bohemia.

'No, Mr Midwinter,' went on Mrs Fanshawe firmly. 'You must have a proper honeymoon, even if it's only a week at the seaside. It is really not fair on Miss Beale to expect her to start her married life with her husband going off all day to sort out his business affairs. At least give her a week of your undivided attention first.'

Mrs Fanshawe, thought Sarah in amusement, could be quite as bossy as Lord Fulmar.

'You are quite right,' said Jack, after a moment's thought. 'Of course we must have a honeymoon. Have you ever seen the sea, Sarah?'

Sarah shook her head.

'I'll show it to you.' And everything else besides.

'I should like that,' said Sarah demurely.

AFTERWORD

Samuel Phelps's *A Midsummer Night's Dream* at Sadler's Wells in 1853 was one of the seminal productions of the mid-nineteenth century. Apart from Madame Vestris's production in 1840—which was condemned for its *'meretricious glitter'*—it was the first to go back to Shakespeare's own text since 1642.

Earlier, in 1847, Phelps had staged the first production of Shakespeare's *Macbeth* for over 200 years—previously Davenant's version had been preferred, which allowed for bevies of singing and dancing witches, and considerable distortions of the text. The *Macbeth* had been hailed as a triumph and, by 1853, the Sadler's Wells theatre was known and respected for its steadfast adherence to Shakespeare's texts; due consideration given to all parts from the meanest to the greatest, and an extremely talented back-stage company who worked together to overcome the problems of an old-fashioned theatre and a limited budget by their sheer inventiveness.

Phelps's determination to put on the play that Shakespeare had written was by no means shared by his contemporaries, where it was not uncommon for a star actor to pinch speeches from another part to enhance his own. The scenery, costumes and lighting are all mentioned in the reviews of the day, as was the carefully rehearsed acting, even down to the 'supers' in the battle scenes. One must conclude that this scrupulous attention to detail was worthy of note.

For Phelps, as many reviewers attested, everything was subordinated to the play, and his own acting was generous and unselfish. A reviewer in *Douglas Jerrold's Weekly Newspaper* wrote, '*There were no false starts, no spouting, no pointed ranting, no mis-directed energy that fires the unreflecting many into sudden admiration. It was all deep, genuine, well-uttered passion and emotion . . .*' Plainly, the Phelps style was unusual enough to be commented on.

In the summer of 1853, the theatre went over to gas lighting (Drury Lane and the Lyceum had done so in 1817, so Sadler's Wells was decidedly behind the times) and Frederick Fenton, Phelps's chief scene designer, was able to use the new medium to its fullest advantage in *A Midsummer Night's Dream*.

Fenton (1817–1898) came from a theatrical family. His father had been stage manager for Edmund Kean and Fenton himself had started work at seven as a page at Drury Lane. He had worked at Sadler's Wells since 1839 and, under the previous management, had been scene painter, actor and occasional writer of pantomimes. He was thus familiar with every branch of the profession. John Coleman, Phelps's biographer, described Fenton as '*a scene painter of indefatigable industry, extraordinary inventive skill and remarkable ability.'*

In 1892, Fenton gave an in-depth interview to J. Moyr Smith about the *Dream* production and how he had got the effects he wanted. The *'blue nett'* (sic) in front of the stage for Acts II, III and IV, the moving diorama, the floating moon and the moonlit pillars at the end of the play are all described, and obviously Phelps had given him a free hand.

Many reviewers comment on the magical quality of Fenton's scenery. Henry Morley, for example, wrote, *'There is no ordinary scene-shifting: but, as in dreams, one scene is made to glide insensibly into another.'* This was echoed by Douglas Jerrold. *'So artistically are the different changes of moonlight, fog, and sunrise produced, that you imagine you have been wandering through an entire forest, with a fresh prospect meeting you unexpectedly at every turn.'*

All the critics agreed that the crowning glory of the production was Phelps's portrayal of Bottom. Phelps chose to play him as a creature of infinite self-conceit. Morley commented, *'Not a touch of comedy was missed in this capital piece of acting.'* *Lloyd's Weekly London News* went further: *'It is a finished work of art that entitles the creator of it to stand henceforth, like a second Garrick, between Comedy and Tragedy.'*

From a writer's point of view, the varied and

prolific source material is a great advantage. Readers might like to know that all the names of the cast and company are accurate. A Miss Beale, for example, was indeed one of Hippolyta's attendants and a Miss Frampton one of Titania's. Mr Frost had been a regular small-part actor for some years, though, for the purposes of the story, he had to break his leg to allow Jack to take over his parts. So far as possible, the costumes, acting and scenery are as they were described at the time; though Theseus's and Hippolyta's costumes are my own invention.

Phelps's promptbook for the *Dream* is in the Folger Shakespeare Library and from it we get details such as lion's tail and stage directions for Puck's appearance and disappearance, for example.

Modern theatre-goers might be bemused by the number of productions on during the season. From the opening of the 1853 season at the end of August until the opening of *A Midsummer Night's Dream* on 8 October, there were ten plays in repertoire. Most ran for two or three nights at a time. Something of the *Dream*'s success can be gauged by the fact that it ran for thirty-six performances in a row, only interrupted by a command performance at Windsor Castle of *Henry V*.

It remains for me to thank various people for their help: David Withey of the Finsbury Library; the Theatre Museum Archive;

Professor Vera Gottlieb, who lent me various books and didn't complain when I kept them for months; Stephen Jenn, who read the typescript from an actor's point of view and made a number of helpful suggestions, and Professor Michael Slater.

Elizabeth Hawksley
London, 1999